P9-BIO-248

LOVERS AND ENEMIES

Recent Titles by Anne Herries from Severn House

A WICKED WENCH
MILADY'S REVENGE
MY LADY, MY LOVE

Writing as Linda Sole

The Country House Series
GIVE ME TOMORROW
A BRIGHT NEW DAY

The London Series
BRIDGET
KATHY
AMY

THE TIES THAT BIND
THE BONDS THAT BREAK
THE HEARTS THAT HOLD

THE ROSE ARCH
A CORNISH ROSE
A ROSE IN WINTER

FLAME CHILD
A SONG FOR ATHENA

LOVERS AND ENEMIES

Anne Herries

This first world edition published in Great Britain 2005 by
SEVERN HOUSE PUBLISHERS LTD of
9–15 High Street, Sutton, Surrey SM1 1DF.
This first world edition published in the USA 2006 by
SEVERN HOUSE PUBLISHERS INC of
595 Madison Avenue, New York, N.Y. 10022.

Copyright © 2005 by Linda Sole.

All rights reserved.
The moral right of the author has been asserted.

British Library Cataloguing in Publication Data

Herries,   Anne
    Lovers and enemies
    1.   Great Britain - History - Civil War, 1642-1649 - Fiction
    2.   Love stories
    I.   Title
    823.9'14 [F]

    ISBN-10 : 0-7278-6268-5 (cased)
                    0-7278-9155-3 (paper)

Except where actual historical events and characters are being
described for the storyline of this novel, all situations in this
publication are fictitious and any resemblance to living persons
is purely coincidental.

Typeset by Palimpsest Book Production Ltd.,
Polmont, Stirlingshire, Scotland.
Printed and bound in Great Britain by
MPG Books Ltd., Bodmin, Cornwall.

One

Caroline was smiling as she woke. Her dream had been so pleasant for it was of children playing in the meadow. As she threw back the covers and got out of bed, walking across the smooth wooden floorboards towards the window, she was remembering. The dream was not only a dream, but something that had happened in her childhood.

Opening her window, she looked out on the extensive gardens of her father's house. Her mother's spaniel dogs were barking excitably as they hunted for rats beneath the box hedges that made up the formal knot garden. They were unlikely to find their quarry, for the servants were assiduous in their work, but the dogs never tired of their game. They were much like the children who had played through her dreams, Caroline thought, smiling softly as she turned back from her window.

The dream was in truth a memory of the carefree days she had known as a little girl in this quiet English village. Sometimes, Caroline thought that her whole life had passed as a dream, for if there had been unrest in other parts she had not known of it. Only in the past year or so had she become aware of trouble between the King and Parliament, and that had seemed so far away, another world. Of late though rumours had begun to intrude into her serenity, stories that made her wonder if the King's quarrels would destroy the peace they had all enjoyed for many years.

Caroline thrust the thought from her mind for such things made her uneasy and she preferred the sunlit dream of her childhood. She recalled it perfectly now. They had been playing, the four of them, in the meadow that lay between

1

Hillgrove and the village of Thornberry. Caroline, her brother Rupert and the Mortimer brothers, Harry and Nicolas.

She smiled as she remembered their games. They had run and leaped, sung and danced as freely as the village children around the maypole, for their parents were friends and no restrictions were placed on their friendship. It was Nicolas Mortimer who had put Caroline up on his pony and taught her to ride.

But the dream was of another time when she was but nine years old and Nicolas fifteen. The daisies had grown tall and strong that year for it had rained all spring and the summer had been hot.

Harry had been organizing a ball game. He was always full of restless energy and would have them at it for hours, as if he were a king and they his subjects. But the others had grown tired of being organised that day and flopped down in the long, sweet grass, which blossomed with daisies and other meadow flowers.

Caroline had sat for a time with her face to the sun, her eyes closed. When she opened them it was to see Nicolas nearby making a daisy chain.

'What are you doing?' she asked, and he had smiled, getting up to kneel beside her.

'I have made a coronet for a beautiful princess,' he told her and placed the circlet of daisies on her head. 'I crown you Princess Caroline.'

Caroline had laughed and jumped up to kiss his cheek.

'Then you shall be my prince – if you can catch me!'

She had run laughing and screaming through the long grass as Nicolas pursued her, but it had been Harry who caught her. He had stepped out in front of her, catching her about the waist and laughing in triumph as he claimed that he had won.

'You cheated,' Nicolas said.

''Tis true,' Caroline agreed. 'You shall not be my prince, Harry, for you did not play fair.'

Caroline frowned at the memory as her maid entered bringing hot water for her to wash. She had denied Harry then, but it was he to whom she would be betrothed on her next birthday.

Their fathers had arranged it between them some years ago.

Caroline was not sure how she felt though she knew she should obey her father's wishes. Besides, Harry was Lord Mortimer's eldest son and would inherit Thornberry Manor, while Nicolas had only a small estate left to him by his late mother. And Nicolas had changed of late from the merry boy who had crowned her with daisies, becoming more serious, sterner. Sometimes now when he looked at her, Caroline was frightened by what she saw in his eyes.

'Lady Saunders said to remind you that 'tis today that Mistress Waldegrave is expected, Mistress Caroline,' Tilly said.

The girl's words brought Caroline swiftly from her reverie.

'I had forgotten for the moment,' she confessed. 'I must hurry for there will be things that my mother would have me do . . .'

Nicolas saw his brother speaking with the village wench, revolted at what he was seeing. How could he use his time so ill when he was promised to Caroline Saunders? He waited until Harry left the girl and came up to him.

'You are a fool,' Nicolas said. 'What do you think Caroline would say if she heard that you were messing around with that wench?'

'And who is to tell her?' Harry's eyes were full of contempt as he met his brother's furious stare. 'Will you run to her with the tale, Nicolas?'

'You know that I shall not,' Nicolas retorted. 'I have never gone behind your back, but I shall not see you hurt her, Harry. Be warned that I shall find a way to stop you.'

'You have become a prating Puritan,' Harry mocked him. 'Father may not be best pleased with me, brother – but he will be even less pleased when he discovers that you are a traitor to all that he holds dear.'

'At least I am honest in my beliefs,' Nicolas said, his eyes narrowed in anger. 'It is my intention to make my position clear to our father but do not forget, Harry, I shall not let you hurt Caroline.'

'I have no intention of hurting her,' Harry said with a careless shrug. 'That girl is but a passing fancy – and a man must have his pleasures after all.'

Nicolas threw him a look of disgust. He had no patience with Harry over this, but his brother was right about one thing, he must speak to his father about his intentions before he discovered it from someone else.

'You make me ashamed to own you as my flesh and blood,' Lord William Mortimer ranted at his son. 'Damnation, Nicolas! Supporting that rabble against His Majesty – and in public! – what did you mean by it?'

'That I agreed with them, sir,' Nicolas replied as he tried to explain. He had known that his father would not be pleased, but he had not been prepared for such anger. 'These taxes the King would have had us pay were iniquitous. I know that he hath been forced to abolish ship money but for how long can he be trusted not to impose another such tax? I merely said that I admired John Hampden for his stance against such taxes, which are properly the prerogative of Parliament.'

They were standing in his father's library, the only room in the manor house to have been panelled with oak, and therefore, warmed by the huge log fire that burned in the hearth, the most comfortable. Yet neither of them appreciated the comforts afforded them as they stood, face to face, the air sparking between them.

'God's Body, sir! You would try the patience of a saint. Have a care, Nicolas, your words could be seen as treason and you may find yourself lodged in the Tower one day.'

The dissent between King Charles and his Parliament had rumbled on for many months, and the King had that January removed to the North, having lost all patience with the stubborn men that plagued him.

'I am no traitor, sir, but there are those who say that King Charles is a traitor to his people. He listens to his queen too much and pays secret homage to the Pope. Rumour has it that he treats with the Irish Catholics and the French king.

Had he the money he would no doubt dismiss Parliament once more and rule as he pleased.'

'You are a rogue, sir!' Lord Mortimer thundered. 'I will hear no more of this. His Majesty rules by divine right and no man hath the power to gainsay his rule. Indeed, I am no Catholic as well you know, but I will hold to the King for, by my faith, he is our sovereign and I have sworn an oath to him.'

'And for that I honour you, Father,' Nicolas replied in a quiet, steady tone. He disliked having a breach with his father but believed passionately in the cause for which he was prepared to fight. 'But I cannot but agree with Hampden, Pym and the others of like mind. I am for the freedom of the people and for Parliament.'

'Then should it ever come to a trial of strength we shall be on opposite sides.' Lord Mortimer turned his face away in disgust. 'Take yourself from my sight for a while, Nicolas, for I might say or do something I shall regret.'

'I am sorry I have distressed you, Father, but I think this king unjust and unless he can be brought to see his mistakes I cannot respect him. Therefore I have no choice but to take up arms against him if it should come to a struggle.'

Lord Mortimer waved his hand in dismissal. Nicolas bowed his head, turned on his heel and left the library, where his father had already returned to the study of his accounts. Perhaps it had been unwise to disturb Lord Mortimer at his work for Nicolas knew all was not as it should be. Harry's gambling debts had been a thorn in his father's side for the past year, and a poor harvest the previous summer had made things difficult all round. Some of their best tenants had been unable to pay their rent in full. Lord Mortimer had considered dispossessing three families for debt but both Harry and Nicolas had argued against it, and for the moment they had won.

However, the family fortunes were at a low ebb, something that should be mended when Harry married Caroline Saunders. The betrothal was due to take place in two months when Caroline reached her seventeenth birthday, and their wedding would follow within a year.

Nicolas was frowning as he left the house. He was not

sure why the thought of his brother's marriage disturbed him. It had been arranged that the two would marry some years previously and it would help to restore the Mortimers' fortunes for Sir John Saunders was a wealthy man.

Yet the uneasy feeling lingered at the back of Nicolas's mind. He was not sure if his charming, handsome brother was worthy of Mistress Saunders. Harry's gambling and other aspects of his behaviour made him an unsuitable husband for Caroline, though she seemed happy enough with the arrangement. And he was certain that she had no love for himself, Harry's younger brother – younger by one year and heir only to a small estate near Ely, which had been his mother's dower.

A wry smile lingered on Nicolas's mouth as he strode towards the stairs. Mistress Saunders was very capable of ordering her own life and would not thank him for his concerns.

His booted feet rang on the stone steps as he clattered down them. He would be glad to shake the damp and depression of this ancient pile from his feet. It was a rambling manor house, built at the time of King Henry VIII, and its stone walls were both crumbling and damp; even in summer it was never warm. Its turrets and towers brooded over a dried-up moat, an air of neglect pervading its walls, and, in Nicolas's opinion, it would be better to tear the whole place down and rebuild a smaller, more comfortable house. Unfortunately, Lord Mortimer would hear none of it and by the time Harry inherited their fortunes would probably not allow rebuilding.

He thought himself fortunate to have been left the much smaller but more comfortable house by his mother. He would never be lord of the manor like his brother, but at least his fields brought him a reasonable income and he could be warm on winter nights. One day he would marry himself . . . but the thought of marriage gave him no pleasure. He was not sure why, unless it was that the woman he admired above all others was forbidden him. But he would not allow himself to think of her. He had forced all thoughts out of his mind and it would be foolish to let her creep in again.

He had been bidden to take himself off and would do so, first to his own estate, situated just north of the Isle of Ely, and then to Ely itself, where he had friends who were of like mind. He knew Master Cromwell well, and had met John Hampden when in the company of others who opposed the King's unjust taxes, and he had been invited to visit when he chose. A few days sojourn at his estate would serve well enough to keep him out of mischief and his father's eye.

''Twas exceeding kind of your mother to send us this fine ham,' Mistress Abigail Blackwell said to the young woman seated at her kitchen table, partaking of a raspberry cordial. 'You must thank her for me, Mistress Caroline. The Reverend Blackwell hath been unwell this past sennight but being partial to a good ham he may be tempted to have a bite for his supper.'

'That was my mother's hope,' Caroline Saunders replied. Tall and slender, she was a pretty girl of some sixteen summers with auburn hair and green eyes that held a merry twinkle in their depths. 'She was sorry to see him so poorly in church last week and hopes he will soon feel better.'

'He hath at times a weakness of the chest, but nothing that a good goose-grease poultice will not cure,' his wife told her. 'You may assure Sir John and Lady Saunders that the Reverend will be well enough to attend his parish duties soon enough.'

'My parents will be pleased to hear it, ma'am,' Caroline said. 'And now I must take my leave of you as we are expecting a guest. She is a distant cousin, for her mother is cousin to mine. Her own mother died quite recently and Lady Saunders invited her to stay with us.'

'Then you must be at home to welcome her. 'Twas good of you to walk all this way when you are needed at Hillgrove.'

'We have been preparing for days and there was nothing left for me to do,' Caroline said. 'But I shall not linger for I would wish to be there to greet Mistress Waldegrave on her arrival.'

Leaving the Rectory, Caroline set out to walk the short distance to her home at a brisk pace, her empty basket over her arm. She had welcomed her mother's request to walk down to the village for it was a fine spring day, though the breeze was cool. Yet she had been pleased with the exercise for her dream had made her restless, uneasy in her mind, a little dissatisfied perhaps, which she should not have been for she had everything to look forward to.

Her future betrothal to Harry Mortimer was occupying her mind much over these past days, for she knew her family eagerly anticipated it. Indeed, she had thought it would content her well enough, and in truth there was no reason why she should doubt it.

Harry Mortimer was a fine young man, handsome, strong and possessed of a charming manner, which made him popular with most people. Caroline liked him very well and at first she had been happy to accept her father's plans for her, though recently some doubts had begun to creep into her mind. There was nothing specific, just a slight unease when she was with Harry that made her wonder if she would be truly content as his wife. Yet she must accept it for it was her father's wish and she had ever been dutiful.

Somewhere a labourer was whistling the air to 'Cherry Ripe', and she could hear the clear laughter of children. It was such a peaceful scene, a blackbird trilling at her from the branches of a May tree.

As she left the village streets behind her, she saw the black-smith's daughter, Rowena Greenslade. Rowena had been gathering herbs and roots from the hedgerows for her mother used them to make cures and potions. She called a greeting but Rowena merely looked at her and did not answer. It was a little odd for the girl had been friendly enough until recent weeks.

Hearing the thud of a horse's hooves somewhere ahead of her, Caroline moved to one side of the narrow country lane, which was bounded on each side by tall hedges. As she waited on the verge for the horseman to pass by, she realized that it was Nicolas Mortimer, Harry's younger brother.

He had seen her and slowed his horse as he approached, doffing his hat to her but not smiling. She inclined her head to him but neither spoke as he passed. Caroline did not know why but Nicolas always sent a shiver down her spine when he looked at her these days. There was something very intense about him, he was so different from his charming brother. She thought that, had he been intended as her betrothed, she would not have felt easy in her mind.

He was as unlike his brother as it was possible to be, taking after his father while his brother favoured their long dead mother. Nicolas had hair so dark it was almost black and eyes like the night sky. Sometimes the look in his eyes seemed almost to burn her, and his manner made her tremble, though she knew not why. But today he had hardly glanced her way, his mind clearly elsewhere.

She knew that Nicolas and his father often quarrelled for they were alike in temperament as well as looks, whereas Harry knew how to gain his own way with a smile.

Just why did Nicolas sometimes look at her as if he might devour her? Yet at other times his look was so harsh that she thought he must disapprove of her. Caroline pondered the problem for a moment. As a child he had been as carefree and merry as his brother. What had changed him?

She paused to pick a few violets she saw growing under the hedge. They smelled lovely and she was smiling as she straightened up, her troubling thoughts forgotten as she began to think of other things.

Then, as she turned the bend that wound up the narrow lane to the top of the hill, she saw a wagon approaching along the high road from St Ives. She thought that it must be bringing her mother's cousin and that she must hurry or it would reach Hillgrove before she could.

Caroline was breathless as she entered the house, her chest heaving as she fought to recover herself.

'Mercy on us,' Lady Saunders said as she came into the hall and saw her daughter, her long hair hanging down her back in untidy spirals, skirts awry. 'What ails you, daughter?'

'I saw Master Carter's wagon as I came from the village,' Caroline replied. 'And ran all the way so as not to be late.'

'Goodness gracious,' her mother said with a shake of her head. 'I had not expected them for another hour. The coach from Huntingdon must have been early for once.' Lady

Saunders was a petite lady, rather stout and not as handsome as her daughter, but she was good-natured and much loved by her family. She nodded to her daughter. 'Go up and tidy yourself, Caroline. I shall greet Mistress Waldegrave and you may tell Martha that we will have our refreshments in the parlour.'

'Yes, Mother,' Caroline said, and fled up the stairs. At the top she met her brother Rupert, who was looking particularly furtive. He was just a year her senior and forever in trouble with his tutor. 'And what are you about, sir?' she challenged him, a teasing glint in her eyes. They had been good companions as children, always in some scrape, for which Rupert invariably took the blame, though his sister was often as mischievous as he. However, he was too gallant and too loving a brother to let Caroline take the whipping, and bore his father's justice with a smile and a shrug of his shoulders.

'Have you seen old Trotter?' Rupert asked in a low voice. 'He set me some Latin verse but I have promised to meet someone in the village. We are going to hunt for otters by the river.'

'Father will not be pleased if your tutor complains about you again, Rupert,' his sister warned him, for though she had grown out of childish disobedience, he had not. 'He said that he would send you away to college if you did not attend your studies.'

'If only he would,' Rupert said and grinned at her. Like Caroline he was tall, his hair a fiery red that put hers to shame, his eyes more blue than green. 'I dare say there would be some fun to be had at Oxford. Trotter is a dry old stick, Caro, and I grow bored listening to him. You haven't seen him lurking, have you?'

'No, I have but this minute come from the village, and just in time. Mercy Waldegrave is arriving . . . that must be her now and me not ready. I must go . . .' Caroline fled along the hall to her bedchamber as she heard voices in the hall downstairs.

The room she called her own was large and comfortable, and well furnished. There was a bed with a half tester and curtains that hung about it, an oak coffer for her personal things, a fine linen press for her clothes, a side table where her brushes and mirror were kept, a three-legged stool and her virginals. The walls were panelled with oak and there were woven rush mats on the floor to make it feel warmer. In winter she often had her own fire in the small grate for the east winds could be very cold and Hillgrove was exposed to the elements on all sides.

She picked up her pretty, silver-backed hairbrush and drew it quickly through her curls, bringing back some semblance of tidiness to the disarray caused by the breeze, for she had worn no hat on her walk to the village. It was a fault in her, and one her mother was forever scolding her over, but she liked to feel the wind in her hair.

Glancing in her small hand-mirror, she saw that she looked respectable once more, and, having smoothed her skirts, tied a clean falling band at her throat and settled her petticoats, she went downstairs to the kitchen to ask for the refreshments her mother had requested.

This small task accomplished, she made her way to her mother's best parlour, stopping at the door as she heard voices inside. Mercy was answering Lady Saunders's questions, her voice low and husky – rather pleasant, Caroline thought as she opened the door and went in.

Her first thought on seeing their guest was that she was beautiful. Mercy was not as tall as Caroline. She had long dark hair, though it was only her ringlets that were visible for she wore a plain white cap that framed her lovely face. However, it was her eyes that were so remarkable, Caroline thought. They were very dark, lustrous, the whites very clear, and they held a sadness that was almost haunting.

She must still be grieving for her mother, Caroline felt, her heart touched with pity for the other girl's loss as she went towards her, her hands outstretched.

'Mistress Waldegrave,' she said. 'I have been looking forward to meeting you so much. I am your cousin, Caroline.'

Mercy turned towards her, those dark eyes dwelling on Caroline intently for a moment, and then she smiled. If she

11

had been beautiful before, now she was glorious. Caroline felt drawn to her immediately.

'Caroline,' Mercy said. 'Will you not address me as Mercy? We are cousins and I hope we shall be friends.'

'Yes, of course,' Caroline replied and went to exchange a kiss with her. 'Did you have a good journey? The coach from Huntingdon was early I believe?'

'I do not know for I did not come by coach,' Mercy said. 'My stepfather does not hold with such luxury. He arranged for me to travel by wagon. A neighbour was bringing goods to market at St Ives and kindly offered me a lift as far as the crossroads, for it was only a little out of his way. I was able to find transport for this last part of my journey at the inn, as Lady Saunders told me in her letter.'

The journey from her home in Huntingdon was more than a three hour journey, and by wagon that must have been uncomfortable indeed. Caroline knew that it had been agreed that Mercy should be taken up on the coach when it stopped at the busy market town where she lived. The fare was no more than one silver shilling and it seemed hard that she should have been forced to accept the charity of a neighbour, when she could have travelled more comfortably.

'But I sent monies for your journey,' Lady Saunders said, clearly distressed by the idea of her cousin travelling on a farm wagon all that way. 'I do not understand.'

'My stepfather would not accept charity,' Mercy replied, and her smile had vanished, the sadness deepening in her lovely eyes. 'He gave me your gift and bade me return it to you.'

'Well, you shall not, you shall keep it to spend as you wish,' Lady Saunders said on a note of indignation. 'It was my gift, not his, and I would be offended if you returned it to me.'

'You are kind, cousin,' Mercy said, her soft mouth quivering at the corners. She was unused to receiving such kindness and it affected her deeply. 'I shall keep it by me for any expenses while I stay here.'

'You are our very welcome guest. Your mother was dear

to me when we were girls,' Lady Saunders said. 'I hope that you and Caroline will like each other well enough. You are of an age to be good companions. We want you to be happy with us, and to stay as long as you please.'

'Thank you,' Mercy said, her eyes so bright that she looked as if she might weep. However, she blinked and raised her head a little higher. 'I shall try to cause you no trouble, ma'am.'

'What trouble could you cause me?' Lady Saunders asked. 'No more of this nonsense, child. I am delighted to have you with us—' She broke off as her servant brought in a huge silver tray, upon which were placed delicate glasses, a Venetian flask filled with sweet wine and a plate of biscuits. 'Thank you, Martha. There, now we shall sit and have our refreshments and you shall tell me what you like to do, Mercy.'

'I do not understand you, ma'am?' Mercy looked puzzled. 'I shall be pleased to do whatever you would have me do. I am a good plain seamstress and I can cook—'

'Goodness me,' Lady Saunders said and shook her head. 'You are my guest, child. I do not want you to work for your keep. I meant what would you like to do – for pleasure? Do you like to walk or ride? Do you enjoy reading, music or fine embroidery?'

'My stepfather did not allow such pleasures,' Mercy said, a slightly guilty expression on her face. 'However, I like to sing in church and I love to read – though my stepfather has no books other than the Bible. And of course my mother used to love to embroider. I remember watching her when my father was alive . . . but he died ten years ago and then my mother married again. After that our lives changed.'

Lady Saunders frowned. It was clear that she did not find this story pleasing, but she was too good mannered to speak openly of her disgust. It seemed that Mercy's stepfather, Sir Matthew Lisle, was a hard, stern man, and in her opinion the girl had come to them none too soon.

'Well, my dear,' she said as she poured a glass of the fine wine and passed it to her guest. 'I believe you will find that your life has changed once more, and this time I trust it will be for the better.'

Mercy glanced around the room to which her cousin Caroline had conducted her, understanding at once that she had been given what must be one of the best guest chambers in this big house. It was furnished with everything she might need, the linen chests too large for her sparse wardrobe, for she had only two plain grey gowns and a black one, for church, with a white linen collar.

She had never expected her mother's cousins to live in a house like this, or that she would be welcomed as an honoured guest. Her stepfather had told her that she must be prepared to wait on her relatives and that she must behave with propriety, for he would not take her back if she disgraced him. To be received with such kindness, to be given wine such as she had never tasted and delicious sweetmeats, and asked what she liked to do for enjoyment, was beyond her dreams.

Lady Saunders had been so kind that Mercy had almost wept. She had learned to live with harsh words and unkind acts since her mother married Sir Matthew Lisle, a man of strict principles and cold eyes – and yet there were times when his eyes had held a different expression when they looked at Mercy. It was a look that had frightened her terribly, especially since her mother's death, and she had prayed that God would send her deliverance. The letter from her mother's cousin had been as an answer to her prayers, for she had feared what might happen if she was left to live with her stepfather and his two young sons. However, Sir Matthew had recently made plans to marry again, and therefore had given his grudging consent to her visit.

'I might have asked you to remember your duty to me, Mercy,' he reminded her in his harshest manner. 'However, it may not suit Sarah to have you here. Therefore you may go, but remember that your duty is to me and that you must return should we need you.'

Mercy had promised that she would respond to his

summons, for a sense of duty was strong in her, though in her heart she sometimes rebelled. There were moments when she knew she hated him, and felt sorry for the young woman who was to wed him, but as a good devout member of her stepfather's church, she knew that such thoughts were wicked and tried to subdue them. She had prayed for guidance and God had answered her prayers, for he had sent her here, away from her stepfather's house.

A shudder ran through her as she recalled an incident from a few weeks before she had left her stepfather's home. He had come into her room while she was washing herself one morning. Mercy had been wearing her shift, her foot up on a stool as she wiped the cloth over her legs and up under her linen, for she had been taught that it was a sin to be naked even in the privacy of her room. A woman's body was the temptation of the devil, she had often heard her stepfather say. But from the hot, lustful look he had given her she knew that his words belied his thoughts, which were surely sinful. She had swiftly pulled her shift down to cover her legs, facing him proudly, anger making her forget her fear.

'Your pardon, sir, but I did not hear you knock,' she said. His eyes had seemed to devour her hungrily as they dwelled on the shape of her slender body, which clearly showed beneath the thin material of her shift. 'Please leave my room at once!'

He had retreated before her indignation, but the look in his eyes had frightened her. As a child she had heard her mother weeping after he had left their bed, and there was something about him that made Mercy feel unclean when he looked at her. She suspected that he was not a good man for all his strict observance of the Lord's day.

She could only hope that she would be allowed to stay here and that she need never return. Indeed, she thought that she would rather die than live in her stepfather's house again.

'I hope you will not find it too quiet here,' Caroline said to Mercy when she came downstairs later that afternoon. 'You have been used to a market town and there is little to do here, other than walk – though the fair visits next month.'

'Do you attend the fair?' Mercy looked at her in surprise. 'Do your parents allow it?'

'We all go together,' Caroline replied. 'It is something to look forward to and my father gives my mother and I money to spend as we wish. Have you never been to a fair?'

Mercy frowned as she tried to remember. 'I think my father and mother took me once when I was very small, but my father died when I was but six years and my mother married again a year later. My stepfather does not believe in such things. He says that they are the work of Satan.'

'But that is so foolish,' Caroline said impulsively and then halted as she realized what she had said. 'Forgive me, cousin, that sounds rude – but fairs bring a day of pleasure into our lives and for many of the poor folk there is little else.'

'Do not apologize,' Mercy said and smiled at her. 'I have oft wished to visit a fair but Sir Matthew forbade it and I dared not flout his wishes.' A shiver ran through her as she recalled beatings for childish misdemeanours that had surely not deserved such strict punishment. Time and again, he had seemed to take pleasure from inflicting pain on her, and only her inner strength had carried her though. She had learned to be meek and obedient outwardly, though there was still a spark of rebellion inside her that made her question his teachings. 'He forbade many things . . .'

'Well, you are with us now,' Caroline told her. 'I am sure my parents will visit the fair as always and you shall share my money to buy treats for yourself.'

'I do not know why you and Lady Saunders are so kind to me.'

Caroline's laughter was warm and spontaneous. 'It is but common kindness we would show to any guest or friend, Mercy. You may repay us by being happy while you are with us.'

'I could not fail to be happy here,' Mercy said in such a simple manner that Caroline knew it was sincerely meant. 'Please, tell me how I may be of use to you and Lady Saunders.'

'Oh, I dare say we shall find little tasks for you,' Caroline said and gave her a mischievous look. 'My dearest mother is forever tangling her embroidery silks and someone has to sort them for her. And we like to read from the works of Master Shakespeare while we work. We take it in turns to read aloud, and you may share the task with us.'

'Oh, I should count it a privilege. For me it would be a pleasure to read such books,' Mercy replied at once. 'And your mother does such beautiful work, for I think she must be responsible for the drapes in my bedchamber and the prayer hanging above my bed.'

'Mother certainly made the drapes, and the tapestry cushions were also her work, but I made the hanging above your bed, Mercy. I put it there to comfort you lest you felt lonely away from your home.'

'Oh, no, I could not feel lonely here with you and Lady Saunders,' Mercy said and looked at her hesitantly. 'Do you think you could teach me to do work as fine as yours, Caroline? I have been permitted only plain sewing and I would so love to use those lovely silks.'

'But of course,' Caroline felt pleased that she could be of help to her cousin. 'I have many spare canvases and you may take your pick of them and my silks. And when the fair comes we shall buy some of your own choosing.'

'Thank you. Perhaps one day I shall be able to repay your kindness, Caroline.'

'Do not think of repayment, only of being my friend. And now I must tell you that we are to have a special dinner this evening in honour of your visit. Lord Mortimer and his sons Harry and Nicolas are to join us. I am soon to be betrothed to Harry Mortimer. We wait only for my seventeenth birthday.'

'Oh, how exciting for you,' Mercy said. 'I should like—'

Mercy's thoughts remained her own for at that moment they were joined by Sir John and Lady Saunders. A sweet wine was served to the ladies in the parlour, Sir John preferring a dry sack, and the conversation became general until their guests arrived.

Lord Mortimer was a large, stout man with a ruddy complexion. He talked heatedly and in a loud voice, which seemed to dominate the company. His son, however, was very different. He was as tall as his father but his hair was the colour of ripe corn, his eyes a deep violet blue that seemed to twinkle with merry laughter. He greeted Caroline with a chaste kiss on her cheek, asked her if she was well and told her that she looked beautiful. His gaze moved restlessly about the room, as if seeking something, coming to rest on Mercy and dwelling there.

Mercy found herself blushing beneath his direct stare, for she had never met with such a man before. Sir Matthew's friends were all stern, dour men who would think it wrong to look too closely at woman, unless betrothed to her. Harry Mortimer was so handsome in his fine clothes, a beautiful jay that made her more aware of her drab colours.

'You must be Caroline's cousin,' he said as he bowed to her, his eyes seeming to hold a challenge that made her tremble inwardly. 'I bid you welcome, Mistress Waldegrave.'

'Thank you, sir,' she said, lifting her head a little, for despite her modest manners, she was proud. 'I am happy to be my cousin's guest.'

'I am sure both Lady Saunders and her daughter are pleased to have you. Caro will enjoy the company, will you not?'

'Yes, indeed,' Caroline said, and then to save Mercy's blushes, 'Your brother was in a hurry as we passed earlier today. He did not accompany you here this evening?'

'Hush, Caro,' Harry warned with a glance at his father, who was fortunately not listening. 'My brother has taken himself off to his estate. He hath fallen out with my father and 'tis best not to mention him for the time being.'

'I see,' Caroline said and thought that would explain the reason for Nicolas's black face as he thundered past her. 'And you, sir, are you settled here for the summer or do you plan to return to the court?'

'That depends much on His Majesty's plans,' Harry told her. 'I accompanied him to the North after the situation in London became critical, but was given leave to return home.

I shall return to him if needed, and I believe there will be some kind of a struggle. His Majesty must teach these rebels a lesson!'

In January of that year the King had tried to arrest five members of Parliament, stubborn men who had dared to oppose him openly. However, they had been warned of his intentions and made their escape. In a fury at this further treachery, Charles had taken himself off to reflect on what to do next.

'Indeed?' Caroline frowned. Harry was employed at court in a junior position in the Lord Chancellor's office. It was, she understood, an office that troubled him little and he was free to come and go much as he wished, though he might be summoned to attend State banquets and any similar event. 'I am sorry to hear it, sir. I had hoped that things would go better now that His Majesty had recalled Parliament.'

'As did we all,' Harry said looking angry. 'There are obstinate men behind these plots, Caroline. Yet I think the King will deal with them and all will be well. It is to be hoped so – but we should not trouble ourselves over such things this evening. I would hear more of Mistress Waldegrave. Tell, me, lady, are you betrothed to some fortunate gentleman?' His merry eyes quizzed her unmercifully.

Mercy blushed as his attention fell on her once more, for she was unused to his manners, which seemed to charm and tease her, and was relieved when the housekeeper came to tell them that dinner was about to be served. However, Harry was not to be cheated of his purpose, and giving one arm to Caroline, he offered the other to Mercy. She was obliged to take it for she did not know how to refuse, though afterwards, when she saw that his father had taken Lady Saunders in, she realized that she ought to have waited for Sir John to escort her. As it was, Sir John walked in accompanied by his son, to whom Mercy had been briefly introduced but who seemed to be in some trouble with his father and had left it until the last minute to come down to the parlour.

Mercy was at a loss to know how to answer Harry's questions, and merely shook her head when he asked again if

19

she were betrothed. She was trembling inside and yet she felt more alive than she had for years, her heart racing wildly. Marriage was something she had hardly thought of in her stepfather's home. She was relieved when she discovered that she was placed between Sir John and Rupert Saunders.

'You should not tease poor Mercy,' Caroline reprimanded Harry as he held her chair for her at table. 'She is not used to it and needs to become accustomed to us before she knows how to deal with a rogue like you, sir.'

Her smile robbed her words of any sting, and Harry gave her a wicked grin. He and Caroline understood each other well, which was why he had been content to go along with his father's wishes in the matter of his betrothal. Caroline would, he believed, make a comfortable, complacent wife, and providing that he did his duty by her and provided her with a brood of children, he would be free to carry on his own independent life.

Harry was not in love with her. As yet he did not know what it meant to love with all one's heart, only with the body. He had bedded his first wench at fifteen, a fresh-cheeked country wife who had initiated him into the pleasures of the flesh. A smile flickered over his mouth as he thought of his current arrangement, which was very much more to his liking. Rowena was very different from that placid farmer's wife, and she would be waiting for him in the woods when he could finally slip away to meet her.

The thought of meeting her later made his loins throb with an urgency that he knew he must conquer. Rowena Greenslade was the blacksmith's daughter and a hot, desirable wench, but she was merely there to serve his lust. Caroline was a lady and would be his wife, and he must not neglect her – even though something about Mercy Waldegrave had aroused a feeling in him that he normally associated with wenches like Rowena.

'Then I shall not do so,' he whispered back to Caroline. 'I thought only to make her feel one of us but I would not displease you for the world, Caro.'

Caroline smiled at him. Harry's words were meant to please

and charm her, but for some reason they only served to make her more uneasy.

She fought to dispel her doubts. Her betrothal had been planned for some years and both families expected the marriage to take place before her eighteenth birthday. To even contemplate refusing what was clearly inevitable was disturbing, for she had no reason – at least there was nothing substantial that she could put her finger on. Her parents would think she had gone mad if she simply told them that she would rather not marry Harry Mortimer.

And indeed, until recently she had been quite content with the idea. She was not sure when the doubts had begun to creep in. Was it a month ago when she had seen Harry speaking with the blacksmith's daughter? He had been laughing and there had been a sly look in Rowena's eyes as she saw that Caroline had noticed them. And yet, Caroline thought that they might even have begun sooner – last Christmastide, when her family had all dined with the Mortimers at Thornberry Manor.

It had been a merry evening, and they had observed all the traditions, drinking spiced punch out of a bowl laced with good French Brandewine and apples, singing carols and playing silly games. Nicolas had given her a forfeit after he had caught her while he was wearing a blindfold. He had asked if she would have a kiss or a forfeit for her freedom and she had chosen the latter, but Nicolas would not tell her what he demanded of her.

'I must think it over,' he had told her with a teasing smile. 'For now you may escape it, Mistress Saunders, but do not forget it is owed.'

His dark eyes had been so intense that she had felt her body shiver deliciously, but she had also been afraid, wishing that she had chosen the kiss, for a kiss would have been soon over. Nicolas had never mentioned the forfeit in the months that had since passed, but sometimes she thought she saw a speculative expression in his eyes and she wondered what he planned.

But it would not do to let her thoughts wander! Caroline

brought them back to the present company, setting herself to talk to Lord Mortimer who was seated next to her.

'Do you go to court this summer, sir?' she asked for she knew that it was his habit to visit most summers. In winter the roads were sometimes so thick with mud that it was impossible to travel by coach, and she knew that he would find it too hard to ride there as his son was wont to do.

'I am not sure, Caroline,' he said with a frown. 'It was always my habit, as you know, but my son is often there and I think that perhaps my days at court are done. As a younger man, I knew King Charles well and was pleased to serve him, but now . . .' he shook his head. 'My wife enjoyed the time we spent in London but I am alone now and it hardly seems worth the trouble.'

Looking into his face, she saw that he still missed his wife, who had died of a malignant fever five summers past, and felt sympathy for him. He must be lonely up in that big house with Harry away so often at court, and Nicolas tending to his own estate.

'Harry says he thinks he shall be at home now for a while so you will have his company, sir.'

Lord Mortimer nodded, making no comment. In truth he feared he knew the reason for his son's return. As yet Harry had not confessed to more gambling debts, but there was an apprehensive look in his eyes at times that made his father wonder. Damn the lad! He would ruin the estate in time, though his father might not be there to see it for he had been experiencing some pain in his chest of late.

'I look forward to the day that my son brings you home as his bride,' he told Caroline, patting her arm. 'My house is a great empty barn and needs a woman and children to bring it back to life.'

'You are kind, sir,' Caroline said, feeling guilty.

How could she even think of asking for her betrothal to be cancelled when so many people were looking forward to it?

Two

'Where are you going, Black Eyes?' Rowena heard the taunting voice and felt the familiar thrill of excitement laced with fear. She paused, turning her head to look at the tall gypsy. Roald Vipurn both excited and frightened her for he had a wicked temper and she knew he had marked her as his woman. Thus far she had resisted him, because she had eyes only for the lord's son. 'Stay a moment and talk with me.'

'Be none of your business where I be goin',' she told him. 'I ain't none of yours, Roald Vipurn, that be sure.'

'Have I not told you that it hath been written for us?' he asked and his dark eyes glittered in the moonlight. 'Blood seeks out blood, Rowena. You belong with us, and one day you will be my woman.'

'You and your riddles,' Rowena scoffed. 'Tom Greenslade be my father and Ma be from Cornish stock. I be no blood kin to you, gypsy.'

'What is written in the stars cannot change,' he replied. 'If you go to meet the young lord you are a fool. He cares nothing for you – you are but his plaything and he will abandon you when he has done with you.'

'You be jealous,' Rowena said, her eyes sparkling with anger. She tossed her head proudly. 'He do truly love me. He will marry me no matter what his father says.'

'If you believe that you are blind,' Roald told her. He watched as she walked on, back straight, hips swaying, and her head held high. Her beauty held him in thrall, though his pride made him want to punish her for her wild ways.

Yet he knew that she would be his at the last for it had been foretold to him.

'You must wait until she comes to you,' old Greta had told him. She had read his future in the bones as well as the stars. 'If you try to enslave her you will lose her for she is as wild as the witch winds, and no man will tame her if she does not wish it.'

Roald squashed the desire to follow her. Had she given herself to the lord's son? His hands curled into tight balls at his sides. If he knew for certain, he might have killed them both. Harry Mortimer was merely using Rowena. She was foolish if she could not see it, but there was nothing he could do. His destiny and hers was written and he must bide his time.

Rowena walked on, unaware of the gypsy's thoughts. She would not allow him to dictate to her, though if she had not fallen in love with Harry Mortimer she might have been more inclined to listen. But with Roald life would be hard as they travelled the roads, working here and there, never stopping long in one place. Rowena wanted more. She wanted the wealth that marriage to a young lord could bring her and she was confident that her beauty would buy it for her.

Harry was mad for her. He had offered her presents and money but she had refused them all, sending him away with a toss of her head, and for a while he had gone, off to London and the King's court, but he had returned to her more desperate than before. Only when he had promised that she should be his wife had she finally given herself to him. She had worried that having lain with her, he might laugh and desert her, but she knew that she had satisfied him as no other woman ever had, and believed that in the end he would wed her.

Seeing him watching for her in their special place, she began to whistle a tune. Harry turned eagerly. She could tell that he wanted her, was on fire to lie with her, and she smiled inwardly. She had lost none of her power over him, and it seemed her mother's potion had worked well. Harry would never leave her while she took it. Head up, body held straight and proud, she walked slowly towards him, knowing that he could hardly wait to lie with her.

'Where have you been?' he demanded. 'I thought you weren't coming.'

'Patience, my lovey,' Rowena teased, feeling a surge of pleasure at his fretful manner. It gave her a sense of power to know that he wanted her so urgently. 'I had to wait until my father went upstairs. If he knew that I was coming to meet you he would be angry. I dare not think what he might do if he knew that . . .'

Harry silenced her as his lips fastened over hers in a demanding kiss. He did not know why his feelings were so powerfully aroused for he usually enjoyed teasing Rowena. This night all he wanted was to feel her lying beneath him, to lose himself in her sweet flesh.

'Quiet, you witch,' he hushed her, drawing her down to the soft grass. 'Lie with me, Rowena. You know I have promised you shall be my wife one day.'

'I hope you be tellin' the truth,' she said as she tangled her fingers in his hair, biting at his lips as their kisses became feverish, ravenous. 'I have a terrible temper when I be crossed, Harry Mortimer.'

'Love me,' he commanded. She would do as he bid her because their passionate coupling gave her as much pleasure as he derived from it. He felt her nails digging into his back through the fine linen of his shirt as he lifted her skirt and began to caress her, seeking out the warm moistness of her femininity. Hearing her moan softly, Harry laughed and nibbled her earlobe. 'Don't pretend that you don't love it, my sweeting. You were made for this, for me. Whatever happens, I shall not abandon you.'

A warning bell sounded in her head but she was too far gone to refuse him now. She loved him, loved what he was doing to her, longed to feel him moving inside her, deep, deep inside her.

'Betray me and you'll be sorry,' she muttered but the

words were lost as he thrust into her, making her scream with pleasure.

Harry was thoughtful as he walked home later. He had enjoyed himself with Rowena as always, but for some reason he felt unsatisfied. Rowena had responded as hotly as ever and their loving had been fierce and hungry, and yet even as he spilled himself inside her, it had been of another woman he was thinking.

Mercy Waldegrave's eyes haunted him. He did not know why, for though she was beautiful she was untouchable and as the stepdaughter of a Puritan gentleman, she was beyond him. He could not seduce her with sweet words and false promises, for she was Caroline's cousin.

Harry knew that he needed the alliance with Caroline's family. His gambling had caused his father some trouble and Lord Mortimer had been forced to raise a loan to tide them over.

Harry saw his father had waited up for him as he walked into the house. He frowned at him, clearly determined to have his say.

'Well sir, what have you to say for yourself? It's money again, I suppose?'

'Forgive me, Father. I am sorry to have lost so much money.'

'You have endangered your own inheritance,' Harry's father replied angrily. 'If things do not improve we may have to sell land. If it were not for your betrothal to Caroline Saunders I might not have been able to raise the loan without selling.'

'Are things so bad, Father?'

'Worse than you can imagine,' Lord Mortimer said gloomily. 'Oh, 'tis not all your fault, Harry. Things have not gone well for us for a few years now. I dare say I neglected my duty to the estate after your mother died. It will be best for all of us if you marry Caroline as soon as her father will allow.'

'Yes, Father. I shall leave it to you to arrange with him.'

'You must speak to Caroline herself. Discover her feelings. If she is impatient for the marriage her father may bring it forward.'

Harry had no particular wish to bring his wedding forward. In a few months he might have tired of Rowena and it would not matter, but for the moment she served her purpose. Or she had until he'd laid eyes on Mercy Waldegrave.

What was it about her that had got beneath his skin? She did not flaunt her beauty, indeed she hid it as best she could, wearing those unbecoming clothes and scraping her hair beneath a cap.

Harry cursed, wishing that he were free to follow his own wishes, for Mercy could not be had without marriage, and he was obliged to marry for the sake of his family. Nicolas was lucky. He had already inherited his mother's small estate and could please himself what he did. Although he spent much of his time at Thornberry, he was not tied to it.

Harry frowned as he wondered what his brother was doing and almost wished that he might change places with him.

'We are not a mindless rabble seeking anarchy for its own sake,' the speaker's deep voice resonated in the secular hall that belonged to the great cathedral nearby. 'We are for King and Parliament, Liberty and Property. What we ask is the right to live our lives in peace and prosperity, to be free of Charles Stuart's petty quarrels and the evil of popery.'

A rousing cheer from the onlookers made Nicolas glance about him at the determined set of faces. These men were in the main gentlemen of moderate means, the stalwart of England; men who would rather tend their fields than fight. However, a mood of resistance was gradually growing stronger. He sensed that, if called upon, these men would take up arms to defend their beliefs, as would he if necessary.

Nicolas sincerely hoped that it would not happen, that the King would return to London and come to Parliament prepared to listen to their just cause. As yet there were few here that wished to see Charles Stuart deposed, though he had heard a few angry whispers and knew that some doubted the need for a King.

'Come, Nicolas,' a voice spoke at his side. 'Let us leave these hotheads to their talk. My family expects you for supper. I hope you do not mean to disappoint them?'

Nicolas smiled at his companion. It was Master Cromwell who had invited him to this meeting, but he sensed that the man he was proud to call friend was not pleased by what he had heard that night.

'I would not disappoint your family for the world,' he replied, and after they had left the hall, walking across the green to the small whitewashed thatched cottage that stood within the shadow of the cathedral, 'You were not pleased with the meeting, sir?'

'Charles Stuart is misguided, influenced by others too easily and inclined to popery,' Oliver Cromwell replied. 'He must be brought to an understanding of his mistakes. Yet he is our King and if we take arms against him we should do it only after long and serious consideration. By that I mean that we should pray for guidance.'

'We should be traitors under the law and if our cause went badly . . .' Nicolas frowned for he had been troubled in his mind since his quarrel with his father. 'Yet I would not stand by and do nothing.'

'It is not the thought of failure that bothers me or its consequences, but of the precedent we set. Before a man takes such a step he ought to look deep inside himself, Nicolas. He must be sure that he acts for the sake of justice and for God, and not be swayed by the eloquence of others.'

'You are moderate in your thoughts, sir.'

'Nay, Nicolas, make not an idol of me, I pray you. I have wrestled with my thoughts for at times they are far from moderate. I have and shall pray for guidance in this weighty matter, sir, but I fear that it will result in a bloody war. Any God-fearing man must hate the idea of war but there are times when it becomes necessary. I may hesitate to take the step, but should I cast my hand in this I shall do all I can to bring us victory.'

'If you raise a troop, sir, I shall be proud to serve with you.'

Cromwell looked at him. 'Your father will not be pleased if you take up for Parliament against the King. You must consider well before you quarrel with him.'

'In this war I fear it will be brother against brother, father against son,' Nicolas said in a sombre tone. 'I would not have war, sir, but if it comes there is only one side for me – and that is justice for the people of this land.'

He thought but did not speak of something that had helped to set him on this course, remembering the desperation that the king's unfair taxes had brought to the family of a friend, and his own feeling of frustration at not being able to prevent the tragic consequences. For his friend's father had been forced to sell his estate and soon after had taken his own life, leaving his widow and teenage son to fend for themselves as best they could.

'We should have government by the people for the people,' he said, frowning at his thoughts.

'Well spoken, sir,' Cromwell approved. 'We have time yet for it will take months to raise an army on either side, and we must hope that in the meanwhile someone can bring His Majesty to his senses.'

Mercy sat on the little stool provided for her comfort and brushed her long hair. It was thick and glossy and she took secret pride in it though she had been forced to hide it beneath a cap for her stepfather said that a woman's hair was sinful and should not been seen by any man other than her husband.

Mercy sighed as she laid down her brush, getting to her feet to look out at the night. The stars were so beautiful and the sky so dark that it touched something within her, making her long for something that she did not understand. Until tonight she had accepted her life, expecting nothing but blows

29

and unkind words, but her gentle hostess had shown her that there could be another way to live. And the look in Harry Mortimer's eyes had made her heart behave very strangely.

She had never thought of marriage and children before, nor a home of her own. She had not dared to even dream of all the things that any young woman desired but now she was thinking of them, imagining golden-haired children held to her breast while their father looked on in the firelight.

Oh, but she was wicked to think of him. Soon he would be Caroline's betrothed. He could never be anything to Mercy or she to him. It was impossible and she must not let herself think of him.

She went to her bed, pulling back the warm quilt to slip in between the cool linen sheets. She was a guest here and she must do nothing to abuse the kindness of the people who had taken her into their home.

'Good morrow, Rowena,' Richard Woodville said when they met the next morning as the girl set out on a mission to pick herbs for her mother. 'You were late home last night.'

'Have you been spying on me, Richard Woodville?' Rowena questioned, smiling a little secret smile to herself, for she knew that he lusted after her, but she had no time for him or his mother who was a shrew with a bitter tongue. She would make the life of any woman foolish enough to marry him a misery, and Rowena did not intend to be caught in that trap. She had better things on her mind.

'I was late myself,' he told her. And I chanced to see you coming from the woods near the Manor.'

'And what business have you there?'

'That is my affair,' he replied sullenly. He had hoped to better himself with the post of secretary to Lord Mortimer but had been refused and brusquely at that. He had been educated better than most yeomen landowners, and though his holding was small he had ambitions. A place in the household of someone like Lord Mortimer would have been the first rung on the ladder that he fully intended to climb.

He would show these self-important men who thought them-selves his betters that he was not to be slighted. He would rise despite them and the time was coming when he might be given his chance. 'You would do well to smile on me, Rowena. One day I shall be an important man in these parts.'

'I wouldn't lie with you if you be the King himself,' she told him with a toss of her head.

Richard Woodville scowled at her. 'Watch your tongue, bitch. You may be sorry one day that you slighted me.'

He walked away, her laughter ringing in his ears. Rowena turned as she heard her mother calling to her from their cottage. She went reluctantly towards her for she wanted to be away. Roald would be up in the woods now and despite her determination to have Lord Mortimer's son, she liked to tease the gypsy.

'What were you saying to that man?' her mother demanded. 'You should keep away from him, Rowena. He will bring no good to you, believe me.'

'He be after me,' Rowena answered, 'but I told him he be the last man I would lie with.'

'You be sure of that,' her mother told her. 'Woodville be a dangerous man. He and his family be cursed. Have naught to do with him, girl.'

'Did you curse him?' Rowena looked at her curiously for her mother had many secrets.

'He be cursed. It be enough for you to know that,' her mother said. 'Off with you now and be sure you bring the things I need. I must make that cure tonight as the moon's waning, if 'tis to work as it should.'

Rowena walked off, as eager to leave as her mother was to see her go. She wondered about the warning as she made her way towards the woods that belonged to the Manor. Just why was her mother so particular that she should have nothing to do with Master Woodville?

'You have such pleasant gardens,' Mercy said as she and Caroline walked together that afternoon. A little sigh escaped her, for she had been here almost a month now and had come to think much of her surroundings and her new friends. 'And this is such a lovely day, Caroline.'

'Yes, it is beautiful,' Caroline said and smiled at her. Both girls were carrying baskets for they were cutting flowers and herbs from the garden, some to be used in preserves, others to adorn Lady Saunders' parlour. At their heels two small black and white lap dogs followed, short stubby tails wagging for pleasure. The scent of approaching summer was in the air, the sound of birdsong all around them. 'And the day after tomorrow it will be the first day of the fair . . .' She broke off as she saw a man walking towards them, for it was Harry and she was a little displeased with him. He had promised her that he would not tease Mercy and yet he did so continually.

'Well met the day and two ladies fair,' Harry said, a playful smile on his lips. They made a lovely picture indeed, the one so bright and pretty, like a rose, the other neat and darkly robed but beautiful beyond compare. A pale lily, perfect and forbidden. 'I see you are picking flowers – but who needs them when such beauty graces this garden in your own selves?'

'You are a wicked flatterer,' Caroline reproved him immediately. Poor Mercy was blushing and clearly upset by his teasing; she had never met with such compliments from anyone else and did not know how to answer him. 'Shall we send him away, Mercy? It is what he deserves, yet he may serve his purpose. For he shall carry our baskets and he shall meet us at the fair and treat us to some sweetmeats.'

'It was for this that I came,' Harry answered cheerfully. He took Caroline's basket from her, but Mercy shook her head as he offered to carry hers. 'I know that you usually attend the fair, Caroline, and I came to tell you that I shall be there at your service. Mayhap I shall win a prize for you.'

'We want no prizes, sir,' Caroline retorted, and tossed her head. 'Or none that we cannot win for ourselves. But you shall escort us to see the bearded lady or the two-headed dwarf, if they be on show this year.'

'They are all nonsense and meant to deceive,' Harry scoffed. 'The year before last I won ten golden sovereigns in the wrestling. It was that contest I thought to enter.'

'Then we shall not own you,' Caroline told him with a toss of her head, though her eyes sparkled with mischief. 'For 'tis a vulgar sport and fit only for common folk.'

'Oh no . . .' Mercy said and then blushed in confusion. 'I mean . . .'Tis a test of strength is it not?' Wrestling would be a sin in her stepfather's estimation, but she had begun to reject his teachings, to step out of the shadow of fear that he had cast over her and bask in the warmth of the sunshine she had found in this house.

Harry's eyes quizzed her. 'There,' he cried, well pleased with his champion. 'You are routed, Caro, for if Mistress Waldegrave says it is a fine, brave thing then you cannot in justice gainsay it.'

'Oh, Mercy,' Caroline groaned in mock reproof. 'Why must you encourage him? Last time he won he was like a bantam cock preening his feathers for weeks afterwards and there was no talking to him.'

Mercy looked at her uncertainly, saw that she was laughing and smiled. She understood that she was being teased, something that had never happened to her until she came to this house, and she discovered that she liked it very much. Especially when it was Harry Mortimer doing the teasing. Her uncertainty fell away from her like an ugly cloak, bringing a shine to her eyes. In that moment she was breathtakingly lovely, and Harry could not take his eyes from her face.

Caroline could not fail to notice his expression, which confirmed a growing suspicion in her mind. She was certain that Harry was more than a little attracted to her cousin, and felt a certain pique. He had never once looked at her as he was looking at Mercy, and if she had been a jealous individual it would have made her turn against the other girl. However, it was not Mercy's fault that Harry chose to flirt with her, and Caroline knew she had done nothing to encourage him.

Yet it made her own dilemma harder to fathom. There was now only one month until her seventeenth birthday, and then she would be betrothed to Harry. How could she marry him knowing that he did not love her as a husband ought? Her own feelings for him were mixed. She had believed for a long time that it would be pleasant to be his wife, but now she had begun to think that it would not suit her. Besides, it was unfair to Harry himself if he loved another. She had no idea how Mercy felt about him, but if she cared for him . . .

Caroline brought her thoughts back to the present as she realized that Harry was speaking to her. 'Forgive me, I did not hear what you said just then, sir.'

'Your thoughts were far away,' Harry said with a little frown. 'I was saying that the day after the fair I must leave for York. I have been summoned to the King, though I shall return in time for our betrothal, Caro.'

'My father says that His Majesty is raising an army,' Caroline said. 'I do not think that he agrees with this way of solving the quarrel between the King and Parliament. He says that His Majesty would do better to return to London and treat with the people, than to cast the country into civil war, which would be a shameful act.'

'You mean go cap in hand to those arrogant men who believe that they know better than His Majesty?' Harry's eyes narrowed and his face hardened in a way that Caroline had never seen before. 'He rules by divine right, and by heaven I swear he shall never bend the knee to such tyrants while I and others of like mind have breath to defend him.'

'Harry, do not speak of such things,' Caroline said, looking at him in distress. 'You cannot want war – not a war that would tear this country apart and set neighbour against neighbour?'

'It was those stubborn men that began this,' Harry said and his eyes were flinty. 'Had they not forced His Majesty to give up Stafford and humiliated him, it would not have come to this, but when the five members were warned it showed the King that he could not trust any of them. He has set up his court in York and those who would fight for him are gathering now to pledge their support.'

A little shiver ran down Caroline's spine, for she had heard her father arguing with Rupert over the affair. Her brother was all for the King and Sir John had reacted angrily, telling him that he was a fool and too young to understand the causes of the trouble.

'Well, we shall miss you,' she said for she wished an end to the conversation. 'But we shall enjoy ourselves tomorrow, Harry, and will hear no more of this matter if you please.'

'Your wish is my command, my lady,' he said, but his eyes were on Mercy, who had bent to add a small rosebud to her basket. He noticed that her gown had caught on a thorn and bent to free her before she had noticed it. 'I fear your gown has snagged a little, Mistress Waldegrave – but tomorrow you may buy cloth for a new gown, and I pray you, let it be blue or green for those colours would be more worthy of you than this dull grey you favour.'

'I wear grey for my mother, who is not more than six months dead,' Mercy said quietly. 'But my stepfather does not approve of bright colours for a woman's gown. He says it is immodest.'

'Be damned to his prating,' Harry muttered. 'And all such men, for they would have us on our knees the day long and see no beauty in anything. Give me a lovely woman, a jug of good wine and the leisure to enjoy them both. I will not apologize for enjoying such things for without them life would not be worth the living.'

Mercy's cheeks blushed scarlet, her lips moved as if she would reply, but then she shook her head and turned away to Caroline. 'I think we have cut enough for Lady Saunders' needs,' she said. 'I shall take the baskets up to the house and leave you to talk to your betrothed, Caroline. If you please, sir.' She held out her hand for the basket Harry carried, and something in her manner made him relinquish it to her without protest.

'I think Mistress Waldegrave is displeased with me,' Harry

said as she walked away, her back very straight. 'I believe I have offended her.'

'You should be ashamed of yourself,' Caroline scolded. 'Mercy is not used to your ways, Harry. I know you mean no harm by them, but she is still in mourning for her mother.'

'I had forgot that for the moment,' Harry said and looked thoughtful. 'Do you not think she would look better in blue or green?'

'Yes, of course she would,' Caroline said. 'She is beautiful – far more beautiful than I am. Even in her dull gowns she is remarkable, but dressed as you would have her she would be glorious.'

'Yes, she would,' Harry agreed, and then realizing what he had said, 'But you misjudge yourself, Caro. You are also very lovely.'

'I thank you for the compliment,' Caroline said and laughed for she was not a vain girl. 'I am pretty enough but I know that I could not hold a candle to my cousin. However, I do not mind that, for I am fond of her – very fond, Harry. I should not like it if someone were to hurt her.'

Harry heard the odd note in her voice and understood that she was warning him, very gently, subtly, but still a reminder.

'I am sure that I would never wish to hurt her,' he said. 'I am content with my future as it stands, Caro – but a man may look, may he not?'

'Yes, certainly,' Caroline agreed. 'I should be a fool if I did not expect my husband to look at a pretty woman, Harry – but I should be most upset if it went beyond that.'

Harry was silenced, his smile gone for the moment. It was the first hint that he had had from her that she was not quite the complacent wife he had imagined she would be.

Caroline had been to the village with gifts for a poor woman that lived alone, and of whom her mother had recently heard worrying reports.

'You must take Mother Edwards some good beef broth and a wedge of ham,' Lady Saunders had told her daughter earlier that morning. 'We have so much, and it is our duty to be charitable to others, especially those in need, and I hope you will remember that when you are mistress of your own house, Caroline.'

'Yes, Mother,' Caroline had replied, for like her mother she had a tender heart and it distressed her to hear of anyone in need.

Having delivered her mother's gift to the old woman, and spoken to the neighbour who was kindly seeing to her fire and feeding her, Caroline began her journey home. She felt sad for she had sensed that the old woman would not survive long and there was nothing that she or her mother could do to prevent it.

As she crossed the meadow where the fair was to be held, she saw that the gypsies had begun to set up camp there, and she paused to glance at their caravans and horses. She saw an old woman together with a young girl gathering mushrooms that often grew in a damp corner of the meadow, and they looked up from their work as Caroline approached.

'Good morrow,' she said, smiling at them in a friendly way for she had no fear of the gypsies, who had been coming to her village for as long as she could recall. 'Have you found some good mushrooms? I picked some yesterday and they were delicious.'

'Good morrow, Mistress Saunders,' the old woman said. 'I thank you for your enquiry – and yes, we have been lucky.' She showed Caroline her basket, which was filled not only with the meadow mushrooms but other fungi that was found only in the woods.

'Those look good,' Caroline said. She was about to walk on when the gypsy woman laid a skinny hand on her arm. 'Did you want something?'

'Would you have me tell your fortune?'

'I have no money with me,' Caroline said. 'I thank you for the offer but . . .'

'You do not need money,' the woman said. 'You do not yet know it but you have what some call the gift of *sight*. It will not always be a blessing, but it will grow as you grow older.'

'I think you mean to tease me,' Caroline said, but could not help but feel fearful for already she understood what the old woman meant. There had been times when she had sensed something was about to happen, but she had always dismissed it, finding excuses in her own mind when it did. 'Surely you are the one with such a gift?'

'Aye, that which I have is stronger than yours, mistress, but you have it for those you love whether you wish it or no.'

'If you know so much,' Caroline said, a sceptical look in her eyes, 'tell me if I shall gain my heart's desire?'

'You do not yet know your heart's desire,' the woman told her. 'I shall tell you that your life will be long and happy, but there will be one happiness denied you . . .'

'Only one?' Caroline's laughter was like the sound of church bells on the air. 'How fortunate I am, Granny. I thank you for your fortune telling and I wish you good health and prosperity.'

'My blessing goes with you, mistress.' The gypsy gave her a toothless smile. 'Your husband will be a lucky man . . .'

Caroline was laughing softly to herself as she walked on. For a moment the gypsy's words had chilled her, but the rest was all nonsense, the kind of thing that women parted with their money for at the fair, and she dismissed the small incident from her mind.

Mercy was at her sewing. She had mended all the things she could find, and now, feeling that she could not be blamed for doing what she liked best, she was embroidering a pretty tapestry that Caroline had given her. It would be used as the cover for a cushion in the large front parlour and was one of a set, which meant that she was being very careful. She would not want it to be less beautifully worked than those Lady Saunders and Caroline had done themselves.

Her thoughts had been wandering and she pricked her

finger. A tiny spot of blood came to the surface and she sucked it so that it would not spoil the work, but it would not stop so she got up and went to wash her hands in cold water in the little basin provided for her ablutions.

She paused to look out of the window, across the meadow to the fair beyond. Then, as she saw Caroline approaching, she turned and went downstairs to greet her cousin.

'Oh, Mercy, such fun,' Caroline told her. 'I so wished that you were with me so that you could have heard . . .'

'What do you mean, cousin?' Mercy asked, for she could see that Caroline was laughing. 'I thought you went to see a sick old woman?'

'I did and she, poor thing, is quite ill. I do not think she will live long,' Caroline said, her laughter fading. 'But it was as I was walking home that I met a gypsy in the meadow. She insisted on telling my fortune for nothing. She said that I would have a long and happy life, though there would be one thing that I desired which I should not be granted. If I shall lack only one thing I must be happy indeed, do you not think so, Mercy?'

'Yes, indeed,' Mercy said and gave a little shiver. 'I am glad you can laugh, Caroline. I do not care for gypsies. One of their kind came to my stepfather's house once and . . .' She shook her head. 'No, I shall not say it for it was nonsense.' The gypsy had foretold a terrible tragedy that would fall upon her but she had put it from her mind, refusing to believe the woman's tales.

Caroline thought that she looked upset and wished that she had not told her. It was clear that Mercy's fortune had not been as pleasant as hers.

'Well, it is all nonsense anyway,' she said. 'Now tell me, dearest. What have you been doing while I was gone?

Rowena saw that the gypsies had camped in the far meadow where they stayed every year at fair time. She knew that Roald would be with them. He was a prince of the true Romany blood, though he often travelled alone, for he was a gifted singer and made a living entertaining people at the inns wherever he stopped, returning to his people only at times like these when they gathered together for a special reason.

As she lingered near the camp, a girl and an old woman came over to her. The girl was young, perhaps fourteen, a pretty slight thing with a friendly smile.

'Would you like my grandmother to tell your fortune?' she asked. 'Come to our fire and join us in a meal.'

Rowena hesitated, then went with them. A stew was cooking in a large black pot over the fire and its smell was tantalising. Her stomach rumbled hungrily for it was some hours since she had eaten.

'What would you have of me for the reading?'

'For you there is no charge,' the old woman said. 'Give me your hand, girl. I shall tell you where your future lies.'

Rowena held out her hand, her heart racing nervously as the long dark fingers curled about it, the nails yellowed and curling like a hawk's talons. For a moment she was tempted to pull it back but something in the woman's eyes held her.

'Blood will to blood,' the woman said. 'Though you fight your destiny it will come to you. What you desire shall also be yours but it shall end in bitterness. Only when you accept your blood shall you be free.'

'You talk in riddles,' Rowena said. There was something mesmerising about the old woman's eyes that made her afraid. She felt coldness at the nape of her neck and for a moment she smelled death, the decaying stink of rotten flesh. She jerked her hand away, turning and running across the meadow as the fear rippled through her. She did not stop running until she reached the highroad, and even then the fear was still in her.

Mercy looked about her at the bright stalls and the games taking place in the far end of the meadow. She could see that the wrestling ring was surrounded by people and could hear the cheering. To one side of the wrestling arena the tug-of-war was taking place between the villagers of Thornberry and some of the travelling men. In the far field the gypsy folk were camped, their wagons drawn up in a circle, the horses tethered and cropping the rich grass.

She and Caroline had already visited the sideshows, which, thankfully, in Mercy's opinion, did not feature anyone with two heads, though there was a very fat bearded lady. Mercy was not certain that the beard was real but she did not mention her doubts to her cousin, for Caroline had been full of pity for the woman.

There was also a tent in which you could have your fortune told. It seemed that there was always someone waiting to hear what the gypsy had to tell them, but Mercy was glad that her cousin did not suggest that they should have their fortunes told. She still recalled what she had been told by a woman who had come to the house, and it had haunted her for a time, because it had foretold death. No, she would not think of it! She was here to enjoy herself and she meant to do just that.

They had seen a dancing bear, horses performing all manner of tricks, and a collection of birds of prey, some of which were allowed to fly free and returned to the hand of their master lured by fresh meat. There were all manner of stalls, such as apples on strings to be eaten with the hands tied behind the back, and these were attracting the children, also shooting arrows into a barrel, throwing dice for trumpery prizes, and bowling for a pig.

But the stalls selling various goods were those attracting most of the attention, and the girls wandered from merchant to merchant, examining the fine cloth, lace and trimmings to be found. Besides the cloth merchants there were tinkers with pots and pans, trinkets from foreign lands, religious relics, and cheap toys for the children – little peg dolls and flags on sticks. And to be avoided at all costs unless in dire need, there was also the booth of the man who pulled out rotten teeth.

There were also the pie stalls and others selling honey and

sweetmeats, all kinds of preserves and cakes, potions, cures – and a love potion that was offered to young ladies with a sly look. Caroline bought some candied fruits and shared them with Mercy. At first she was shy of eating them because it was not good manners to eat in public, but Caroline ate hers and everyone else seemed to be munching on something, so Mercy tasted hers and found it delicious. She ate one with relish, but kept the others in a kerchief for another time.

'Mother said we were to purchase enough cloth for a gown each and also the trimmings we desired to compliment it,' Caroline told her as they came to the end of their first walk down the line of merchants' stalls. 'I have seen some green silk that I like very much – and I saw a pale grey that I thought you might like, cousin.'

'Do you mean the very pale, pearly grey that seems to have colours in it when the light catches it?' Mercy had noticed it too and liked it at once, but she had hesitated to mention it for she feared it must be costly.

'Yes, I thought it would make a suitable dress for the evenings,' Caroline said. 'It is grey and therefore in keeping with your mourning, but very attractive. Did you not think so?'

'I thought it lovely,' Mercy said. 'But are you sure Lady Saunders would sanction such a purchase? It must be expensive and there are plainer cloths that I might choose.' Indeed, she ought not to be tempted for her stepfather would not have allowed it, but the cloth had caught her eye.

'My mother would certainly approve – but here she comes and you may ask her for yourself.'

Lady Saunders came up to them. 'Are you enjoying yourselves?' she asked. 'And have you chosen the cloth yet?'

'I think so,' Caroline replied. 'We shall show you, and then you may give us your opinion.'

As she had expected, Caroline's mother immediately approved their choices and ordered the cloth to be delivered to her house. They spent another half an hour choosing lace, beads and ribbons with which to dress their new gowns, and then moved towards one of the large tents where refreshments were being served.

To reach the refreshment area, they had to pass by the wrestling ring and Mercy noticed that Harry had just won his bout. He was standing in front of the crowd, his arms in the air and stripped to the waist, enjoying the cheering that came his way. Catching Mercy's eye, he bowed to her and winked, bringing a flush to her cheeks and making her heart race wildly.

She followed hastily in the wake of Lady Saunders, wishing that she had had the modesty not to look as she passed the wrestling ring. It was very wrong of her to have hoped she might see Harry Mortimer. He was soon to be betrothed to Caroline, and he was also a Royalist by choice. He stood for everything that she had been taught to despise. She ought not to like him, and she knew that he could never be anything to her, but despite being taught to disapprove of such things, which were surely sinful, she could not help feeling pleased that he had won his contest.

After she had partaken of ale and cinnamon cake, Mercy was surprised and startled to see Harry coming towards them, his arms full of things he had bought from the fair. Her heartbeat rose as he bowed to her, mischief in his eyes.

'I won as I promised,' he announced, 'and I have brought presents for two beautiful ladies.'

His gifts included a silk neckerchief for both her and Caroline, besides some beads and embroidery silks from the peddlers. None of these were of great value, but the neckerchiefs were pure silk and soft to the touch. Hers was a dark emerald green, with fringes of black and spangled with coloured beads. It was a wonderful gift and she hardly knew how to thank him for it.

'You are too generous, sir,' she whispered, not daring to look at him for fear that her eyes might give her away. 'I shall treasure your gift.'

'I hope you will wear it for it will suit you,' Harry said

and then turned to Caroline. 'I hope that you like your gift, Caro?'

'You know that I do,' she replied, for hers was a bold crimson trimmed with a dark gold fringe. 'Thank you, sir. You are wasteful with your money but we shall not scold you for it.'

'I won ten golden sovereigns in the wrestling ring,' Harry said and grinned at her. 'What better way to spend it than on those who deserve it most?'

'You have a silver tongue, sir,' Caroline chided him, but she was smiling. 'We do thank you for your generosity.'

'So it has been a successful day all round,' Lady Saunders said. 'I think we shall go home now, my dears, for I saw Sir John leaving a while ago.' He had not looked too pleased about something and she was a little worried that he might have been quarrelling with someone, for he had not been in the best of moods that day. She believed that he and Rupert might have had words before they left for the fair earlier that morning.

'Shall we see you before you leave, sir?' Caroline asked of Harry, remembering that he had said he was leaving them.

'I think not,' he replied. 'But I shall write to you if I have the time.'

'Very well,' Caroline said. 'We shall meet again in a few weeks from now.'

'Until then . . .' Harry bowed over the hand she gave him and kissed it. He glanced at Mercy but she merely inclined her head and looked beyond him, her cheeks slightly heated.

Harry frowned as he watched them walk away. His betrothal was fast approaching, and the nearer it came the less he liked the idea of it. Catching sight of Rowena Greenslade he felt his spirits lift. He had not met her for some days now, but he would this night. He would give her a gift, something pretty that would make her grateful. Perhaps a neckerchief similar to the ones he had given Mercy and Caroline.

He smiled to himself as he made his way back towards

the silk merchants. He would buy a small gift for Rowena and arrange to meet her in their special place that night.

'You will have no more to do with that family, do you understand me, madam?' Sir John looked angrily at his wife as she stood in dumbfounded silence. 'After what has passed between us this day, my friendship with Lord Mortimer is at an end.'

'You cannot mean it?' Lady Saunders found her voice at last. Summoned to her husband's library on their return from the fair, she had not expected this. 'What of Caroline? She was to be betrothed to Harry on her birthday.'

'That is ended,' Sir John said coldly. 'I will not have my daughter marry a scoundrel. His father made it quite clear where he stood today, and it seems Harry will also fight for the King.'

'But . . . you have always said that it was best we had a king,' his wife said, feeling bewildered. This was all so sudden that she could not take it in nor begin to understand what had happened. 'I know you were against the taxes he imposed and you disagreed with the Court of Star Chamber, but you were for the King himself.'

'That was before I heard that he plans to hire Irish Catholic mercenaries to fight against his own people. If Charles Stuart hath his way we shall be brought under the heel of the Pope before many months hath passed.'

'Surely not?' Lady Saunders was upset by the news for she had heard from her own mother as a child of the cruelty that Queen Mary had imposed upon the people in the name of Catholicism. Indeed, her grandfather had been tortured for refusing to give up his faith, though saved from the fire by payment of a large fine. 'You cannot believe that, husband? It is just a tale put about by those who hate His Majesty.'

'It is oft and truly said that there can be no smoke without fire,' Sir John said. A man of mild temperament and courteous manners, he could be stubborn when aroused, and he was smarting from the quarrel with his neighbour. It was not only the politics involved, but also Lord Mortimer's manner that had aroused his anger to a pitch beyond bearing. Mortimer had shown no respect for Sir John, and when he had tried to put his own point of view he had been shouted down. 'I believe that His Majesty may have made mistakes, but I shall not be told that I am a bigoted fool by any man. You know that I have no time for these canting Puritans, Lady Saunders, but the King must be made to see that he rules by the consent of the people, not as a right. He should consult with Parliament to bring justice for all.'

Lady Saunders was saddened for she knew how stubborn her husband could be, and sensed that this quarrel with an old friend had offended and hurt him.

'I agree with your views, husband,' she said quietly. 'But to forbid the friendship – and with Caroline's betrothal so close . . .'

'I believe it is the best thing,' Sir John said frowning. 'It was my dearest wish as you know, wife, but I have recently heard whispers of a nature I find unpleasant concerning Harry Mortimer. I was considering whether I should investigate the matter further before having a word with Harry, but this will put an end to it.'

'You are sure you will not reconsider?'

'My mind is set. I shall not change it.'

'For myself I do not mind the breach,' his wife said, 'but it will be distressing for our daughter. Caroline has been expecting this match for so long now that it would come as a shock to her.'

'I think you will discover that she does not mind so very much,' Sir John said, looking thoughtful. 'I am not at all sure that it was Caroline's wish to marry into that family. Indeed, I believe she may be relieved that it is no longer considered her duty.'

'But . . . there is no one else suitable living close by.' Lady Saunders was not particularly surprised by his statement, for she too had noticed something in her daughter's manner of late. 'How can we arrange another match for her?'

'Give me a little time,' Sir John said. 'I have not yet had the leisure to consider. Perhaps we shall take her to visit one of our friends. Mayhap to a relative or some good family where there is the possibility of a connection. Do not fear, my dear. Caroline is a pretty girl with a sweet if lively manner, and she will inherit a decent portion besides her dowry for there is more than enough for our son. Therefore I do not think it impossible that another match be found to please her. Indeed, I am certain that we may do something for her – she is too pretty to remain unwed for long.'

'I am sure you are right,' Lady Saunders said and looked thoughtful. 'Yes, you *are* right, husband. We must give this matter our consideration. After all, there is no particular hurry. Caroline will be but seventeen next month, which is young enough to look elsewhere for a husband.' Indeed, she had never been sure that his choice of a husband for their daughter was a good one, but she had never questioned it openly.

'It is best that you go and tell her,' Sir John said. 'Make it plain that there must be no contact between the Mortimers and our family, none at all. I shall make the position clear to Mortimer myself by letter. He must understand that all idea of the betrothal is at an end. There is no need for Caroline to suffer embarrassment.'

'Yes, of course, if that is your wish.'

Lady Saunders left him to contemplation of his wine, knowing that his anger would abate and that regret would set in. Such a shocking turn of events had upset her and she was at a loss as to how to deal with it for the best. It might be that her husband would change his mind in time, but for the moment they must all obey his wishes.

She could only hope that he would relent in time, for the families had been friends too many years for it to end this way.

Three

'You are forbidden to speak to Harry?' Mercy stared at Caroline in shocked disbelief. 'But how can this be? You were to have been betrothed soon . . .'

'My father hath quarrelled with Lord Mortimer,' Caroline said. She was still feeling stunned and did not know whether she ought to be upset or relieved. Of late she had begun to think that it would not suit her to wed Harry, but now that she had been forbidden to speak to him she felt rather strange. 'Mother hopes that my father may relent but somehow I cannot think it. He must be terribly angry or he would not have ordered us to break all contact with the family. We have been friends for so long that it seems odd.'

'I do not know how you can accept this so calmly,' Mercy said, tears in her eyes. 'It is so very cruel. You must be heart-broken, cousin.'

'I am upset, of course,' Caroline replied. 'But I do not believe that my heart is broken. I think Father will feel this breach more deeply than I shall. He has been a close friend of Lord Mortimer for so many years. It is a shame that this quarrel between the King and Parliament should cause such trouble between old friends.' Her brow creased in a frown for she was deeply upset, for her beloved father more than her own self.

Mercy looked at her sadly. 'I think you are very brave. Had it been I who must lose my betrothed I should have wept bitter tears.' As it was she felt like weeping for she could not bear the thought that she might never see Harry again.

Caroline was silent for a moment, then, 'Perhaps it is you

who will suffer from this estrangement more than I, Mercy.'

'What can you mean?' Mercy said looking embarrassed. 'I have lost nothing.'

Caroline gave her a straight look. 'I shall not tease you, cousin, but I have wondered if you felt some fondness for Harry – and he for you?'

'You cannot think that I would abuse your kindness by encouraging any attention from your intended?'

'No, indeed, I know you would not, ' Caroline said. She could sense Mercy's distress but would not add to it. 'However, had Harry not been intended for me it might have been otherwise.'

'I – I do not know,' Mercy said, her cheeks pale. 'I would not allow myself to think of . . .' Yet she had dreamed of it, seeing herself as Harry's wife.

'I know that you have done nothing to harm me,' Caroline assured her. 'Do not look so upset, Mercy. This is none of your making and may prove to be a blessing.'

'Do you truly not mind?' Mercy was still shocked by Caroline's calm acceptance of the situation.

'I feel empty at the moment,' Caroline confessed. 'I have been accustomed to the idea of living at Thornberry as its mistress, and I am fond of Harry and his father. However, I am not in love with Harry Mortimer.'

'Yet you have lost much, Caroline.'

'Friendship, yes. The consequence of being Lady Mortimer one day, but that means nothing. As yet I do not know how I shall fill my life, but no doubt I shall learn to be content . . .' She smothered a sigh. 'But for now I must remember to behave with dignity. Mother has asked me to walk down to the village with a message and I shall oblige her.'

'I could go in your stead if you wished to be quiet for a while,' Mercy offered.

'Thank you for the thought, cousin, but I believe the air will do me good. I should be restless at home but walking will help me to think clearly.'

Mercy nodded and said no more as Caroline left her. She

was still distressed by the news and believed that her cousin was being brave, hiding her feelings.

But if this ban were true it altered things. Harry was no longer bound to Caroline and there might be a chance for Mercy . . . but no, she must not allow herself to hope. Such a match could never take place. Her stepfather would forbid it even if she dared to defy the people who had treated her so well.

A sob rose in Mercy's throat. She was foolish and wrong to care for Harry Mortimer. She must put him from her mind at once.

Alone with her thoughts, Caroline admitted to having mixed emotions. She had known Harry for such a long time and Nicolas too. The ban imposed by her father must also extend to him. A sharp pang of regret made her eyes sting suddenly as she realized there would be no more Christmas celebrations at Thornberry; no more foolish games of Blind Man's Buff.

How foolish of her to regret such childish games! She must not allow herself to continue in this fashion for it would do no good. She lifted her head as she set out to walk to the Rectory with her mother's message. Lady Saunders had decided to invite the Reverend and his wife to dine in an attempt to lift their spirits, though it could only make them more aware of their loss, for the Mortimer family had been cheerful company. It was not only she who had lost by this, Caroline knew, for her parents would miss their nearest neighbour.

As yet no word of the quarrel between Sir John and Lord Mortimer had reached the village and she was able to carry her head high, which might not be the case in future. She knew that one consequence of her father's actions might be that she would be pitied, for some might believe that she had been jilted. She would find such speculation distasteful, Caroline thought, but must be ready to accept it.

Her intended betrothal was of such long standing that it must be widely known, and it might mean that no other gentleman would think of asking her to marry him. While no fault was attached to her, some might wonder and she could suffer a loss of reputation.

Her visit with Mistress Blackwell was brief but pleasant. However, as she returned from her errand, Caroline saw the blacksmith's daughter standing outside the forge. Rowena Greenslade was carrying a basket over her arm, which looked as if it contained wild herbs. It was well known that she often picked such things from the hedgerows or the woods. Her mother made cures and potions that were said to help many illnesses and Caroline had heard it whispered more than once that Sally Greenslade was a witch – that she could ill wish as well as cure folk.

Such whispers could mean trouble for the woman so named for in times of unrest folk looked for someone to blame. However, the village of Thornberry was peaceful enough and its inhabitants were in good health. Besides, Master Greenslade was a large, powerful man and had a terrible temper. Very few would dare to speak out openly against his wife.

'Good day, Mistress Saunders,' Rowena said as Caroline approached her. 'Did you enjoy your day at the fair?'

'Yes, thank you, Mistress Greenslade,' Caroline replied. She noticed that the girl was wearing an expensive silk neckerchief very like the ones that Harry had given her and Mercy. 'I see that you visited the silk merchants yourself.'

'Oh no,' the girl said, eyes bright, a contemptuous smile on her cherry red lips. 'This neckerchief be a present from my intended. I be goin' to marry soon.'

'Indeed? That is good news. I wish you joy, Mistress Greenslade.'

Why did she feel that the girl's black eyes mocked her? Caroline wondered about it for a few moments as she walked on, conscious that Rowena was watching her. And then she forgot the girl as her attention was taken by children playing a game, hopping on one leg from one square they had drawn in the dust of the road to another. She stood and watched for a moment, a smile on her lips, exchanging a word with an old man driving his pig along the street. As she left the tiny cottages behind, she was thinking of reaching her home and helping her mother to sort the linen chests.

It was as she was crossing the meadow that bordered her father's estate that she saw a rider coming towards her. She thought it might be Harry and suddenly realized that she was on land that belonged to the Mortimers. She had often used this shortcut to her home in the past, but she ought to have taken the longer route. She hesitated as she saw that the rider had seen her, and then, as he slowed his horse to a walk, her heart began to race as she realized that it was Nicolas.

For a moment she found it difficult to breathe and she wondered what she ought to do, for it was clear that he meant to speak to her.

''Tis a fine day, Caroline,' he said smiling down at her. 'Have you been to the village?'

'On an errand for my mother,' she said, her cheeks pink with embarrassment. 'Forgive me, I . . .' She hesitated as she considered how best to extricate herself. It was no use; she could not simply ignore him! 'You have been away. Perhaps you have not yet spoken to your father?'

'Is something amiss?' Nicolas frowned.

'I fear 'tis so. Your father and mine have quarrelled and all friendship is at an end between our families. Father has forbidden my mother and I to speak to any of you . . .'

'Forbidden . . .' Nicolas stared at her for a moment in silence. 'But you were to have married Harry . . .'

'That too is forbidden,' Caroline said and bit her lip. 'My father would be angry if he knew that I had ignored his wishes by stopping to speak with you like this but I could not just ignore you, sir. We have been friends for so long.' To her dismay a tear trickled from the corner of her eye and she had to catch her breath for the breach had suddenly become painful, more painful than she could ever have imagined. All at once she did not know how she could bear it.

Nicolas slid down from his horse's back as he saw her distress. The tears were falling now and she could not prevent them, her body trembling as he reached out and drew her close, stroking her hair as she let her emotions free, her head against his shoulder, sobbing.

'Surely he will relent?' Nicolas murmured as he held her. 'No father would willingly see his daughter break her heart. You have been robbed of your happiness.'

'No . . .' Caroline detached herself, wiping a hand across her cheeks. 'No, it is not that I mind so very much if I do not marry your brother,' she whispered. 'But we have all been such good friends.'

Nicolas looked down at her, handing her his kerchief to wipe her cheeks. 'You were not in love with my brother?' She shook her head wordlessly. 'But you would have married him?' He was surprised for he had thought her happy with the arrangement. It was the reason he had been so stern with himself, for as his brother's promised wife she had been forbidden him.

'It was arranged,' she said in a whisper. She offered him his kerchief but he shook his head and she slipped it into her bodice. 'And I liked him well enough. I – like all of you.'

'Even me?' Nicolas's eyes held a questing expression. It was said in a careless way and yet she sensed his tension as he waited for her answer.

'Yes, of course.' She blushed and could not meet his eyes. 'It was only when I thought of losing . . .' Realizing what she had been about to say she stopped. 'I must go. My father would be angry if he saw us speaking like this.'

Nicolas stood back, allowing her to pass, but then he ran after her, catching her arm, swinging her back so that she looked up at him in surprise. 'He will relent,' he said and his eyes had such an intent expression that Caroline shivered. She felt the simmering passion he held inside. 'He must and shall relent. Believe it, Caroline.'

She gazed at him, confused as much by her own emotions as the look in his eyes, the intensity of passion he was battling to suppress. However, he released her almost immediately and she walked on, her heart thudding. How was it that he had made her aware of how much she would miss her friendship with him and his family in a way that the cancellation of her betrothal had not?

She had not cried for Harry's loss, but seeing Nicolas, speaking to him, had caused her heart to ache. Caroline could not understand why she was suddenly feeling so miserable. It was Harry she was to have married not Nicolas. And yet, it was the thought of never being able to speak to Nicolas again that was causing her so much pain.

It had rained overnight and the hedgerows were dripping when Rowena saw the gypsy girl that morning. She was picking wild herbs, her basket almost full. She hesitated, waiting as the girl came up to her, seeing that she too had been gathering twigs and berries.

'You were frightened by my grandmother's words,' the girl said without waiting for her to speak. 'They were meant to warn you not to frighten you.'

'It was just the . . .' Rowena paused, knowing that she could not speak of the stench that had seemed to come from the old woman, the stench of the open grave. 'I was frightened for a moment but I am not now. My name is Rowena. You did not tell me yours?'

'I am Carlina,' the girl said. 'I knew your name for Roald has spoken of you. He wants you as his woman.'

Rowena saw something in her face then, guessing that she wanted the Romany prince for herself, that she envied her her hold on him.

'I do not want him,' she said. 'There is another I love. If you are patient he may turn to you.'

The girl shook her head. 'It is not written for me,' she said. 'My destiny is short. I cannot change it. But I wanted to see you, to speak to you, for I know that you will bring luck to our people. Your son will return to his blood and the fruits of his labours shall be good for us.'

'I have no son. 'Tis all nonsense,' Rowena said. 'Did your grandmother tell you this?'

'Greta is wise. She knows that I have but a short time to

live and I have accepted her words for she told me that when death comes I shall embrace it.'

Rowena shivered. She felt as if she were in the middle of a cold wind that carried her with it despite her will.

'I say it be naught but faery tales,' she declared. 'You be young and strong. Your time cannot be soon.'

Yet even as she spoke the words she knew that the girl did not believe her, and in truth she did not believe herself.

Mercy was in the gardens that morning when she saw Harry Mortimer coming towards her. She paused in the act of picking a rose, her pulse racing. Her hand trembled, her eyes darting here and there as if seeking escape. What was she to do? If she spoke to him it would be in direct disobedience to her host's wishes, and she would not offend Sir John for the world, for he and his family had been so generous to her. Yet something inside her was urging her to stay and at least exchange a greeting with Harry.

'Good day, Mistress Waldegrave,' Harry said. There was a grim line about his mouth, the merry smiles he had previously given her noticeably absent. 'I pray you, where might I find Caroline?'

'I do not know, sir,' Mercy said truthfully. 'I believe she went out with Lady Saunders earlier this morning.'

'Then you may deliver a message for me, for I have no time to tarry. I must answer His Majesty's summons – but you will please tell Caroline that I shall return for our betrothal as arranged. This estrangement is none of my making. If she will not marry me I would hear it from her own lips.' Harry was furious over his father's ultimatum, not least because he had been relying on her fortune to settle debts he had not yet dared to tell his father he owed.

'But . . .' Mercy was flustered and became more so as she heard an angry shout behind them, and then Sir John was striding towards them. 'How dare you come here, sir?' he demanded of Harry, his face dark with temper. 'As for you, girl, into the house with you. Have I not told you that you are to have nothing to do with this scoundrel?'

Mercy threw a look of apology at Harry and moved away towards the house, her eyes stinging with unshed tears. Behind her she could hear the men shouting at each other. Sir John was in a fine rage and though she could catch only a few words, she knew that he had said terrible things to the man Caroline was to have married. It did not all concern Harry's intention to join the King either. There was also some mention of a woman called Rowena Greenslade.

Mercy's thoughts were in confusion as she went into the house. It was not she who had been robbed of her betrothed, but Caroline. She had no reason to feel so distressed – but she did. It was very wrong of her. All her instincts, her upbringing, were against it, but her heart told her that she had fallen in love with Harry Mortimer. He was a Royalist and, if she had heard right, a wicked flirt for he had betrayed Caroline with this other woman. Even if he cared for Mercy enough to offer marriage now that he was free of his promise to Caroline, her family would never accept it.

Her heart was aching as she went up to her room. How foolish she was to care for a man who could never be hers.

'It is finished I tell you,' Lord Mortimer thundered at his younger son. 'The friendship between our families is ended. Harry will not marry Saunders' daughter and you will oblige me by not mentioning this subject again.'

'But you were all for the match,' Nicolas persisted though he could see the angry flush spreading up his father's neck. 'I thought you were counting on her dowry to pay some of the estate's debts?'

'We must sell land, that's all there is to it,' Lord Mortimer replied. 'I sought to keep the estate intact for Harry, but it was he who brought us to this sorry state and he who must take the consequences.'

'Would it not be better to mend fences?' Nicolas asked. 'Harry told me what passed between you and Sir John, and

I believe you were most at fault, Father. It should be for you to apologize.'

'Go cap in hand to that prating fool?' Lord Mortimer's face had turned dark red. 'Be damned to you, Nicolas! I'll see the estate brought to ruin first. Do you know what he said to me? The disrespect he showed toward His Majesty? And besides, it was in his mind to delay the betrothal. He had heard that your brother had gambling debts and that he had been foolish over a common wench. He had the effrontery to demand that Harry apologize and mend his ways.'

'Sir John knew about . . .' Nicolas halted as his father's eyes narrowed. 'Yes, I knew, Father. I had spoken to Harry, warned him that he was a fool to risk so much, but he would not listen.'

'Had you thought to inform me, I might have done something before it came to this,' Lord Mortimer thundered. 'And where have you been all this time, sir?'

'You told me to take myself off,' Nicolas reminded him. 'I visited the estate that was Mother's.'

'And – what else did you there?' his father demanded. 'I am not a fool, Nicolas. I know you have friends in Ely – men I would not care to know.'

'Master Cromwell does not wish for war, Father,' Nicolas said. 'He asks only for the reform of various laws and the right of Parliament to play its proper part in those reforms.'

'He is of the Puritan persuasion,' Lord Mortimer replied. 'God knows that I have no love of Catholics, though I can live peacefully with them. But those damned Puritans would have us all bound by the knees, Nicolas. Mark my words, if they should gain the upper hand you will live to regret it. There will be no joy left in this land.'

'Surely you misjudge them, Father?' Nicolas said with a frown. 'I ask only for justice for the people, for tolerance. I have no wish to force them to worship in a way that is abhorrent to them.' In his inner thoughts Nicolas believed that something must be done to bring the King to a more reasonable frame of mind. He did not wish for a divisive war but knew that he was prepared to fight for his beliefs if necessary.

'You may not think to force your will on others, but there are those you follow who will,' his father told him. 'You may think me a fool now, but one day you may realize that you were wrong. God forbid that it comes to it, but I have a terrible fear that we may all suffer in ways we have not dreamed.'

'We must pray that the King will come to terms with his people.'

'Damn you, boy!' Lord Mortimer roared. 'Do you never listen to a thing I say? Have done with these rogues or the time may come when I ask you to leave this house for good.'

'I should be sorry if that happened, Father,' Nicolas said. 'I honour you and would not have a breach between us, but I must do what I believe is right.'

Lord Mortimer shook his head and then dismissed him.

Nicolas left him to the contemplation of his accounts. It was a sorry thing that they should be at odds with one another, but he could not deny the cause that was so dear to his heart. The King was wrong to abandon Parliament and rule alone. He must be shown the error of his ways. Nicolas did not wish for war, but if he were forced to take sides, it would be for Cromwell and Parliament that he declared.

However, at the moment, he had other things on his mind. He had refused to admit his feelings for Caroline before this, because she had been promised to his brother, and he had believed that she was well content to marry him. Angry at the situation, which he had in honour been unable to change, he had withdrawn into himself, becoming silent and sometimes harsh. Now all was different. The betrothal would not take place and Caroline had admitted that she did not love Harry.

Was he wrong to think that she might have warm feelings towards him? Or had he imagined it? Were her tears only because the long-standing friendship between them was at an end?

Nicolas had felt her tremble in his arms, had seen a look in her eyes that made him think otherwise. But even if she did have some feelings for him there was little he could do.

His father had forbidden the match for one son and would
not countenance it for another – and Sir John must have been
very angry to forbid his wife and daughter to speak to any
member of the Mortimer family. To go against them all
would be to cut themselves off from family and friends,
perhaps forever. While Nicolas would be prepared for such
an eventuality, he could hardly ask it of Caroline.

He frowned in frustration, accepting that he was still
hampered by circumstances and unable to break free of the
restraints that hedged about him. For years he had known
that it was expected that she would marry his elder brother,
and he had battled against the feelings of jealousy and resentment the knowledge aroused in him. He had held back in
his dealings with Caroline, and the pain that had festered
inside him had made him harsh. Now all the longings that
he had repressed these past years rose up in him, making
him burn to hold her in his arms, to kiss her and tell her that
he had loved her for longer than he dared admit.

There had been a dreadful storm in the night. Thunder and
lightning had rent the air, and the rain had lashed down,
beating against the windows so fiercely that it seemed as if
it would break through the tiny panes of glass. Glancing out
of her window, Caroline saw that the wind had wrought
havoc, all kinds of debris scattered across the courtyard.
Already the servants were at work, clearing the mess, but
there was no doubting that it had been a wild night.

As she watched, she saw a horseman canter into the courtyard and then dismount, shouting at one of the servants to take
his horse before striding towards the house. Once a gentleman
visiting on his horse might have meant that Nicolas or Harry
had come to call, but that was something she must forget.

Caroline was thoughtful as she walked down to the hall.
She imagined the caller had come to see her father, but when
she entered the parlour it was to see that her mother was
receiving a visitor. He was plainly dressed in a dark coat and
breeches, his dark hair cropped close to his head, and he

carried a black steeple-crowned hat. She was in time to see him make his bow.

'Good morrow, Lady Saunders. Is Sir John at home?' the gentleman asked, smiling at Caroline as she joined them in a way she did not care for. She hardly knew Richard Woodville, though she had seen him in church on a Sunday with his mother. This was the first time he had ever been admitted to her mother's parlour. 'You look very well, Mistress Saunders.'

'You are kind, sir.' Caroline inclined her head but did not smile. She had had an odd feeling of foreboding as she'd surveyed the aftermath of the storm and it increased as she looked at the harsh features of their visitor. She glanced at her mother. 'If you will excuse me, Mother. I must fetch something for my sewing.'

She left the room with dignity, a feeling of unease overcoming her. Something in Master Woodville's eyes a moment earlier had made her distinctly uncomfortable. It was foolish of her for his business must be with her father. She had spoken but half a dozen words to the gentleman in her life, and he could want nothing of her – and yet there was that look in his eyes, knowing, somehow predatory.

She went up to her bedchamber, delaying there for some twenty minutes or more until one of the maids came to find her.

'Mistress Caroline,' Tilly said. 'Sir John would like to speak to you in his library. He asks if you would go down to him now.'

'Thank you, Tilly,' Caroline replied with a smile. 'I shall go immediately.'

She walked down the stairs, wondering what it was that her father would have of her. Sir John seldom sent for Caroline, choosing to leave his daughter's well-being to her mother. Pausing at his door, she listened for voices but there was only silence so it seemed that his business with Master Woodville was done. She knocked softly and entered when Sir John's voice bade her do so.

'Ah, Caroline my dear,' he said and smiled at her. 'Thank you for coming so promptly. I hope I did not take you from something important?'

'What could be more important to me than a request from you, Father?' she asked and smiled at him lovingly.

'You are a good child,' he said, 'and you have not once reproached me for spoiling your hopes.'

'I have nothing to reproach you for, sir.'

'Good, I thought your feelings were not too badly bruised,' her father said. 'And indeed, there is no need for it – for we shall find you another husband in good time. This very day I have refused a request for your hand in marriage from Master Woodville.'

'Master Woodville?' Caroline stared at him in shocked dismay. Her stomach churned and she felt sick at the thought. Now she understood that look in his eyes! 'Why should he ask such a thing, Father? We do not know him.'

'I have had some dealings with the gentleman in the past, and he is a decent honest man,' Sir John said looking thoughtful. 'However, I have turned down his request. It is too soon after . . . and I do not think him a suitable match, though I did not say it to his face. You deserve more, Caroline, and I believe we shall soon find a good match for you. Your mother and I are giving it some thought and you may have a special treat coming your way soon, my dear.'

'Dearest Father, what can you mean?'

'We are planning to take you on a visit, my child. Mayhap to London to visit old friends of mine, though no arrangements have yet been made. However, I have decided that we shall all go together, for 'tis time that you saw a little of the world, and perhaps it was remiss of me not to take you before. Yes, perhaps I should not have been so ready to accept what was at hand.'

Caroline caught the sad, slightly wistful note in her father's voice but made no comment. She knew that he was suffering from the loss of a friendship that had been dear to him, but there was little she could say to comfort him.

'Well, daughter, that is all I have to say,' her father told her. 'I thought you should know that the offer had been made, and that I had refused it.'

'Thank you for telling me,' Caroline said. 'I am glad that you refused Master Woodville for I do not think I could have been happy with such a match.'

'There is no hurry for you to marry,' her father said. 'Run along to your mother now, Caroline. We shall not speak of Master Woodville again. My mind is quite made up on this. He will not do for you.'

Caroline smiled and on impulse kissed his cheek before leaving the room to seek out her mother. It was very strange that Woodville should have asked for her hand in marriage, and so soon after her intended betrothal was cancelled. She could not help feeling relieved that her father had refused to consider the idea.

'Out of my way, woman!' Richard Woodville demanded. He reined in impatiently as he saw the gypsy and her granddaughter, who had been picking herbs from the hedgerows and were walking two abreast in the narrow lane. 'I am in a hurry . . .'

'Wither would thou go so fast?' the old woman asked, her eyes dark and intent as they fastened on his face. 'You cannot escape your destiny no matter how you try.'

'Be careful, crone,' Richard muttered. He was furious that his offer for Caroline Saunders had been so swiftly refused and in the mood for a quarrel. 'You speak blasphemy for such words are of the devil and may bring you trouble if you do not mend your ways.'

He urged his horse forward suddenly, pushing past her so that she was thrust forward, landing in the hedge at the side of the lane.

'In future make way for your betters!' he called over his shoulder as he thundered off down the lane, the mud flying from beneath his horse's hooves.

Carlina hurried to her grandmother's side, helping her to her feet and looking anxiously at her as she asked her, 'Are you hurt?'

'Do not worry, child,' Greta answered her. 'My time is not yet. I am bruised but it will pass.'

'He is an evil man,' the girl said. 'Why did you not curse him?'

'He is already cursed,' Greta told her. 'I did not need to waste my strength on him. The seeds of destruction are in him and he will bring about his own destiny.'

'Ah, there you are, my dearest,' Lady Saunders said when her daughter came into the parlour that morning. 'Have you seen your brother? He was arguing with his father earlier, and it seems he has been neglecting his studies again.'

'No, I haven't seen Rupert this morning,' Caroline replied. 'Have you any messages for Mistress Blackwell, Mother? I have decided that I should return the book that the Reverend Blackwell loaned to me some weeks ago. It was a history of King Arthur and very entertaining. As it is such a lovely day I thought I would walk down to the Rectory and take it back.'

'Yes, that is a very good idea, Caroline,' her mother said. 'It was exceedingly good of him to lend you the book, which is quite valuable, as you know, and not one that your father has in his library. You may take some preserves with you, for the fruit has been good this summer and I know Reverend Blackwell particularly enjoys gooseberry jelly.'

'I shall go to the kitchen and ask cook for the jelly,' Caroline told her. 'Mercy is mending the sheets again. She asked me if we wanted her to spin some wool for cloth as she did at home. I told her that there is no need for her to do such work, but she will insist on it . . .'

Lady Saunders nodded, an odd expression in her eyes. 'If it pleases her it is no great matter, Caroline. I have wondered – do you think she is happy with us? She hath been very quiet these past weeks.'

'Yes, I think she is happy enough,' Caroline replied for she would not betray her cousin's secret. She had guessed that Mercy was breaking her heart for Harry, but she would not speak of it to anyone else, even her mother. 'I think she misses her mother and there are times when she needs to be quiet.'

'Yes, perhaps,' Lady Saunders said. 'And what of you, my love? Are you happy?'

'I . . . am as happy as you would expect me to be,' Caroline told her with a smile. 'Why should I be anything else?'

Lady Saunders saw the shadows in her eyes but made no comment. She knew that both Caroline and Mercy were suffering their own private grief, and though she might guess at the reason for Mercy's distress she had no idea what had made her daughter so thoughtful of late.

Walking to the village through the quiet country lanes, Caroline was trying to come to terms with the feeling of loss inside her. The peace and solitude of her surroundings had always been enough to calm her spirits, but even the sight of a lark singing high above her could not ease the ache in her heart that day. She had tried not to dwell on her unhappiness for there was no changing things while her father remained stubborn. Besides, even if he were to relent he would expect her to marry Harry Mortimer – and it was not he who filled Caroline's thoughts.

Oh, she must not let herself think of him. It was foolish to pine over something that could not be changed. Caroline was able to dismiss the problem from her mind as she visited with Mistress Blackwell. However, when she left the Rectory almost an hour later, she decided to take the shortcut home through the meadow, and alone once more, her thoughts began to plague her.

If only she had known how she felt months ago. Regret was running through Caroline's mind as she walked, head down, unseeing. Had she spoken to her mother then she might have been betrothed to Nicolas and things might have been different, for his feelings on the matter of the King and the war, which seemed inevitable now, were more in keeping with her father's. And yet Sir John's quarrel was with Lord Mortimer and it seemed there was no way the breach could be mended.

'Good morrow, Mistress Saunders. May I walk with you for a while?'

Startled out of her reverie, Caroline felt a surge of alarm as she saw the man who was blocking her path. It was almost two weeks now since her father had refused his unwelcome offer, and she had forgotten about him. Now she felt a stirring of unease.

'I did not see you, Master Woodville,' she said. 'My mind was elsewhere.'

'You have been to the Rectory,' he said. 'I have long admired you from a distance, mistress. You are a good and devout woman, and I have wanted to speak these many months but I thought my case hopeless.'

'Please, sir, do not,' Caroline said feeling stifled as she heard the passion in his voice. There was something about him then that caused her both alarm and repulsion. 'You must not speak to me so. My father has . . .' She looked at him in embarrassment, unsure of what to do. 'Pray let me go on my way.'

Still he prevented her from walking by, seeming intent on speaking no matter what her feelings. 'So he told you, but you do not understand. Sir John thought it too soon. Perhaps he did not understand the depth of my feelings. I hold you in high regard, Caroline.' He seemed as if he wished to dominate her, to force her to his will.

'No! I did not give you permission to use my name,' she said, her feelings of unease turning to alarm. His manner was so aggressive that it frightened her, and she sensed his bitterness. 'My father refused you, sir – and I beg you not to speak of this again.'

She moved towards him trying to go past him, but he caught her arm, his fingers digging into her flesh. 'Not so fast, Mistress Saunders,' he said and now he was no longer hiding his feelings. 'Your father did not think me good enough for his daughter, but one of these days he may be glad to take my offer. For there are not many that would take Harry Mortimer's leavings . . .'

'How dare you?' Caroline was furious as she struggled to free herself from his grasp, but he held her tightly, his fingers tightly clasped round her arm, bruising her flesh. What was he implying? 'I think you mistake yourself, sir. If you imply that there has been anything improper . . .'

'I have seen you laughing with him in the meadow . . . looking up at him in the way of lovers. A virtuous woman would not behave thus.'

'You are insulting, sir!' Caroline tried to pull away from his grasp and yet still he held her. She cried out and struggled desperately, terrified of what he meant to do, and then suddenly, seemingly out of nowhere, she was aware of a horse's pounding hooves. All she could see was a blur of powerful horseflesh coming at them and she screamed in fear. In another moment the rider had flung himself from the saddle and grabbed hold of Woodville by the coat collar, dragging him away from her.

'Damn you, you rogue,' Nicolas snarled and threw a punch at him, sending him crashing to the ground. His eyes flashed with temper as he stood over his hapless victim. 'How dare you lay hands on Mistress Saunders? By God, I am minded to kill you. If I see you upsetting her again I'll thrash you.'

'Nicolas . . .' Caroline cried. Relief mixed with the shame of what Master Woodville had said to her earlier. 'Thank goodness you came.' Her eyes stung with tears and she was trembling, though she would not give way to her emotions, lifting her head proudly.

Richard Woodville had struggled to his feet. His eyes went from her to Nicolas, his hands clenched at his sides as if he wished to strike back at his assailant but did not quite dare. Nicolas Mortimer was the lord of the manor's son and his father had the power of privilege. To strike Nicolas might mean that he himself could be arrested by the justice and cast into a prison cell to await trial at the lord's pleasure. It was not a fate that appealed to Woodville, and he knew that soon there might be altered circumstances, a chance for him to take a better revenge on the family.

'Be off with you, Woodville,' Nicolas ordered, every inch the aristocrat he was, his eyes cold, nostrils flaring arrogantly. He might have been a Viking marauder or a Saracen prince so magnificent was he in his fury. 'You have no business here.'

'Oh Nicolas,' Caroline said, catching a sob, as the other man took himself off across the meadow, clearly still frustrated at his inability to strike back. 'He said such terrible things to me.'

'Damn his impertinence,' Nicolas said. 'Do you want me to go after him, teach him a lesson?'

'No, please don't,' Caroline said, laying her hand on his arm. 'I would rather forget it happened. He was angry because my father refused his offer of marriage for me.'

'The devil he did!' Nicolas looked furious. 'How dare he presume to think of such a thing? It is sheer insolence. He is not your equal in any way, Caroline.'

'He thinks . . .' Caroline shook her head, her cheeks hot. 'No, I cannot say it – but it seems I am damaged goods.'

'I'll thrash him!' Nicolas exploded. In that moment he was so like his father that it made her smile inwardly. It was the reason he quarrelled so often with his father, she thought, for they were too much alike. 'Woodville shall not say such things to you. It is a damned lie and if he dares to speak it elsewhere I shall punish him severely. I would kill him rather than have harm come to you!'

'Please do not offer him violence,' Caroline said. She had begun to recover and wished only to forget the unpleasant incident. 'It would only cause a terrible scandal. And I am not even supposed to be speaking to you . . .'

'Has your father not relented even a little?'

'No, I do not think so,' Caroline replied. 'He is terribly upset. I know it hurts him to be at odds with your father but he is so stubborn. He says that your father was at fault and it is not up to him to apologize.'

'Father will never do so.' Nicolas caught the reins of his horse, turning to accompany her, the fine thoroughbred walking docilely beside him. 'You know that I care for you, Caroline. I would defend your honour with my life and count it a privilege.' He longed to say much more but knew he dared not do so and his expression was harsher than he realized.

'Nicolas . . .' She was feeling much calmer now and inclined to think that she had made too much of the incident. She smiled at him, a teasing light in her eyes. 'I do not think it will come to that, do you?'

'I wish that it might,' he said, his expression suddenly intense as he looked at her. 'Then you might understand the depth of my feelings for you.' He broke off, believing that he had said too much.

'You must not . . .' Caroline caught back a sob. 'How can we? It would never be allowed.'

Nicolas stared at her, seeing the way her eyes had darkened with emotion. 'Caroline, if your father could be persuaded . . .'

'You must not try, not just yet . . .' she breathed, her heart jerking as he moved towards her. Oh, this was so foolish but she could not help it for she was swept away on a tide of feeling. He took her hand, raising it to his lips, kissing the palm. 'Nicolas . . .' She was overcome and could not go on, for she was caught up in the moment, lost to all reality. He reached for her, drawing her into his arms to kiss her on the lips, softly at first and then with hunger as he felt her respond.

'Caroline my dearest. You must know how much I care for you?'

'No, Nicolas . . .' She broke from him in distress as she realized what had happened. Harry had never done more than kiss her hand or her cheek even when they believed they would marry one day. Nicolas's kiss had aroused feelings in her that she did not understand, a wild, hot longing for something that was beyond her comprehension. It frightened her. 'We must not . . .'

She turned and ran across the meadow. Nicolas let her go, standing where he was to watch until he saw that she was safely within the gardens of her home. He was thoughtful as he turned to mount his horse, his mood one of exultation. Until this moment he had not dared to believe that she could feel as he did, but now he knew that she loved him too. She might not even realise it yet herself, but he had felt her surrender as he kissed her, felt the way she allowed herself to melt into him, to become one with him. For a few moments she had been his completely, but then she had remembered all that stood between them.

But now that he knew her heart, Nicolas would leave no stone unturned. He would strive to bring about a reconciliation between his father and hers – because he was going to have her one day. Caroline would be his wife. She loved him as he loved her and nothing should be allowed to keep them apart.

Yet he must act carefully for unless he could bring two stubborn men together he would have to steal Caroline from her home. Knowing that she loved her father and mother dearly, he was loath to take that step. So for the moment he must be patient.

'Caroline!' Lady Saunders came to meet her as she entered the house. 'Thank God you are come. I am at my wits end and hardly know what to do.'

'What is wrong, Mother?' Caroline looked at her in alarm for she was in a state of extreme agitation. 'Why are you so upset?'

'Your father hath had a seizure,' Lady Saunders told her. 'It happened soon after you left the house this morning. He and Rupert had been quarrelling. Your brother . . .' She caught her breath on a sob. Her fingers trembled as she pressed them to her mouth. 'Your brother has refused to pay attention to his tutor or to go to university this autumn. He says that there will be a war and he is determined to join the King at York.'

'Oh, no,' Caroline said, her throat catching with emotion. 'He must not do this foolish thing; he cannot – he is too young. And it would break Father's heart.'

'I fear that he may already have done so,' her mother said anxiously. 'We sent for the physician and he is with your father now, but . . .'

'Hush, Mother. Do not weep, dearest,' Caroline said and

put her arms about her. 'Father is very strong. He will recover. I am certain of it.'

'We must pray that you are right,' her mother said. 'For your brother rode off in a temper not knowing that he had broken his father's heart, and if he dies . . .' She shook her head. 'I do not know what we shall do.'

Mercy read the letter from her stepfather. It had come that morning and she had been afraid to open it lest he demanded that she return at once. Her heart was beating wildly as she read the cold, precise words. He had merely written to tell her that his wife was with child and that he hoped she would be content to make her life with her cousins, because his wife did not want her in their house.

She closed her eyes as the relief washed over her. She would rather die than return there after the freedom she had found in this house. Besides, while she remained with her cousins there was a chance that she might see Harry again, might see him smile at her, feel the touch of his hand again, as she had when he had helped her remove her skirt from the rose thorns.

Surely Sir John would not continue his ban forever? It could not be that she would never be able to speak to Harry again, for surely her host would relent in the end.

But she was selfish to be thinking of herself when Sir John lay ill, Mercy scolded herself. There would be much to do for Lady Saunders would need to spend time at her husband's bedside. The least Mercy could do was to perform small tasks that would ease her cousin.

Caroline was being very brave, but how could she not feel her loss deeply? Mercy knew that in her position she would have been wretched. Indeed, she would have been ready to run away with the man she loved rather than lose him . . . but then, she had no love for her stepfather and did not wish to return to him. Caroline's parents had been so good to her that it made it impossible for her to think of disobeying them. She wished that there was something she might do to help Caroline, but she was powerless to interfere.

Four

'Your father is feeling a little better this morning,' Lady Saunders told her daughter some weeks later. 'We were able to talk properly for a while and he has made up his mind, Caroline. He is not well enough to take you to London as we had hoped, and of course I cannot leave him while he is so ill. Therefore, you and Mercy are to visit a relative of mine. Margaret Farringdon is a widow of some means. She has written often to inquire if we would visit her and it is my intention to ask if she will have you and Mercy to stay with her.'

'Stay with Margaret?' Caroline vaguely recalled the lady visiting them some years previously. She was a bright, attractive lady, had a merry smile and was in her late twenties when she was widowed. 'It would please me if we had all been able to visit – but how can I leave you while Father is so ill?'

'You must go for his sake,' her mother told her. 'He is fretting because of what has happened, Caroline. He feels that he has robbed you of your chance to make a good marriage. At Oxford you will meet many people and you may find someone you like. Margaret will take care of you and make sure you mix only with her friends. I know I can trust her to keep you safe, dearest – and it would ease your father's mind to know that you are enjoying yourself.'

How could she leave at such a time? She had been helping her mother to care for Sir John, carrying things to his room and reading to him from Master Coverdale's Bible, which was the first to be written wholly in English, and therefore

71

easily accessible to anyone who could read and was able to buy or borrow a copy. She felt that she would have preferred to continue to help instead, but if her father wanted her to go, she had no choice. Caroline smothered the protest that rose to her lips.

'If it is what Father wants,' she said with a little sigh. 'But you will write to me? You will tell me if I am needed here?'

'Of course.' Lady Saunders smiled at her affectionately. 'But I believe that your father will mend now, my dear. As you said, he has a strong constitution. It was the grief of his breach with Lord Mortimer and then that dreadful quarrel with your brother that brought him so low.' She caught back a sob. 'And still we have no word from Rupert. It is too bad of him to worry us all like this!'

'It is all the fault of this war,' Caroline said. 'For the King has set up his standard and his supporters are flocking to him. Poor Father. It must be hard for him to bear.'

'Sir John hath always been a man of mild habits,' his devoted wife said, her eyes weary from weeping and lack of sleep. 'These quarrels have upset him deeply, as does the thought of war. As you know, your father is not of the Puritan persuasion. Yet he cannot agree with the King's attempts to destroy the authority of Parliament. He would have peace and common sense prevail.'

'Perhaps it will all be over soon,' Caroline said to soothe her. ' A battle in the North and then they will surely come to terms?'

'We must pray it is so,' her mother said. 'But we shall not change things no matter what we say. Now, my love, go and find Mercy and tell her what is to happen. I think a visit with Margaret may lift her spirits for she hath been very low of late.'

Richard Woodville stared resentfully at his mother. Her sharp tongue had been like a scourge to him all his life, and he sometimes felt like breaking her scrawny neck, and yet she served her purpose for she kept the house in good order and the servants were too afraid of her to leave their work undone.

''Tis time you found yourself a wife,' she told him, her voice like the lash of a whip, stinging him on the raw. 'A good decent girl who would look after me.'

'You may look after yourself,' he muttered in a surly tone. He wanted a girl of good family so that he could rise in the world, not a common slut who would be a slave to his mother.

'You never listen to me,' she muttered. 'You might have taken a girl from the village before this and then I should not have to do everything myself.'

He walked from the house, his anger rising to boiling point for he had not recovered from the double insult offered him by Caroline Saunders and her father. If he could have made such a match his dreams of becoming a gentleman might have prospered. His blood was good enough, for his father had been the younger son of a country gentleman, but he had small fortune and he was tired of his lowly status.

His mother's complaints followed him from the house as he left, his stomach tying itself in knots as he thought about getting his revenge on all those who had sneered at him and treated him as nothing. One day he would show them all – especially Caroline Saunders and Nicolas Mortimer. Between them the families ruled the village and the area for leagues about it, lording it over everyone else. But the time was coming when they would learn a sorry lesson. Oh yes, the time was coming . . .

Ahead of him, he saw a girl walking with a basket over her arm. He thought that it might be Rowena Greenslade and a smile touched his mouth as he set out to follow her. He must wait for revenge against Saunders and Nicolas Mortimer, but he could teach that little bitch of the blacksmith's a lesson in manners and enjoy it.

Oh yes, he would enjoy it very much.

'If you go now, you leave my house for good, Nicolas,' Lord Mortimer told his son. His mouth was hard, tight with anger, a dark flush spreading up his neck. 'I had hoped you might have come to your senses ere this.'

'Forgive me, Father,' Nicolas said. 'I would not willingly have this breach between us, but I must do as my conscience bids me. I cannot fight for a King I despise, nor can I stay at home when the country is to be plunged into bitter war.'

'His Majesty will soon teach that rabble a harsh lesson,' Lord Mortimer said with a sneer. 'They are ill trained and quarrelling amongst themselves already. It may go ill with you in the future if you choose the wrong side.'

'If we are defeated I shall accept the consequences.'

'I never thought to see my son turn traitor to his king!'

Nicolas's mouth drew into a harsh line. 'If I fought for a cause I believe unjust I should be a traitor to myself. This king, through Archbishop Laud, sought to bring back the Bishops and treated good men ill at the Court of Star Chamber. Had Hampden, Pym and some of the others not stood up to him, he would have ruled as a despot. For pride, decency and honour, I can do no other than take up arms for Parliament.'

'Then you are no longer my son,' Lord Mortimer said. 'I do not wish to see your face again. Take your belongings and go.'

Nicolas looked at him in silence for a moment more, then inclined his head. 'So be it,' he said. 'But remember, this breach was not of my making.'

Lord Mortimer got up from the oak table at which he had been seated writing up his ledgers, going to the heavy carved buffet in which he kept items of value locked away. He took a large iron key from his coat pocket, his back to his son as he removed something and stood, head bent, studying the close script.

The interview was clearly at a end. Nicolas walked from the room, his boots echoing on the stone floor. His fists were clenched at his sides as he fought to control his emotions. It was not just of his father to behave thus for he had never given him cause.

He would take nothing from this house but a change of clothing. He had the estate, which was his mother's legacy, and needed no more.

There was some business he must attend to at his estate before he joined the troop that Master Cromwell was raising, but he would return to Thornberry soon. Not to his father's house but to see Caroline – perhaps for the last time.

He pulled his cloak tighter about his neck for the wind had begun to get up and he sensed that there might be a storm before long.

Mercy stood looking out of the window. She watched as the dark clouds gathered overhead. There was going to be a storm. She was not frightened, though her mother had always been terrified of thunder. Yet it was the lightning that could be dangerous and by the time you could hear the thunder, the danger was past.

She turned away from the window, taking up the neckerchief that Harry had given her, and putting it about her throat. She pinned it with a little silver brooch that Caroline had given her, then sighed as she prepared to go downstairs and join the family.

Harry was with the King now. He would have forgotten all about her by the time they met again – if they ever did.

Rowena hurried her steps for she felt that a storm was due and she wanted to be home before it broke. She had lingered in the woods hoping that Harry might come to meet her, for though he had said he was going to the King, she had hoped that they might meet one last time, but he had not come, and now she was late. She would likely get a thrashing from her father and suffer a black eye as her mother had done two days earlier. Sometimes she hated him with a fierceness that made her wish him dead, but she did not dare to lay a hand on him in anger for he would kill her.

Hearing a girl's screams just ahead of her, Rowena paused. What was that? She heard it again – a girl crying

75

for help and a young girl at that. What was going on?

Her heart was beating wildly as she made her way carefully towards the sound, and then she stopped, sick to her stomach as she saw what was happening. A man was raping a girl – a girl of no more than fourteen summers. It was Carlina, the girl she had spoken to in the woods, and the man . . . the man was Richard Woodville.

What could she do? Rowena felt the anger surge inside her and she looked about her for a weapon, but even as she did so, she heard a cry of rage and suddenly another man rushed into the clearing. He grabbed Woodville by his hair and yanked him to his feet, shouting and hitting him with his hammer fists as he hurled insults at him.

'You are a filthy beast like your father before you,' Blacksmith Greenslade yelled angrily. 'He raped her just the way you raped that girl . . . left her for dead. He hoped she would die so that none would know of his crime, but I found her and I took her back with me. I made her well and I married her!'

'You lie!' Richard Woodville cried. He was beside himself with rage. 'Foul lies that you learned from a whore . . .'

Rowena watched in terror as the men exchanged blows, her heart catching with fright as it seemed to veer one way and then the other. But surely the blacksmith would win? She knew his strength, knew his violence. Yet Woodville was standing up to him, giving blow for blow. And then, when she thought that this nightmare would never end, she saw Richard Woodville had something in his hand. It seemed to be an iron bar, and she watched in horror as he brought it crashing down on the blacksmith's head, again and again, until he slumped to the floor and lay still.

She could hardly keep from crying out as she stood there, hidden in the bushes, the vomit in her throat as she realized that she had witnessed bloody murder. It had been a fair fight at the first, but in the end murder had been in Richard Woodville's mind.

For what seemed an eternity but could only have been

minutes, Woodville stood looking down at his victim. Then he suddenly realized what he had done and threw the iron bar into the trees, turning and making off into the darkness as swiftly as he could.

Rowena waited for a moment or two until it was safe, then she crept out of her hiding place. She went first to the blacksmith but knew from his staring eyes that he was dead. Hearing a small moaning whimper behind her, she turned to see that Carlina was conscious and staring at her, a look of horror on her face.

'I tried to resist,' she whispered. 'But he was too strong for me . . . too strong . . .'

'He is an evil monster,' Rowena said. She hurried to the girl, assisting her to rise. 'Come home with me. Let me help you. My mother will give you something to ease the pain.'

'No,' Carlina said. Her face was pale, her eyes dark with misery, and yet she was calm, accepting of her fate. 'You mean well, but leave me be. 'Tis my destiny as it was written and I must go to my blood. Greta will do all that is necessary.'

'You won't . . . you won't do anything foolish?' Rowena knew that in Carlina's place she would have been torn between anger and shame.

'Take my own life?' The girl smiled at her oddly. 'The time is not yet. It is written in the stars and I must follow it – for your destiny and mine are linked. It was written that you would be near at my worst hour and I shall be near at yours.'

Rowena watched as the girl walked away, back straight, head up.

All this talk of destiny was foolish superstition, and yet she was shivering from head to toe. She started to run as the first huge spots of rain began to fall.

'I have had bad news,' Lady Saunders told her daughter when she came into the parlour the next morning. 'The Reverend Blackwell came this morning especially to tell us.'

'Do you mean that Nicolas hath quarrelled with his father?' Caroline asked for she had heard it from Martha Roberts who had had it from the boy who brought fresh meat from the farm that morning.

'No, though that is bad enough,' Lady Saunders replied with a frown. 'Nicolas is not prepared to fight for the King it seems and his father bade him leave his house – but this news is far worse, Caroline. Indeed, it is quite shocking and it made me feel quite ill. There has been a murder. Master Greenslade was found at first light this morning with severe wounds to his head.'

'That is terrible,' Caroline agreed, feeling stunned. 'How can such a thing have happened?'

'No one knows. He was discovered in the woods near Thornberry Manor and carried home, but he was already dead.'

'How sad for his wife and daughter,' Caroline said and a shiver ran through her. 'They will find life hard without him, Mother.'

'Yes, I fear you are right,' Lady Saunders replied with a little shake of her head. 'Mistress Greenslade is not much liked. While her husband lived . . .' She hesitated and looked grave. 'I think it may go ill for them in times like these. Would you feel able to visit them and ask if there is anything we can do to help, Caroline?'

'Yes, of course,' Caroline answered readily. 'We must do what we can to aid them, Mother.'

'Sally Greenslade might like to work in the kitchens here. There is always room for another pair of hands and her daughter may make herself useful in some way.'

Caroline looked thoughtful. 'Yes, though when I spoke to her recently, Rowena told me that she expected to marry soon.'

'It would be best for her,' Lady Saunders agreed. 'It may be that they do not need our help, Caroline. But it is an act of charity to ask and the sooner the better.'

Caroline agreed, for her mother had always done what she

could to alleviate the plight of those in need or sickness, giving them food or clothing and sending simple cures to ease their ailments.

'Then I shall not delay,' Caroline said. 'It will do no harm to ask.'

'You should take your cloak,' her mother advised. 'The weather hath changed of late. There was a terrible storm last night, and there is a touch of autumn in the air this morning, though August is not yet out.'

'It is still warm despite the clouds,' Caroline laughed softly. 'But to please you, I shall take my cloak.'

She set out for the village almost at once. It was alarming to hear of such a shocking murder happening so near to Lord Mortimer's home. Who could have done such a wicked thing and why?

Most people in the village had been afraid of the black-smith, for he was a huge man with thick arms and a bull neck, and he had a violent temper. Some people said that at times he hit his wife and blacked her eye, and perhaps his daughter too. There were few who would have willingly picked a quarrel with him. It must have been a stranger passing through, Caroline decided, and perhaps more than one. And yet what had Master Greenslade been doing in woods that belonged to Lord Mortimer? Those woods were the property of the lord of the manor and the penalty for poaching game there was severe, resulting in either a term of prison, which many did not survive for the conditions were harsh, or hanging.

Yet if Master Greenslade had been poaching, the game-keepers were more likely to take him alive so that an example could be made, and his punishment be seen. They could have shot him in the leg or simply sent the militia to arrest him at his home. The kind of beating he had received seemed to have been done in anger.

Reaching the village, Caroline approached the forge, a strange feeling in the pit of her stomach as she saw that it was closed and empty, the fire that had always been kept burning allowed to die out. The villagers would miss him, she thought, for it was a walk of some three hours to the next forge.

She passed by, feeling a sense of foreboding, a chill creeping over her, as if an unseen menace hung over the place. There was no smoke issuing from the blacksmith's cottage either and she suspected that this too was empty even before she knocked at the door. There was no answer but she knocked twice more before turning away.

'They be gone, Mistress Caroline.' An old crone hobbled across the street to her. She was bent, her hair long and greasy as it straggled about her face. 'I saw them leave with all their belongings not half an hour ago. They had a hand-cart with them, their pots and bedding too. Gone they are, and good riddance too!'

'Why do you say that, Granny Sorrell?'

'Sally Greenslade be a witch. She wished her husband dead and now he be dead.'

'But you cannot think she killed him?'

The woman glanced over her shoulder, crossing herself furtively. 'Who knows what she and that bastard child of hers might do?'

'I do not understand you. Why do you call Rowena by that name?'

'Sally had her in her belly when she were wed. She came here from nowhere and that great fool wed her, though none but me knowed the truth. She warned me she would put a curse on me if I told a soul but she be gone now.'

Caroline felt cold all over, for there was malice in the old woman's face. 'You ought not to speak ill of her, Granny Sorrell. It is not kind of you.'

'Kind or not it be true. And you be a fool if you think other. That whore was a carryin' on with the lord's son behind your back for many a month. Blacksmith Greenslade must 'ave knowed and gone to find her – and there he met his death. God rest his soul!' She crossed herself superstitiously.

Caroline would not answer such a charge. She walked away, her head high, cheeks flaming. Instinctively, she knew that this at least was true. She had sensed it long ago. It was one of the reasons she had begun to doubt her feelings for Harry.

What was happening in their village? For years the local people had lived in peace and friendship and a certain prosperity. No one would have thought of speaking to Caroline in such a manner, but she had sensed a change. Always when she visited the village before she had been greeted by smiles and nods from the goodwives, and a cheery wave from the men as she passed by, but now people looked at her warily, as if they were afraid.

Was it because of the murder – or because the fear of war had cast a long dark shadow over the land?

She knew that some of the men in the village had begun to take sides. Harry had taken six men from his father's estate when he rode off to join the King, but Caroline believed that most of the folk in the village were on the side of Parliament. Charles had made himself unpopular with the freemen and landowners alike, many of whom had been forced to pay taxes they judged unfair.

The feeling was running high against him, especially in London, where gangs of armed apprentices roamed the streets with clubs, ready to fight for the slightest excuse. However, here the people were more cautious, slower to change. At the moment the majority were waiting until they saw which way the wind was blowing and they watched their neighbours with suspicion.

Caroline decided she would visit Mistress Blackwell before returning home. It was possible that there was more news. Perhaps they might have discovered who was responsible for murdering the blacksmith.

'No, I have heard no more on that subject,' Abigail Blackwell told her. 'But there is more shocking news, Caroline. 'Tis a terrible thing to rob a father so!'

'What do you mean?'

'Lord Mortimer's family jewels have been stolen,' the Reverend's wife told her relating the tale with some considerable distress. 'It happened the same night that Master Nicolas quarrelled with his father and rode off in a rage.' The same night that the blacksmith had been murdered!

'You are not suggesting that Nicolas would steal his family's heirlooms?' Caroline said horrified. 'No, madam, I cannot believe that he would do such a wicked thing. Those jewels were valuable and should rightfully be kept within the family, to be handed down to the elder son.'

'They say he took them in revenge for his father disowning him.'

'No! Nicolas would never steal from his father. I do not believe it.' Caroline felt a surge of anger mixed with disbelief. 'It is rumour and cruel rumour at that.'

'Well, 'tis what I've heard,' Mistress Blackwell said. 'Like you, I should be sorry to think it of Master Nicolas. He hath always seemed such an honest, decent man.'

'And so he is,' Caroline told her. 'If the jewels have been stolen it was someone else.'

'I do not know what things are coming to,' the older woman said with a shake of her head. 'One minute precious jewels are stolen and the next Master Greenslade murdered . . .'

'You cannot think that they are connected?'

'Who knows? Perhaps Master Greenslade knew who had taken the jewels and was going to tell Lord Mortimer?'

'And was murdered to prevent him from doing so?' Caroline shuddered. 'It is too horrible. I cannot bear to think of such things!'

'But it would make sense of what has been done here. I think the magistrates should be made aware of the possibility and I shall speak to the Reverend about it.'

Caroline looked grave. It seemed that one shocking thing after another was happening, and she did not know what to think – though she believed that the blacksmith may have been in the woods for a very different reason. 'It sounds very odd,' she said. 'And yet why else would anyone want to murder Master Greenslade?'

They could not think of any reason for such a deed, and Caroline was left feeling uneasy. Murder was such a wicked, evil thing. Mistress Blackwell had suggested something that might explain what had happened, but that could not make it any more acceptable.

'Did you know that Master Woodville took himself off this morning to join with Lord Manchester's army? There were three men from the village went with him, but most would not join him for he is not well liked. His mother is a mean-mouthed old thing and the family has lived here no more than twenty years. They are not true village folk.'

Caroline hid her smile for she knew that it took a lifetime to be accepted by the villagers. She felt pleased that Master Woodville had left the village, for she had not forgotten the day he had insulted her and had wondered what might have happened if Nicolas had not come to her rescue.

Her feelings were in turmoil as she walked home. It had been shocking enough that a man had been murdered in Thornberry woods, but that Nicolas was suspected of stealing his family's heirlooms was hurtful. She would never believe that!

'A letter has come from Margaret Farringdon,' Lady Saunders said as she greeted Caroline as she entered the parlour one morning two weeks later. 'She will be delighted to welcome you and Mercy to her home, Caroline. She begs that you will join her as soon as it may be arranged – and your father says you shall go on Monday.'

'So soon?' Caroline was aware of her foolish reluctance, which she struggled to overcome.

'There is nothing to delay you,' her mother told her. 'Your things may be packed on Saturday ready for the carrier and your father will send you in his own coach. You shall have three grooms to accompany you there and your maid of course. Would you prefer to take Tilly or Lucy?'

'May I have Tilly, Mother? She is sensible and reliable, and besides, Lucy is courting the gardener's eldest son. It would be unfair to take her away just yet, though she may have to part with him soon if he joins one of the troops of local militia.'

'Pray do not speak of it,' her mother begged. 'Cook was in tears this morning. She hath two sons, both of whom worked on this estate. One hath declared for the King, the other for Parliament. She fears that they will kill each other.'

'It is the same everywhere,' Caroline said. 'Oh, I do wish this wicked war would not happen. It is changing everything and I fear nothing will ever be as it once was.'

'I pray that it will not happen,' her mother told her and touched the strings of her white lace falling band, her hand trembling. 'It seems that the whole country hath gone mad.'

Caroline sat brushing her hair for some time before she went to bed that evening. She was restless, her mind filled with vague fears that she could not justify. Everything she had known and trusted suddenly seemed to have become uncertain and she knew not what to expect of her life in the future. It had all been so settled and now . . .

Her thoughts were interrupted by something rattling against her window. Startled, it was a moment or two before she got up to investigate, and then it happened again. Moving over to the small-paned casement window, she opened it to look out, her heart beating wildly as she saw who stood beneath it.

'What are you doing, Nicolas?' she asked in a hushed whisper. 'You know you should not be here.'

'Come down,' he said urgently. 'I must speak with you.'

She hesitated for a moment, then placed a finger to her lips as he would have spoken again. She had not yet undressed for the night and was still clad in the mantua gown she had worn that evening. She took her cloak from where it lay across a settle. Throwing it about her shoulders, she opened her door as quietly as she could and looked out. The hall was empty, almost in darkness, for the candles had been extinguished. She would not light them and was just able to see her way because of the bright moon that shed its light through the landing window. Fortunately, her bedchamber was some way distant from that of her mother or father, the nearest to her being Mercy. She held her breath as she removed her shoes and walked carefully down the stairs, her heart racing as she listened for sounds within the house.

Nothing seemed to be stirring and she reasoned that the servants must have retired to bed. Making her way to a side door, she drew back the heavy bolts and went outside into the garden, hurrying to where she knew Nicolas would be waiting.

He came to her at once, a smile of welcome on his lips. He looked so tall and strong, dressed plainly as he was in a dark doublet and grey wool breeches, a short cloak slung over his shoulders, his sword belted low on his hip. Caroline's heart did a rapid somersault and she felt a surge of happiness, which she knew was madness. She was insane to have come down to him, for if she was discovered it would cause endless trouble, and yet she knew that nothing would have kept her from him.

'Caroline,' he said and his voice throbbed with a passion that made her feel weak. 'Forgive me for coming to you like this, but I had to see you – to tell you that tomorrow I am joining Cromwell's troop.'

'Oh, Nicolas,' she breathed. 'Must you? I fear this wicked, senseless war will destroy us all.'

'Hush, my sweet.' He pressed a finger to her lips. 'You do know that I care for you, Caroline? You must know it in your heart for it has always been there between us, an invisible bond that held us whether or not we wished it and now 'tis too strong to be denied. I shall come back when this is over and then I shall claim you for my own – my wife. Promise me that you will give yourself to no other?'

'Nicolas . . .' Her mind protested that it was impossible, that too much stood between them, but she could not say

the words when he looked at her that way. Now she understood why his intensity had always frightened her; she was
not frightened of him but of the feelings he had aroused in
her, of this mindless, aching need that seemed to possess her
body and soul. She looked at the cast of his proud face, the
stern and yet sensuous mouth, the eyes that could hold her
like a bird with a broken wing, fluttering and yet unable to
fly from his grasp. 'Yes, of course I shall wait,' she said in
a choked voice, for she could scarcely breathe. 'You know
I love you. I think it was always you but I was afraid to
admit to such feelings. It would have been easy to marry
your brother but . . .'

She could not go on for he had her in his arms and as he
looked down into her eyes she felt herself drowning in a
fierce, hot desire which left her helpless and needy. His lips
touched hers, softly, sweetly, the kiss deepening slowly with
a demanding hunger that swept them both away.

Caroline melted into him, her senses swimming as she
gave herself up to his kisses, shivering with delight as they
travelled from her lips and down the line of her throat, stopping at the little hollow at the base. His touch scared her
and yet she wanted it, she wanted him to go on and on, to
possess her utterly so that she was his alone.

'Oh, Nicolas,' she moaned against his shoulder as his
mouth released hers and she felt the deep shudder run through
him. 'My dearest love . . .'

'I want to make you mine,' Nicolas said in a voice hoarse
with desire. 'I want you so much, my darling, but I shall not
take advantage of your sweetness this night. For we must
part and if there should be a child from our loving it would
shame and harm you.' His fingers traced the line of her face,
the slender arch of her white throat, his thumb smoothing
the soft curve of her mouth. 'You are so precious to me,
Caroline. Promise me that you will never doubt me whatever happens?'

'I could never doubt you,' she said. 'Even though some
say you took your family's heirlooms when you left

Thornberry, I do not believe it, Nicolas. I know that you would never ...' She broke off as she saw his expression of shock and disbelief. 'You did not know?'

'My father – was he harmed in this attack?'

He looked so anxious that Caroline put her fingers to his lips. 'Why should he have been harmed? The theft was only discovered in the morning when he went to his cabinet and found it open.'

'But ...' Nicolas broke off and shook his head. The key to his father's strongbox never left his side. It was strange that it could have been taken from him without his knowledge. 'You said that you did not doubt me, Caroline. I swear to you now that I know nothing of this theft.'

'You do not need to swear,' she replied with a smile. 'I know it for the truth, Nicolas, and shall never believe ill of you.'

'I thank you for that,' he said but there was a brooding expression in his eyes. 'Though it seems that others may not have your faith in me – but no matter. One day the truth may be known.' He banished the shadows as he looked tenderly at her. 'I must leave you now, my love, for the longer you stay the more likely you will be discovered. Think of me sometimes, and pray that we may be together soon.'

'I think of you always,' she told him and suddenly threw her arms about him, pressing her lips to his once more in a desperate kiss of farewell. Then she broke from him and ran towards the house, stopping briefly at the door to lift her hand in one last salute.

Nicolas stood for a few moments as she went inside. The moment of parting was bittersweet, for he had kissed his love and she had confessed her love for him, but he did not know when they might meet again. This war would claim him now and it might be that he was never able to return.

Turning at last, Nicolas walked away from the house. His thoughts wrenched from Caroline to his father, and the theft of precious jewels. He believed that Lord Mortimer had been considering selling some of them to pay his debts and their loss would be a severe blow.

Again, he wondered how they could have been stolen when the key to the cabinet was placed beneath his father's pillow at night. Although the large oak cabinet was solid enough in itself, there was another cabinet made of iron inside it. To have forced that must surely have made enough noise to waken the house!

It was a mystery, but not one that Nicolas had leisure to solve now. He had broken his journey to see the woman he loved but now he must continue. He must keep his promise to join Master Cromwell and take up this struggle against the King, which he believed was now very close.

Standing at the landing window, Mercy had seen the two figures embrace. Unable to sleep, she had heard a door closing downstairs and risen from her bed to investigate. Now, she was troubled by what she had seen. It had not been Harry Mortimer that Caroline had been embracing but his brother.

'Mercy . . .' She turned at the sound of her name to see Lady Saunders coming towards her. 'Is something the matter? Why are you at the window?'

Mercy thought fast. If Lady Saunders saw Caroline in the arms of Nicolas Mortimer there might be serious trouble for her. She knew that whatever happened she must prevent that somehow.

'I . . . am unwell,' she said and walked towards her hostess, then bent double as if in pain. 'I think it must be my time of the month a little early unless it is something I ate?'

Her heart was beating wildly for it went against her nature to lie to someone who had been so good to her, but she could not betray Caroline.

'Oh, you poor child,' Lady Saunders said. 'Come, I shall take you to your room and then I shall fetch something to ease your pain.'

'Thank you.' Mercy smiled gratefully, accepting her help and taking her time. If she could delay her hostess long enough Caroline would be able to return to her room without fear of discovery. 'You are so kind and I am a wretch to trouble you.'

'No, indeed, how could you be?' Lady Saunders said. 'Now, come and lie down, my dear, and I am sure you will soon feel better.'

Caroline bent to kiss her father's cheek. He was able to rise now and sit in a chair of solid oak, made comfortable with cushions at his back and a blanket over his legs. He smiled at her and pressed her hand as she straightened up.

'I wish you a safe journey, my child,' he said. 'It grieves me that I could not take you myself as I promised, but you will be safe enough with Widow Farringdon. She is a good, respectable woman and she will take great care of you for the love she bears your mother.'

'I remember her staying with us once when I was but twelve,' Caroline said. 'She seemed a cheerful, pleasant lady. I admired her gown for it was of the finest silk and very elegant.'

'I dare say,' her father replied and released her hand. 'She is a wealthy widow. Go now, daughter, and God be with you. I know you will not disgrace me and I bid you to be happy if you can.'

'I love and honour you, Father,' she said with a choke in her voice. 'I shall write to you and Mother when I can.'

'Do not waste your money on too many letters. It will be enough for us to know that you are settled and well.'

'I shall write once a month,' she promised and turned away before her eyes filled with tears. It was a wrench to leave her home, and particularly her father at this time, but she knew it was what he wanted of her and to refuse would have been churlish.

She went down to the hall to find her mother with Mercy. Lady Saunders was pressing a small purse of money on the girl, though she looked embarrassed and tried to refuse it.

'You must take it, Mercy,' Lady Saunders said, 'for otherwise I shall worry about you.'

'But you have already done so much.'

'Pray let my mother give you her gift,' Caroline said. 'You will need it for there are bound to be some expenses and we cannot expect Margaret to pay for everything.'

'Oh no, indeed,' Mercy said and blushed, then darted a kiss at her benefactor's cheek. 'You are very kind, ma'am. I do not know how to thank you for all you have done for me.'

'It was very little,' Lady Saunders said. 'We must see how you feel when you and Caroline return, but I hope that you may be persuaded to make your home here with us, my dear.'

Caroline saw that the other girl was overcome with emotion, and took her arm, propelling her out to the waiting coach. She had said her own goodbyes to her mother earlier, and there was no point in delaying further.

Once they were settled in the coach, Caroline leaned out of the window and waved at her mother, closing the leather curtains afterwards, for she did not wish to be stared at by strangers they might meet upon the road. Mercy left hers open, her eyes dwelling on the house they were leaving until it could no longer be seen.

She sat for a while, lost in her thoughts, and started when Caroline spoke to her. 'Mother means it, you know. She is only sending us away so that my father's mind may be at rest. Our visit will be for a few months and then we shall return.'

Mercy nodded, then raised her eyes to meet Caroline's. 'But will your father relent? Will he allow us to renew our friendship with the Mortimer family?'

'That is something I cannot tell you,' Caroline replied and bit her lip for it had taxed her mind these past few days. 'We can but pray that one, or better still, both of them have a change of heart.'

Mercy nodded, then fiddled with the small bead-trimmed purse in her hands. 'And you really do not wish to marry Harry Mortimer?'

'I really do not wish to marry him, nor shall I.'

Mercy seemed to accept it, and from something in her

manner Caroline suspected that she might have seen her meeting Nicolas when he came to the house.

She gave her a direct look. 'Did you see me with someone?'

'I . . .' Mercy stammered. 'I did not mean to spy on you, Caroline, but I was at the window and happened to look out. Something had woken me . . . a door being opened perhaps. Forgive me. I ought not to have looked.'

'Anyone might look from a window,' Caroline said. 'I trust you will keep my secret?'

'Yes, of course, with my life,' Mercy said fervently. She did not tell her cousin that she had already saved her from exposure for she was a little ashamed of her deceit. 'I do sincerely wish you happiness.'

'I wish that I might hope for it,' Caroline replied with a sigh. This past few days her spirits had soared and then plummeted as she swayed between the delight of being in love and the knowledge that nothing could come of her hopes.

'But Nicolas is not a Royalist,' Mercy said. 'If your father knew that you wanted to marry him he might change his mind and allow it.'

'Perhaps,' Caroline agreed. 'I can only pray that time will soften his heart but for the moment we are forced to be apart. Nicolas must fight for Parliament, for those things that he believes in, and I must wait until he returns to me.' Pray God that he did! she thought.

'It will be the same for most women,' Mercy said looking distressed. 'It is always thus in times of war. I fear that wives and sweethearts, mothers and sisters, will all be forced to wait in hope and dread for their loved ones to return.'

'As you do for Harry?'

Mercy blushed. 'I do not know that he will come back for me.'

'And yet you know that he loves you?'

'He has not spoken of it but . . .'

'You feel it?' Caroline declared as the other girl was silent. 'I sensed it long ago, Mercy. I am sure that when Harry returns he will tell you of his love.'

'Even if he should . . .' Mercy broke off on a sob. 'My stepfather would not hear of it. He is a strict Puritan and he would not approve of Harry. Besides, your father has forbidden us to meet.'

'It is all the fault of this wicked war,' Caroline told her. 'It cannot be long now before this country is torn apart. It fills me with terror. Not for myself so much as for those we love who must fight.'

Mercy nodded. Reaching across, she took Caroline's hand in hers.

'At least we have each other,' she said. 'We shall make a promise now, Caroline. Whatever happens, we shall be friends – do you agree?'

'Yes, of course,' Caroline told her. 'And now we must try to forget our worries for we are supposed to enjoy this visit and I would not distress Mistress Farringdon for the world.'

Mercy nodded her agreement, sitting back in her seat. Until now she had struggled to hold her thoughts of Harry Mortimer at bay. It would have been sinful of her to try to take his love from Caroline, but if she truly did not love him . . .

A little smile lit the depths of her lovely eyes. Perhaps there might be a chance for her to find a happiness she had not dreamed could be hers.

Five

They had been travelling for four days when the leading pole suffered a break and they were forced to get down and make their way to the nearest inn on foot. Fortunately, the accident happened almost immediately after they had passed the Turnpike Inn, and so they had only a few minutes walk to a place of safety.

'It is a nuisance for I had hoped to go further today,' Caroline said as they reached the inn. By its very nature it was rather busier and noisier than the inn that her servants had been intending to stop at that night. However, there was little choice but to ask for rooms since they could not continue their journey that day. 'Let us hope that they can accommodate us here.'

Fortunately, the landlord was able to give them a large room with a double bed, which they were happy to share. A truckle bed for Tilly would be brought out at night so that she could sleep with them. It would mean some overcrowding and was not what they would normally have chosen. However, Caroline decided that they had a good arrangement when a troop of Royalist Cavaliers rode into the yard some minutes after they arrived and demanded they were brought wine and food in the private parlour. They were laughing and shouting, and seemed prepared to take over the whole inn.

The landlord told them that his private parlour was small and already occupied by two ladies and their maid, and the captain of the troop came to the door, doffing his hat with a dashing smile. He was richly dressed, his doublet and crimson breeches slashed with gold thread, his hat wide-brimmed and adorned with a large white curling feather.

'Good morrow, ladies,' he said as he swept them an elegant leg. 'Since you are in possession of mine host's parlour I shall not turn you out – though I would like to share my meal with you.'

Mercy looked anxiously at Caroline, her eyes filled with a mute appeal, but fortunately the landlord's wife came bustling up and sent him off with a few sharp words.

'Some of these soldiers think they own the place,' she grumbled sourly. 'You don't want him bothering you, ladies – and if he should come again, call for my husband. We'll sort him out for you.'

'I do not believe he will return,' Caroline replied with a little smile for she had not been frightened of the Cavalier. He reminded her a little of Harry for his smile held the same kind of devilry. 'I thank you for your help, madam.'

'If it isn't one lot it's the other,' the woman muttered half to herself, her generous chins wobbling. 'Shouting and ordering everyone about. I don't know what the country is coming to and that's the truth.'

Mercy looked at Caroline as the woman shuffled off about her business. 'I am glad she sent him away and yet . . .'

'You would have liked to ask if he has seen Harry?' Caroline nodded, knowing that she might feel the same if the men had been a part of Cromwell's troop. It was impossible to stop thinking of Nicolas, wondering where he was and if he was thinking of her.

'Perhaps we shall see him later,' she said.

However, the troop left an hour or so later and the look of disappointment in Mercy's eyes was plain to see.

For the rest of the evening and night the people who stopped at the inn for food and rest were simple country folk passing through, and the two girls were fortunately not disturbed by more visitors. Both of them slept as well as might be expected in a strange bed, though Caroline was woken early by a cock crowing in the yard. She lay for a while thinking of things that made her restless, then crept from her bed to glance out of the window. The grooms were sleepily going about their business and a coach was at the turnpike, waiting to be admitted.

She dressed without waking Mercy and went down. The landlord's wife was cleaning the parlour and smiled at her as she entered.

'You're early, mistress,' she said. 'I'll bring your breakfast in half an hour if that will suit?'

'Thank you,' Caroline said. 'I would like just some bread and honey if you please.'

She went outside to take a breath of air. Their destination was just a day and a half of travelling ahead if they had no more delays and she would be glad to arrive for she was growing weary of the journey.

'Mistress Caroline.' She had not seen her father's coachman approach and turned as he spoke. 'I wanted to let you know that the pole has been mended, and we can continue when it suits you.'

'Thank you, Walter,' she said and smiled at him. 'We breakfast in half an hour and then we shall be ready to go on.'

Returning to the inn she discovered that Mercy had come down to the parlour and was reading a news sheet which had just been delivered to the landlord, who had given it to her.

'It warns of a dangerous highwayman who hath been working this road,' Mercy said looking alarmed.

'I dare say he will not bother us for we are well protected.' Caroline smiled at her. 'And if he does stop us I have my father's pistol.'

'You would not use it?' Mercy looked even more alarmed now and Caroline laughed as the landlord's wife brought their breakfast, which consisted of freshly baked rolls, butter, honey and a jug of her own cider to quench their thirst.

After breakfast the carriage was brought round and they were off once more. However, they had not been travelling for much more than an hour when they heard a shout and the horses were pulled to a shuddering halt. Mercy gave a gasp of fright and then they heard voices shouting, and glancing out of the window, Caroline saw that a troop of men was blocking the road.

'I do not think it is the highwayman,' Caroline told her. 'It looks like a troop of Cavaliers.'

As she hesitated, wondering whether she should get down, one of the men came towards the carriage. She reached beneath her cloak, her fingers tightening on the small pistol her father had given her. She was not sure she would be able to fire it in need, but at least it might have the effect of making others pause.

As the trooper approached she wondered what best to do but waited prudently for him to speak first. 'Forgive me, ladies,' the trooper said, seeming awkward. 'But would you be willing to take up an injured man?'

'An injured man?' Caroline looked at him suspiciously. 'Who is that man and how was he injured?'

'It is Captain Benedict,' the trooper replied. 'Someone fired a pistol at him from behind those trees up there. Fortunately, the shot missed but it caused his horse to rear up and he fell and cracked his head and injured his shoulder.'

Mercy was looking out of the window. 'It is the man from the inn yesterday,' she cried, and before anyone could stop her she had the carriage door open and jumped down.

Seeing that her cousin was determined to involve herself with the injured man, Caroline also got down and Tilly followed her. When they reached the man, who had now recovered enough to sit with his back propped up against a tree, she saw that Mercy was offering him a flask of Brandewine that had been given them for the journey.

The Cavalier smiled up at her. He looked pale and shaken, but he accepted the flask and took a few sips before returning it to her.

'I thank you for your kindness, lady,' he said and then looked at Caroline. 'I believe we have met before? Please forgive my men for stopping you, but I am in need of help.'

'Yes, I can see that you are,' Caroline replied and sighed. 'Very well, I believe I cannot refuse. Your men may bring you to the carriage – but I will have your word of honour now that neither you nor your men will take advantage of the situation.'

'On my honour as a gentleman, mistress,' he said. 'Indeed, my men shall form a guard for you on your journey, for these are uncertain times, and I have heard that a wicked highwayman haunts this road. Where are you headed, if I may ask?'

'Our destination is none of your affair, sir,' Caroline said, her manner proud and haughty. 'We shall help you as far as the nearest inn and then you must make arrangements for yourself.'

The Cavalier smiled oddly, inclining his head. 'I am grateful for your generosity, mistress. Will you at least tell me your names?'

'I am Mercy Waldegrave,' Mercy said and then looked apologetically at Caroline. 'And this lady is my cousin, Mistress Caroline Saunders.'

Captain Benedict nodded, but two of his men were helping him to his feet and it was obvious that he was in a great deal of pain. He smothered a curse and it seemed as if the effort was almost too much for him, but a little later, settled in the carriage, he gave his benefactress a rueful smile.

'I dare say you must be wishing me to hell,' he murmured. 'I am sorry to be such a nuisance. We are on our way to Oxford and . . .'

'As we are,' Mercy said and then stopped again. 'Oh, I should not have said that . . .'

'It shall go no further,' the Cavalier said and laughed softly. 'I have friends there, you see, and I shall be able to rest and recover before . . .' He stopped as if he had said too much.

'You go to Oxford?' Caroline frowned. She hesitated for a moment, wrestling with her conscience; it was highly improper that he should travel all that distance with them,

97

and she ought to take him no further than the next inn. Compassion won, for it was her Christian duty to help an injured man. 'Then I suppose that we may take you some of the way. The house we are to visit is just outside.'

'You are generous indeed.' He smiled at her. 'It was fortunate for me that you came this way.'

'Yes, perhaps,' Caroline replied, and then, glancing at Mercy, 'My cousin wishes to ask you a question, sir – if you feel able to answer it?'

'I shall surely do my best.'

'Have you seen Harry Mortimer?' Mercy said, the words bursting from her in her eagerness. 'He is Lord Mortimer of Thornberry's son.'

'I know he of whom you speak,' Captain Benedict replied with a slight frown. 'We have met occasionally at court. I fear I can tell you no more. He may already be on his way to join His Majesty. It is my intention to journey there when I have finished my business elsewhere. Would you wish me to mention that you asked after him, mistress?'

'Yes,' Caroline said at the same moment as Mercy denied it with a flush of her cheeks. 'You may tell Harry that we hope he is well – and that we are to stay with my mother's relation at Oxford.'

'I shall be happy to do so,' Captain Benedict replied. 'Would you forgive me if I closed my eyes for a few moments, ladies? I have a fearful headache.'

'Of course you must rest,' Caroline said. 'Sleep if you wish. You are safe with us, sir.'

He smiled and closed his eyes. Mercy looked across the carriage at Caroline, but she placed a finger to her lips, silencing her. She had been reluctant to take their passenger with them, but now that she had she would do all she could to help him.

By the time they reached the next coaching inn, their passenger was feeling much recovered. He dined with them in the host's private parlour and proved to be an entertaining and pleasant companion. He accepted Caroline's offer to go on with them to the inn where they were to stay the night, but there he left them to join his men and the next morning he had gone before they rose. A letter of thanks was waiting for Caroline when she went down. She read the brief words telling her that he was now recovered enough to make his own way, and tucked it into her purse, feeling relieved that the incident was over. She would probably never see Captain Benedict again.

They set out on their journey once more after breakfast and accomplished it without incident, arriving in the afternoon just before dinner. Margaret's house was a large, well-built house dating from Elizabethan times; trails of ivy climbed the walls, which were of soft red bricks that had faded into a mellow rose, and there were many small windows of thick grey glass.

The coachman drove them to the front entrance, helping first Caroline and then Mercy and Tilly down from the carriage, before taking it to the back to unload their baggage. He would be made welcome in the kitchens at Farringdon Hall, and then return to his master's house as he had come, in easy stages.

Margaret Farringdon came to the front hall as a footman opened the door and invited them in. A tall, slim lady of middle years, she retained some of the beauty that had been hers as a young girl, her hair still bright gold, though only a few wisps of it were allowed to show beneath her fetching cap of lace and frills. Her gown was a rich crimson embroidered with gold thread, and she wore a fine lace neckerchief tied at her throat and pinned with a large pearl and garnet brooch.

'Welcome, my dears,' she said, holding out her hands to them. 'I have wished to have you stay with me for many a day, Caroline.' She took her hands, kissing the girl's cheek, and then turned to Mercy. 'And you must be Caroline's cousin. May I call you Mercy, my dear?'

'Yes, of course, ma'am,' Mercy said and bobbed a curtsey to her. 'It is very kind of you to have us to stay with you.'

'Kindness, pouff!' their hostess dismissed it with a puff of her lips. 'It is you who are kind to stay with me. I have many friends but it is always good to have young people about me – and with this dreadful war hanging over us who knows what may happen?'

'Is there any news?' Caroline asked. 'I have prayed that something will happen to prevent it, but I have little hope of it.'

'I fear nothing can prevent it now,' Margaret said with a frown. 'Tempers have been raised and things said that cannot be unsaid. Men are proud creatures, my dears. I doubt it is within their nature to come to amicable terms at this moment. No, they will fight and expect the spilling of blood to appease their anger, but of course it will not.'

A little shudder went through Caroline. 'We must pray that it is soon over.'

'Yes, of course,' Margaret said as she drew them deeper into the house. 'Come into my parlour and we shall take a glass of sweet wine to refresh ourselves, and then you shall go up to your rooms for I dare say you would like to rest before we dine.'

'Shall we not keep your cook waiting?' Caroline asked, for the hour was well past four o'clock.

'We do not dine here until six,' her hostess explained. 'My husband always kept London hours even when in the country and I have followed his example. This evening it will be just the three of us for I thought we should have a little time to get to know one another, but tomorrow I have invited guests and I dare say we shall be invited to dine with various friends. But come, let us take a little wine. I shall not weary you with too much chatter for we have time enough ahead of us.' She beamed at them. 'Now, my dears. You would like to go up and refresh yourselves, I am sure. We shall meet again soon, and I promise you we shall all have a merry time together.'

Caroline was writing a letter to her mother. She sat with her quill in her hand poised over the sheet of fine pressed paper, wondering where to begin. She and Mercy had been residing with Margaret Farringdon for almost a week now and this was the first moment she had truly felt able to sit at leisure for their feet had hardly touched the ground.

After the first evening, when they had dined simply en famille, they had gone from one joyful gathering to the next. Margaret's friends were many and varied, some of them of her own age but most of a younger generation. She had introduced the girls to several young ladies of their own age, besides more than a dozen gentlemen, though most of the men were married or older.

'I fear that a lot of the young men are not here at the moment,' Margaret had told them sorrowfully. 'It is an unfortunate thing that they have other, more important things, on their minds.'

'It does not matter,' Caroline told her. 'We have pleasant company and that is all we require, ma'am.'

They had been into Oxford several times; it was a lovely town with its towering spires and ancient universities, for it had been a seat of learning from the 12th century. There were many beautiful churches, including St Michael's built in the 11th century and St Mary the Virgin, its 13th century sister. At the heart of the town was Carfax or the *quadrifurcua*, meaning four-forked, four main streets that followed the four points of the compass.

One of the best things was the abundance of shops, Caroline thought as she began to write in her careful copperplate hand. In one of the cobbled lanes of the town they had found a stationer's, where she had bought this paper and a beautiful journal in which to keep a record of her thoughts. The shop also loaned books for the deposit of one crown to customers who were accounted trustworthy, and as Margaret's guests, both Caroline and Mercy had been allowed to choose from a shelf of some thirty volumes. These included many of the works of Master Shakespeare besides Ben Johnson and John Donne, as well as others as yet unknown to Caroline. Such riches would prove a source of much pleasure and Margaret had told them that there were other places where they could also borrow books for the cost of a few pennies.

They had also visited a milliner's shop, where Caroline had bought a charming tall steeple hat trimmed with curling feathers for herself and persuaded Mercy to purchase a pretty hat with a wide brim. It was fashioned of green velvet and became her well, lifting the gloom from her habitual gowns of grey and black.

'Harry would think you beautiful in that,' she told Mercy when she hesitated over the purchase, and had persuaded the girl to part with her money, a whole silver shilling and some pennies.

Caroline smiled as she laid down her pen. She had made no mention of the Cavalier they had taken up in their carriage, for it was not necessary. It was unlikely they would meet with Captain Benedict again.

Having finished her letter, sanded and sealed it with wax and her own signature ring, she took it downstairs, for Margaret had promised to send it by the carrier with her own letters. It might take some weeks for Lady Saunders to receive it, but there was every hope that she would do so in time. The carrier was worthy of trust and would see the letter safely on its way.

As she reached the hall, she placed her letter with others on an oak side table in the hall, and as she heard the sound of laughter she made her way towards the parlour whence the sound came. Entering, she stopped in surprise for there were three gentlemen already seated there, enjoying a glass of wine with Margaret and Mercy, who had come down earlier.

Mercy looked up as she saw Caroline. 'We have a visitor,' she said. 'Captain Benedict called to see Margaret and brought some of his friends. He was surprised to see me for he did not know we were staying here.'

The gentlemen had got to their feet as Caroline entered. Captain Benedict turned to her, making her a respectful bow and smiling.

'It was a most pleasant surprise, mistress,' he said, his

eyes bright with laughter. 'I had not thought to find such charming company – though Mistress Farringdon always keeps a welcome for us.'

'Sir,' Caroline said and frowned for she was not as certain as Mercy that he had been surprised to find them here. 'I trust you are recovered from your accident?'

'I am very well, ma'am,' he said, 'which must be in part due to your kindness in allowing me room in your carriage when I was injured.'

'It was nothing. I could not refuse to help in the circumstances.'

'You were exceedingly kind to this sad scamp of a nephew of mine,' Margaret told her. 'Had I known I should have thanked you for it at once, Caroline.'

'Captain Benedict makes too much of it,' she replied and sat down on the settle close to the fireplace so that the gentlemen might also be seated.

'But I am remiss,' Captain Benedict told her. 'My friends – Captain Lord William Bolton, and Captain Henry Marsh, all at your service, ladies.'

Caroline inclined her head. 'I am pleased to meet you, gentlemen.' Margaret Farringdon seemed to be very much of the Royalist persuasion, although she had not thought it until this moment. Sir John had not known it or he might not have permitted this visit.

'I should scold you for not visiting me before, Walter,' Margaret said but she was smiling affectionately at she looked at her nephew. 'You have been here for nigh on a week and this is the first time you have thought to call on me.'

'Forgive me,' he replied. 'I had other business – business that takes me away on the morrow, aunt. However, we shall be pleased to dine with you today if you will have us?'

'Need you ask?' Margaret said, looking at him indulgently. It was clear that he was high in her estimation, and could do little wrong. 'I am sure Mercy and Caroline will be pleased to keep you company until then. You must excuse me now while I see to some business.'

A small silence followed her exit from the room, and then Captain Benedict got up from his seat and came to sit on a padded stool next to the bench where Caroline was seated.

'Would you care to walk in the gardens until dinner?'

'It is a pleasant enough afternoon,' Caroline said. 'Would you like to walk, Mercy?'

It was agreed that they would all take a stroll in the gardens. Caroline and Captain Benedict found themselves side by side, while the other two gentlemen accompanied Mercy. It was clear that at least one of them had been stunned by her beauty, for she had chosen to wear a pale grey velvet gown that morning, trimmed with a falling band of lace that Caroline had made for her as a gift. She had begun to wear her hair looped up about her face with ribbon knots and to leave off the plain caps that she had worn in the past, and the change in her was stunning.

'Do you and your friends go to join His Majesty?' Caroline asked for she was very conscious of the man walking beside her as they strolled in Margaret's large and formal gardens.

'Yes, on the morrow.' He glanced at her. 'When we first met I thought your cousin of the Puritan persuasion, but I may have been mistaken?'

'Mercy's stepfather is indeed of that persuasion, but she is more liberal in her views, as is my father. We do not take sides in this quarrel, sir, and would have peace between the King and his people – all his people.'

'I fear there is little chance of that, mistress. I believe we must teach this rabble a lesson if the King is to be master of his own country.'

'Would it not be better to talk than spill the blood of your own countrymen?'

'I am sorry that it must be,' he replied, and yet she was not sure that he was sorry at all and thought he merely spoke softly to please her. A gleam in his eyes told her that he looked forward to the fight and believed that the Royalists would secure an easy victory. 'But there are times when men must do their duty.'

'Yes, perhaps,' she said. 'It may be well that I am merely a woman and can play no part in this conflict.'

'Women are meant for kinder work,' he replied. 'You have beautiful hands, Mistress Saunders. They should not be soiled with blood.'

Caroline was not sure that she liked his compliments and did not answer him. Instead, she remarked on the garden. It was set out with well-trimmed hedges that formed squares, within which different plants were displayed. Some were set with roses, beautiful, full-blown and fading now as the summer gave way to autumn. Others held scented herbs, lavender that had been shorn of its perfumed harvest, honeysuckle and rosemary. She remarked on a bed of pure white lilies and Captain Benedict confessed to an interest, for at home, like many others of his class, he took pride in such things. Caroline was able to give an informed opinion of various plants and shrubs, for her father too had been a collector in his time.

In this manner they whiled away the time until it was dinner, when they returned to the house. The others made a merry company, and Caroline was pleased to see that Mercy seemed to be enjoying herself and that Captain Marsh had the knack of making her laugh.

It was pleasant to hear for she had not laughed much in recent weeks. And yet Caroline was aware of an unease within herself, and was aware that her father would not care to see her in such company.

It was clear that Margaret was delighted with the young men's company and kept them there as long as she could. However, Caroline was not sorry to see them leave, and though Captain Benedict bowed over her hand and thanked her most sincerely for her kindness to him when he was injured, she could not truly like or trust him. She was certain that his business in Oxford had been for the King, for though there was a strong Royalist faction in the town many of the ordinary townsfolk were for Parliament.

After they had taken their leave, the ladies retired to their own rooms. For a while Caroline wrote in her journal for she could not easily sleep. Her thoughts were with Nicolas and she felt close to him, almost as if he were nearby. Putting down her pen, she went over to the window and looked out. It was a dark night and she could see nothing in the garden clearly, just the shapes of bushes and trees. Sighing, she returned to her desk but the desire to write had gone.

She believed that Nicolas might have been thinking of her as she was of him that was why she had felt him close to her. Had he meant it when he said that he would marry her when the war was over, no matter what? She stood up and began to pace the room for she had only the memory of that passionate kiss to sustain her. Nicolas had sworn that he cared for her and she believed him, but there were so many obstacles in their way. How could she wed him when her father had broken all contact with his family?

If she stood against him in this it would mean a breach between them – but if she did not marry the man she loved it would break her heart. But she could not give him up. She would not!

Still restless, she returned to bed and blew out the candle, drifting slowly into a deep and peaceful sleep.

Nicolas lay on his hard cot thinking of Caroline as he had last seen her, of her smile and her sweetness, and the way her eyes sparked when she was piqued or aroused. There were other women as lovely, her cousin was said to be beautiful, but it was the woman inside that called to Nicolas now as he lay, contemplating the night through the window of the inn at which he was staying.

Sometimes it was the waiting that seemed the worst. Cromwell had spoken to him earlier of his belief that it must begin soon, and of the urgency that most men felt.

'If we cannot win this first battle,' he had told Nicolas, 'then 'tis likely to be a long and bitter struggle. If the fools would but agree together . . .'

Nicolas knew that it irked him because the generals in

command of this army, Fairfax, Essex and Manchester amongst others, were arguing between themselves. The men who had flocked to answer their call were often untutored, common folk who had never wielded a weapon in their lives, being more used to a ploughshare than a sword. Most were undisciplined, badly trained and ignorant of what lay ahead. On the other hand, most of the King's Cavaliers were gentlemen, trained to ride, shoot and use their swords from an early age.

'We need strong clear thinking,' Nicolas said, understanding his colonel's frustration. His own troop had been taught to obey his command and were beginning to gain a reputation for their discipline. 'But our cause is just and surely we must prevail – however long it takes?'

'Aye, that is true,' Cromwell replied with a wintry smile. 'I fear it will cost men's lives before the fools listen, but in the end I dare say we shall have our victory.'

Nicolas's eyes were dark with emotion as he rose from his bed, unable to sleep. He prayed that the victory would come soon so that he might return to his home and claim Caroline as his wife. Looking out into the darkness of the night, he wondered if she too was sleepless. Sometimes he felt her so close that he could almost reach out and touch her. But if she was here he would not be restless, for they would lie together and this burning need, this aching deep in his loins, would be banished by her lips.

His mouth twisted in a rueful smile. He would not sleep and there might be those amongst the men who were also restless, dreaming of home and family. He would go down to them, join them, pray with them, for most were devout, good men who had been driven to this fight by conscience.

Harry sat drinking wine with his friends. The four of them were the only ones left in the inn for it was late into the night, and the landlord was yawning behind his bar as he waited for them to leave. They had been playing cards for most of the evening and for once he had actually won.

'I think my luck is in,' he laughed as their entertainment

ended for the evening, standing up and yawning. His doublet was open to the waist, his shirt gaping at the neck, the frills of lace, usually so pristine, awry. He had drunk several glasses of wine and yet his head was clear for with the battle looming he had not been able to drink himself into the oblivion he craved.

He left the inn at which he and his friends had been whiling away the hours, looking towards the Royalist camp. He could see the fires burning, the smoke drifting, mingling with the rancid smell of horses, unwashed bodies and fear, and knew that the men would be restless before the battle. He ought perhaps to join those who served with him, yet he too was restless and did not feel like mouthing the false platitudes that would be expected of an officer.

He walked into the darkness, his thoughts returning to his home and the night that he had left it with his father's blessing. A twinge of conscience struck him as he recalled his crime, for he had stolen from his own father to pay more debts. It was not something he was proud of but he had seemed to have no choice, for it was urgent that he paid the most pressing of his debts.

He was a damned fool! He swore softly in the darkness. It might be better if he were killed in battle for he was in such a predicament that he did not know how to extricate himself. His father would give him nothing more. Indeed, he would be hard pressed to keep the estate running. More land would have to be sold, and there would be little left of the fortune that had once belonged to his family. And most of that was his fault.

He should have come to his senses long since, Harry thought ruefully. He had placed all his hopes on his marriage to Caroline, but it seemed that that was at an end. Unless, he thought, his optimism reasserting itself, he could persuade her to marry him despite the quarrel between their fathers.

Rowena stood looking at the spires of Oxford, feeling a spiral of excitement curl through her. She and her mother had had no thought of their final destination when they left their cottage. It had been a hurried leaving, for Rowena had told her mother that she had witnessed the murder of her father, and Sally Greenslade had told her something that had shocked her.

It was a secret that her mother had kept for many years, and only now that the violent husband she had feared was dead did she dare reveal it to her daughter – for it was the name of her true father.

But the truth was so shocking and so terrible that Rowena had wanted to flee from Thornberry. However, in the weeks spent wandering, she had come to see that one day some profit might be got from her secret knowledge, for it seemed that she was the daughter of a yeoman landowner and that something might be owed her by his family.

She and Sally had hitched lifts whenever they could for they could not afford to pay to ride on the coach. The last one had been with a man carting goods for the army. He had made it plain that he lusted after Rowena and she had strung him along with vague promises and sighs, finding excuses all the while why she could not bed with him.

In the end she had sent him off with a pretence of outraged modesty, boxing his ears and crying as if he had insulted her. They had been walking for the last week, sleeping rough and eating whatever they could mange to find in the hedgerows, sometimes buying a loaf or meat pies from a market seller to supplement their meagre diet.

But now they were in Oxford, and if the evidence of her own eyes was true, there were Cavalier soldiers aplenty here. Harry Mortimer might be here, but if he was not there would be others. Rowena had denied her favours to the rough soldier who had given them a lift on his wagon, but if she found an officer to her liking she might not be so reluctant to lie with him. Her mother had spoken of finding work at one of the many inns, but Rowena had no intention of working for her bread unless she was forced to it.

She had come here because they had heard that the

Royalists had been gathering nearby in force, and she hoped that she would find Harry Mortimer amongst them. Failing that, she might be forced to find another rich lover, one that had money to spare and would give her presents.

Caroline was finding it difficult to sleep at nights for Nicolas seemed to walk often in her thoughts, and she often lay wakeful wondering when they would see each other again. There had been rumours every day for the past week that the fighting would begin soon, and now it was rumoured that a battle was to take place imminently and somewhere not too far distant from them, for both armies had gathered in Oxfordshire and were preparing for a fight.

When the news came on the morning of the 24th of October, Caroline heard the shouting from outside her window. She opened it to hear more of what was said, and her heart began to race wildly as the gardeners working in the formal beds below began to cry out the news of a victory for the King.

Victory for the King! Caroline's stomach clenched with fear as she wondered if Nicolas had been wounded in the battle, and how many were dead. Had Rupert been caught in the fighting? He was so young and inexperienced that her heart ached for him. What terrible scenes had he witnessed and how was he faring?

Within minutes of the news reaching the house, Mercy came hurrying to her room, full of what she had been told, her eyes wide with anxiety.

'They say there has been a terrible battle at Edgehill,' she said in a voice breathy with fear. 'And it has ended in victory for His Majesty.'

'I pray God that neither Nicolas, my brother or Harry were wounded,' Caroline said and Mercy agreed. 'Perhaps now this nonsense will be at an end.'

'I pray it will be so,' her cousin said.

However, when they went downstairs together, it was to hear news that made such a swift ending unlikely.

'His Majesty was victorious,' Margaret told them but she

110

was frowning and not as elated as Caroline had expected. 'However, it seems that Essex rallied his troops at the end and instead of our troops finishing them off once and for all, it ended in what might more truthfully be called a stalemate.'

Even as she spoke, a man came striding into the parlour and Margaret gave a shriek of delight as she fell upon his shoulder, for he was clearly unhurt and elated by the partial victory.

'Walter,' she cried. 'God be praised you are safe. 'Tis well you have come for now you may tell us the truth of it; there are so many tales that we do not know what to believe.'

'It was my purpose in coming,' Captain Benedict replied and smiled at her. 'The battle took place yesterday at Edgehill, a few leagues north-west of Banbury, as you may know. Our armies were drawn up on an elevated ridge and we drove down on them, scattering their ranks and putting them to flight . . .'

'Then 'twas a victory indeed!'

'It might have been had not Prince Rupert given chase and left the field,' Benedict said. 'For Essex rallied his men and prevented what should have been a rout. He was forced to leave the field to us eventually, but had Rupert steadied his men we might have crushed them totally.'

'Well, 'tis still a victory,' his aunt claimed, 'and I am glad to see you safe and well.'

'I may not stay,' he told her. 'I have urgent business in the town. But I wanted to see you, and to give Mistress Waldegrave news I believe she may be glad to have . . .' He smiled at Mercy. 'I spoke with Harry Mortimer after the battle, mistress, and though slightly wounded in his left arm he is well. He bid me tell you and Mistress Saunders that he would see you before too long.'

Mercy's face lit up with a smile so bright that he was dazzled by it. 'Oh thank you,' she cried. 'It was a kindness in you, sir, to bring us that news and I do thank you for it.'

'I shall return as soon as I may, aunt,' Captain Benedict said; he glanced briefly at Caroline as if he wished to say more, then inclined his head respectfully. 'Your servant, Mistress Saunders.'

Mercy could not contain her happiness after the sound of his booted feet had died away. 'Harry is alive,' she said to Caroline, her eyes glowing with happiness. 'And he will soon be here . . .'

'I dare say most of the King's army will soon be here,' Margaret informed them with a complacent smile. 'I have it on good authority that His Majesty intends to set up his capital here for the duration of the war. It is to this end that my nephew visited Oxford a few weeks ago. It is a good place strategically, not too far from London, and may be easily fortified with a string of garrisons.'

'The King is to come here?' Caroline was shocked by the news that she knew would not please her father, but what could she do? It would be foolish to attempt to return home at this moment, for now that the war had actually started, the countryside would be teaming with soldiers from both armies and it could be dangerous for two women travelling alone. She would simply have to bide her time and wait, she thought. And, as she saw the glow in Mercy's eyes, she knew that she could not have dragged her cousin away at this moment, for it was obvious that she was longing to see Harry again.

'Is it not good news?' Margaret said, looking pleased and clearly unaware of Caroline's thoughts. 'We shall have a wonderful time this winter for Oxford will be filled with young men, and it is doubtful that another battle will take place before the spring.'

'I wish that the King might settle things with Parliament,' Caroline said. 'Perhaps then this war might be at an end.'

Mercy sat before the window, gazing out at the night sky. It had been very cold of late and there had been a frost earlier, but that had gone now and there was an odd mildness in the air. Surely the stars were brighter, the heavens a deep midnight blue rather than black – or was it simply that her heart was singing with joy?

Harry was alive and he had promised that he would see them soon. The words were written in her mind in letters of fire, illuminating her world, for the happiness she felt was something she had not known before this. Harry was coming here, and in this house she would be permitted to see him, for Margaret would welcome him.

His looks, his touch, the little intimate whispers he had used to make her smile had surely meant that he cared for her? While he was promised to Caroline he had been unable to speak plainly, but now, now there would be nothing to stop him. If he loved her he would tell her and they would be married.

If only such happiness could be hers! Mercy had expected nothing from life before she came to stay with Caroline and Lady Saunders, but it seemed that anything was possible now.

Her stepfather would forbid the match if he knew of it. Even her kind cousins would think ill of her for going against their wishes in seeing him but she would brave anything for his sake.

She knew that she would defy her stepfather to marry the man she loved. As for Sir John, she could only hope that he would relent and wish her happy. She was on fire with impatience for Harry to return, for surely when he did so he would make his feelings clear. Now that he was no longer bound to Caroline, he would speak to her of the love he bore her instead of merely hinting.

She stood up, sighing as she turned towards the bed. Was she letting herself hope for too much? Harry had never actually told her that he loved her, but surely she had not mistaken that look in his eyes?

Six

'You know that I would still marry you?' Three days had passed since news of the battle had reached them and Harry had come on the afternoon of the third day. They were together in the small back parlour for he had asked to speak to her alone. 'I would honour my promise if you should wish it, Caro. No matter the consequences.'

'I thank you for making the offer,' she said, gazing up into his clear eyes, which were the colour of a perfect summer sky. 'But why do you want to wed me? Pray tell me the truth if you will. Are you in debt, Harry? Is it the money that makes you think I would suit you?'

He gave her a rueful smile, 'I think you know me too well. I am not in love with you, 'tis true, but I think we might have gone on comfortably together.' He liked Caroline well enough, but there was no denying that her fortune would have solved his problems.

'That is not enough for me.' A fire was crackling in the grate and outside the wind howled through the trees, for after a mild period the weather had turned wild of late. She looked at him thoughtfully. She had heard of his gambling from her father and of his entanglement with Rowena Greenslade from Granny Sorrell, but even had he been blameless she could not have wed him now. She would have no other but Nicolas for her heart belonged to him. 'I consider myself free of any promise and you must do the same, Harry. We were never actually betrothed and so neither one of us is legally bound.'

He nodded, for in his heart he knew it was not what he truly wanted, but for the sake of her fortune, which he so sorely needed, he had asked one last time. 'And you will not hate me for deserting you?'

'I could never hate you,' she said with a smile. 'We shall always be friends but I believe there is someone else you may prefer to wed?'

'You mean your cousin?' Harry nodded, for the attraction was strong, but Mercy had no money and neither had he. Once the war was over he would return to find the estate heavily encumbered by debt. Yet he would be quartered at Oxford for the winter and Mercy was truly lovely. There could be no harm in a little dalliance. His mouth curved in one of the smiles that the ladies found so charming. 'I do not know that she cares for me.'

'May I suggest that that is for you to discover?' Caroline said and smiled in return, for in this mood he was hard to resist. She was looking very pretty that day for she wore a short, waisted jacket and skirt of cutwork silk in a shade of blue that became her well. 'And now you must excuse me if you will, for I have promised to meet with friends in Oxford this afternoon.'

Harry inclined his head. 'Then I shall leave you. I dare say we shall meet often in company.'

'Yes, I imagine we may. Mistress Farringdon has many friends and we are invited to sup with them several times a week. She says that there will be small dances and suppers in abundance now that His Majesty is to take up residence here. She and others of like mind believe that even though Edgehill was not decisive the war must soon be at an end.'

Harry did not disillusion her, though privately he had his doubts. 'I shall look forward to seeing you and your cousin very soon.'

Caroline was thoughtful after he had left her. She did not know whether or not it would be right to encourage Mercy's hopes of Harry. She knew that her cousin was deeply in love, for the girl's expressive face could not hide her feelings, but could happiness ever come to her through a relationship with Harry Mortimer?

She sighed and thrust the doubts from her mind. It was for her cousin to make up her own mind and Caroline ought not to try and influence her one way or the other.

Her thoughts returned to a more personal problem. She had asked Harry early in their conversation if he had news of either his brother or her own, but though he had spoken to Rupert once on the eve of Edgehill, he had no news of Nicolas.

'Both sides lost too many men,' he had said with a trace of sorrow. 'I think our leaders were too fond of glory and played a winning hand badly. But I have heard nothing of Nicolas either way. Some lists of the dead came to my hand after the battle. His name was not on them, but that proves nothing.'

Caroline had let it go there. Harry felt his brother was wrong to take up arms against the King, but there was no bitterness between them.

She left the parlour and went upstairs to find her cousin. Mercy was sewing a lace kerchief. It was clearly meant for a gentleman and she put it aside as Caroline asked if she might talk to her.

'Yes, of course. Have you seen Harry?' She looked hopeful, eager, as if expecting he might have asked for her.

'For a few moments. He has pressing business elsewhere,' Caroline said, not quite truthfully. 'However, we have settled it. We are both to consider ourselves free to marry elsewhere.'

There was no mistaking the joy in Mercy's eyes. Caroline felt an odd start of fear as she saw it. Something warned her that her cousin was headed for unhappiness and yet she could not find the words to prevent it. There were none. It might be that Harry truly loved Mercy and to warn her of vague doubts concerning his character would be spiteful and cruel.

'You have not forgot that we are to meet Mistress Partridge and her daughter this afternoon?'

'No, indeed,' Mercy replied. 'Perhaps we may see Harry – or even Rupert. If Harry is here your brother may also have come to Oxford.'

'Harry told me that he had seen him briefly the night before Edgehill. He was with Prince Rupert, for the prince hath taken a liking for him. Harry says that it was unlikely he would have been in the thick of the fighting. Because of his youth and inexperience, he would possibly have been told to help guard the baggage train.'

Mercy nodded, her expression grave. 'And there is no word of Nicolas?'

'None,' Caroline said. There was a tearing pain inside her for she had a feeling that something was wrong, that he had suffered some hurt. 'But I pray that in this instance the lack of news means that he still lives.'

Pray God he did for she did not know how she would bear it if he died!

'It is as I feared,' Cromwell allowed his anger to show momentarily as he spoke with Nicolas. 'We behaved as the rabble they named us and broke before them.'

'Yet all was not lost for we rallied at the end,' Nicolas replied. He eased his shoulder, which was painful from the wound he had received during the battle. He raised his brows quizzically at his colonel, 'What now think you?'

'The King will take refuge in Oxford,' his companion answered thoughtfully. 'I have too much respect for that town to think of storming it even if we could, which methinks would be nigh impossible as things stand. The Royalists are too great in numbers. No, we must wait for the spring and see what happens.'

'Then may I ask leave to visit someone, sir?'

'If your journey is important, you make take three weeks but no more. We must be watchful lest the Royalists try to march on London, though I doubt it for they will regroup and wait for the spring. And we shall not be idle this winter. We must train them hard. Our men will not break and run again if I can prevent it.'

'Our own men stood firm until the last,' Nicolas replied, for he too believed that had their army received the training they needed they might have fared better. 'We shall see the tide turn in our favour before we are done.'

Cromwell nodded, his face hard, hiding his thoughts. 'Where do you plan to go?'

'There is a house on the outskirts of Oxford. The lady I would speak with is, I believe, a visitor there.'

'Oxford? That might prove useful – but you would risk much to see this lady?'

'I would speak with her for I know she will be anxious.'

'You know the dangers?' Nicolas inclined his head. 'Were you taken you might be treated as a spy.'

'I go to see the lady I intend shall be my wife.' A smile touched his mouth. 'Should I happen to see troop movement – the strength of the garrisons – it would be mere coincidence.'

'Then God be with you,' Cromwell replied, though there was no answering smile. 'I would fain not lose one of my best captains, Nicolas. Do not take unnecessary risks.'

Nicolas inclined his head. He knew there was little hope of taking Oxford as things stood. Their army needed to learn discipline, as much amongst its leaders as the men. However, one day the tide would turn and anything he happened to learn now might then stand them in good stead.

Rowena stared sullenly at the pile of pots she was required to wash in the scullery of the large inn where her mother had found employment. She resented being put to work in the kitchens, for when she had agreed to work here she had expected she would be given the chance to serve the men who came here to drink, many of whom were Cavalier officers.

'Don't stand there, Rowena,' her mother chided. 'Fetch more hot water from the stove. We haven't all day.'

Rowena did as she was bid, leaving her mother to do the scouring on the excuse that more water was needed from outside. She took a large pewter pitcher and went out to the well in the courtyard, letting down the bucket by means of a pulley and winding it up again. As she lifted the bucket to pour water into her pitcher, she heard a burst of laughter and saw that a group of men had come out into the yard. It was clear that they had been drinking heavily, and they had come outside to relieve themselves at the far end of the yard, where a muddy ditch ran between the inn yard and a meadow. As they turned and began to walk back towards the inn, Rowena's heart raced with excitement. One of the men was Harry Mortimer!

She resisted the temptation to rush to him, because she was dressed in the homespun gown she used for work and her hair needed washing. If she wanted Harry to keep his promises, she would need to be looking her best, and to smell of the perfume that drove his senses wild.

Now that she knew he drank here she would find a way of meeting him, seemingly by accident. There was no need for him to know that she worked in the kitchens here . . .

Harry stared moodily into the empty tankard. He had won at cards the previous evening, which meant that he was able to pay his way for the moment, but his debts were constantly on his mind. He could see no way out of his predicament short of death, and it seemed that in battle he had a charmed life.

He had fought with courage, always in the thick of it, unmindful of his own safety, and for this he had become something of a hero to his friends. He had no need to buy his own ale for there was always someone to buy it for him.

A wry smile touched his mouth as he wondered what they would think if they understood the reasons behind his devil-may-care attitude. A strange recklessness had seized him on the battlefield, it rode him now, for there was no use in looking back. He could not put right the folly of recent years, but he would live for now – for the time that was left to him. He would take what he wanted and that included Mercy Waldegrave.

His decision made, he put the mood of despair that had

threatened to overcome him from his mind. He was young, Mercy was beautiful and he would have her if he could.

'Are you enjoying your visit, Caroline?' Margaret Farringdon asked when she visited the girl's room as she was dressing for dinner that evening. 'I think that colour of blue becomes you well. You are very pretty, my dear, and I know that Captain Benedict finds you charming.'

'You are too kind, ma'am.'

'I was thinking that you might care to have your portrait painted while you are here? I know of a good artist now living in Oxford whose work is much in the style of Van Dyck. You have heard of that gentleman, I am sure – a favourite with His Majesty, who is a connoisseur of art in all forms. You might have a miniature done and send it to your parents. I am sure it would please them. Or perhaps there is someone else who would wish to have your likeness?'

'I do not know, ma'am.'

Caroline's cheeks heated beneath the speculation in her hostess's eyes. Mistress Farringdon knew that Lady Saunders had sent her daughter to her in the hope that she might find her a suitable husband. Perhaps it was not just coincidence that Captain Benedict had been travelling to Oxford when they met.

'Not at all, my dear,' Margaret smiled knowingly. 'I would not influence you for the world, but Walter would make a charming and considerate husband.'

There, it was out. Caroline had suspected what was in her hostess's mind for a while now. It had seemed a little fortunate that they should meet the captain wherever they went. Not wishing to offend Mistress Farringdon, Caroline merely smiled and gave a little shake of her head, which might mean anything.

She would try to make sure that she gave Captain Benedict no chance to speak to her of marriage. Her heart belonged to Nicolas and she would take no other for her husband,

though she might take her hostess's advice and have a miniature done, for Nicolas might like to have it one day.

When Nicolas saw the troop of men camped in the vale
below he knew that he must go carefully from here on.
Oxfordshire was a country of two upland areas, the lime-
stone heights to the north, and the chalky downs to the south,
and it seemed that most of it in-between was crawling with
Royalist patrols at the moment. At first he had met with only
small groups of men moving from one place to another, but
now it was easy to see that these were larger groups. Naturally,
the Royalists were on full alert in case of an attack on the
city. It looked to Nicolas that they were entrenching themselves, as if they were preparing to strengthen the defences
of the town with a ring of garrisons.

Cromwell had been right to think Oxford well nigh impreg-
nable. It would take a huge force to lay siege here and there
would be much bloody fighting. For the moment it seemed
that there was a stand-off. The King's army was not strong
enough to take London, but his stronghold here was too difficult to breach.

Nicolas lay on the ground watching the camp fires below
for a few minutes before edging back, crawling on his
stomach to a distance where he could not be seen from below.
It would be foolish to risk being caught for he had already
seen enough to confirm his colonel's opinion.

'Stay where you are, you Roundhead dog!'

Nicolas stiffened as he heard the voice behind him. How
had this happened? He had heard nothing. His enemy had
crept up on him unawares.

'Put your hands above your head.'

Even as the voice commanded, Nicolas sensed that the
man was very close. With a recklessness born of desperation, he swung round, and seeing that the Cavalier was of
slight stature, flung himself on him. They struggled for
possession of the pistol, which, by reason of his greater
strength, Nicolas was able to wrest from the other man after

a fierce struggle. Indeed, he was forced to knock the man to the ground, where he lay catching his breath. However, the tussle had aggravated Nicolas's shoulder wound and he felt the sluggish flow of blood staining his shirt.

He touched the wet patch, cursing beneath his breath as he debated whether to kill the winded Cavalier or let him go. Then, as the moon slid out from behind a bank of cloud, lighting the sky, he saw the face of his enemy.

'Rupert! Damn it, lad. I could have killed you.'

Rupert Saunders looked up at the face of the man who had worsted him and knew him. Until that moment he had seen only the suspicious activities of a man he suspected was a Roundhead, though now that Nicolas had lost his hat in the struggle he could see that his hair had not been cut in that fashion.

'Is it truly you, Nicolas? I thought you were a damned Roundhead spying on us.'

'We are on opposite sides in this war, it is true,' Nicolas said and took his finger off the hammer of the pistol. 'But I was merely trying to find a way through your ranks. I am on my way to see Caroline at Oxford.'

'What is she doing there?' Rupert accepted his pistol, returning it to his belt. He could not kill a man he had known and liked all his life. Besides, if he tried, Nicolas was likely to kill him first.

'Your father was taken ill after you left. He sent Caroline to stay with Mistress Farringdon for a few months.'

'In the hope that she would find a husband, I suppose?' Rupert frowned at the news. His quarrel with his father had lain heavy on his conscience all this time. 'But why are you going to visit her?'

'Because I hope to make her my wife one day.'

'Ah . . .' Rupert grinned, the clouds banished from his mind for the moment. 'It's just as well I didn't shoot you in the back then. She would never have forgiven me.'

'In this case I can only agree,' Nicolas smiled wryly. 'However, if you should happen to come across another suspected enemy, keep your distance and call for assistance.'

Rupert rubbed ruefully at the back of his head, which had struck something hard as he fell. 'You knocked me down so hard 'tis a wonder I have not cracked my skull.'

'Forgive me. I thought it was a case of you or I and it was self preservation.'

Rupert nodded, understanding. 'You were truly seeking a way through our ranks and did not think to spy on us?'

'Oxford is too well garrisoned for us to make the attempt,' Nicolas said. 'For the moment I wish only to see Caroline.'

'Then you should ride due east of here along that ridge,' Rupert told him. 'We are here to guard the rivers and the bridges, but there is a spot some leagues in that direction where it is shallow and you may cross easily. I noticed that it was undefended when we came this way, but that may have been remedied by now.'

'I thank you for your advice,' Nicolas said and offered his hand. 'This war has made us enemies but may we not part as friends?'

Rupert hesitated, then grasped his outstretched hand.

'God speed and protect you,' he said. 'But if we should one day meet on the field of battle, be prepared for I shall kill you.'

'I should be very sorry to have to prevent you from doing that,' Nicolas said. 'God keep you, Rupert. '

He turned and walked away, his back an open target had Rupert wished to fire his pistol. He knew it would not happen but their struggle had done him harm. He could feel the burning pain in his shoulder and knew that his wound had opened once more.

Nicolas paused when he reached his horse, taking a clean neckerchief from his saddle pack and thrusting it inside his shirt. A moan broke from him as he hauled himself into the saddle and he thought with regret of the comfortable bed at the inn he had left behind. He would get no such luxury this night, nor yet for some to follow, but now he had come so far he could not turn back. There were as many Cavalier forces behind him as ahead. But he would be on his guard from now on, for if his would-be captor had been any other than Rupert, he might even now be dead.

Mercy was trembling with excitement as she looked at the note that had been left for her earlier that day. She had been out visiting friends with Caroline in Oxford and when she returned it lay there on a pewter plate on the hall table, where all letters were left for collection. Her heart had leaped as she saw it for she knew at once that it must be from Harry.

She opened it with trembling hands, reading the brief message swiftly and then more closely. He had asked her if he might see her privately in Oxford on the morrow. There was something he wished to say to her in confidence.

Mercy kissed the name he had written so boldly at the bottom of the small piece of paper, and the large X that he had scrawled beneath his name. Such a letter could only mean one thing; he wanted to tell her that he loved her.

Mercy read the note once more and then placed it in the small wooden coffer in which she stored everything that was precious to her. It would not be easy to slip away alone, but somehow she would manage it. She knew that to behave in such an immodest manner would be frowned upon by her stepfather, and indeed by others, but she had gone beyond caring in her desire to be with Harry. From now on she would follow her heart and forget her foolish doubts and fears. Harry cared for her and that was all that mattered.

Rowena laughed as she looked up at the face of her lover. How passionate he was, and how hungry for the satisfaction she gave him. He had had her twice that night already and yet now he was eager for more.

'You be never satisfied,' she pretended to grumble for she wanted some advantage from this arrangement and so far she had received nothing more than some food and wine. 'You promised to wed me, Harry Mortimer, and don't forget it. I be your true wife in everything but name, and I want what you promised me . . .'

Harry lay back against the hard bolster of the inn bed, staring at the canopy above his head. It had surprised him to find her in Oxford, but he had not been averse to tumbling her in his bed. However, he had discovered that despite her eagerness to please him, she bored him. Besides, she was as greedy over her desires as she was in bed, and while it pleased him in one way it annoyed him in others. He cursed himself for ever being fool enough to promise marriage, for she was like a terrier after rats and would not let go.

'I have no money,' he told her at last, 'and if I wed you, my father would cut me off without a penny.'

'But you promised!' Rowena pounced on him, pounding at his arms and shoulders with her fists. 'You promised me, Harry. I told you I had a temper. I'll kill you if you break your word to me. I swear it!'

He flung her away from him, tired of her all at once. She had been useful and he enjoyed their bouts in bed, but he would not listen to her threats. And he would never marry her. Besides, he had other plans that did not include Rowena Greenslade.

'You are welcome to try, my sweet,' he told her, and his merry smile was gone, his eyes like ice. 'It might end in tears for you, but that is the chance you take. I like you well enough, Rowena, but surely you never believed that I would wed you?'

She jumped out of bed, throwing herself at him like a wildcat, her nails scoring his bare arms and chest. He caught her wrists, holding her while she spat at him and hurled insults.

'I am bored with this,' he told her and his voice carried the lash of a whip. 'I am bored with you, Rowena. Find yourself another lover. God knows there are enough soldiers here. It should be easy enough for a comely whore such as you.'

She felt as if he had slapped her and stood staring at him for a moment, the pain of his rejection cutting her to the heart like the blade of a knife.

'I hate you, Harry Mortimer.' Her black eyes glittered with

anger. 'I shall put a curse on you! If you throw me off for another, both you and she shall be cursed.'

Harry gave her a push that sent her sprawling to the ground. He bent to pick up his breeches from the floor where he had dropped them earlier in his eagerness, and in that moment she came at him with an iron candlestick. She succeeded in landing a blow on his arm, which made him yell in pain, but in another moment he had her by the arm, twisting it up behind her back so that she cried out and the weapon fell from her fingers to the ground.

'You be hurting me,' she wept. 'I do hate you, and I do curse you. You shall die in grief and agony and so shall she that takes you from me.'

'Be damned to your curses,' Harry said with a snarl as he thrust her from him. He was driven by a devil on his shoulder. Beyond caring. She stumbled and lay on the floor, staring up at him with her black eyes. 'I want no more of you, whore. Do you hear me? Find yourself another lover.' He took a handful of silver coins and threw them on the floor, then picked up his shirt and doublet, buckled on his sword and walked out of the chamber.

Rowena lay where she was until he had gone. Hot tears stung her eyes and her throat was aching and raw with emotion. A bitter curl of hatred rose inside her and she cursed the day she had met him. He was a devil for he had lied to her, encouraged her hopes, and she hated him. But even as she wept bitter tears, she knew that she was lying to herself. She loved him and she would fly to him if he so much as lifted his little finger.

She stared at the coins angrily, her pride telling her to leave them where they lay, but she hated working at the inn and even this small amount of money would help.

What could she do to get Harry back? She had asked for too much. In her heart she had known her dream of being his wife would never come true, but he had given her presents and he had made her feel as if she were special while he loved her.

She would make him jealous, Rowena decided. She would

find another lover as he had bid her, and when he saw her with a fine cavalry officer, he would want her again.

Caroline sat alone in her bedchamber. As so often of late she was too restless to read or embroider. Her anxiety was all for Nicolas, for her instincts told her that he was either wounded or in danger. A premonition of something terrible had shadowed her for days and she could not shake it off.

Captain Benedict had begun to make his intentions clear, his attentions becoming most particular. She did not believe he loved her, but she knew that her fortune had been described to him as substantial. With things the way they were now, and Rupert part of the King's army, it was possible that she might be her father's only heir one day. A fine prize for any that sought wealth.

'May God forgive me for thinking it!' Caroline prayed constantly for news of her brother, her anxiety for him almost as great as that she felt for Nicolas.

Knowing that she could not rest, Caroline decided that she would go down to the garden. It was past two in the afternoon and Mercy had accepted an invitation to meet friends in Oxford. She had asked if Caroline would accompany her, but had seemed oddly relieved when she refused. Caroline wondered if perhaps she was meeting Harry. She thought that they might have met several times of late, sometimes when she herself was one of the party and at other times when she was not, and she worried that she ought to warn her cousin to be careful. Yet surely no harm could come of their meeting in company? Mercy seemed so much happier of late, as if she had cast off the shadows that had hung over her when she came to them. And she would not be foolish enough to meet Harry alone.

Caroline glanced at herself in her dressing mirror. She was wearing a formal bodice in a pale-green satin; boned, it had laces at the back to pull her waist in tightly, her skirts full at the sides but straight in front, and trimmed with parchment lace. Her hair was dressed in ringlets to either side of her face and pinned with love knots of velvet ribbon.

She picked up her cloak as she went out for the wind was bitter that day. For a few moments she wished herself at home sitting by the fire in her mother's parlour, for despite all the kindness of her hostess she missed her parents. If only this war had never happened! And yet were it not for the war she might have been betrothed and bound to marry the wrong brother.

Walking in the formal gardens, she wandered some distance from the house, lost in her thoughts. Oh, where was Nicolas? Was there no way she could have news of him?

'Caroline . . .'

When she heard the whisper the first time she thought it only in her mind, a product of her longing, her desire to bring him to her. Then it came again, and, as she looked about her, she saw him standing near a tall hedge, as if he had sought its shelter. Dressed in black with a white falling band, he was so different from the flamboyant Cavaliers she saw every day. Her heart quickened, her spirits leaping as she went towards him. He was alive: he was here!

'Nicolas . . .'

He placed a finger to his lips and she glanced over her shoulder to be certain that she could not be observed from the windows of the house as she ran the last few steps to his arms.

'My dearest love! How I have longed for you.'

'Caroline, my beloved . . .' He drew her to him, holding her close as their lips met in a passionate, hungry kiss. He felt the pain in his shoulder but suppressed the groan, his need for her more urgent than his wound. However, as they moved apart he saw that a small patch of blood had stained her bodice.

'We must take care,' he said. 'Wipe that off at once for it will stain, Caroline.'

She glanced at the small wet patch, her concern immediately for him rather than her gown. 'You are bleeding. You have been injured?'

'At Edgehill,' he told her grimly. 'It is nothing but it did not heal as it should and now it has opened again. It has been paining me for a while.'

She knew that it must be very painful or he would not have mentioned it. 'I must bind it for you. Come up to the house and . . .' She faltered as she realized that might be dangerous for him. 'No, there may be Cavaliers there for Mistress Farringdon is of the Royalist persuasion. And she would know at once that you are not one of their number. I must go back and bring linen and cures to help you.' She glanced about her, seeking for a place where he might rest, her eye falling on the summerhouse. 'Go there, my love, and I shall bring what you need – fresh bindings and a poultice that will ease the sting. I have some in my room for my mother swears by it and made me bring it in case it was needed. I think she thought that I might help Rupert should he be wounded and I nearby.'

'Your brother,' Nicolas said and smiled, happy to be able to bring her the news. 'When I left him last night he was well. He had not been wounded but was helping to guard the bridges and rivers.'

'You spoke to Rupert?' She stared at him. 'But do not tell me now – go to the summerhouse and wait. I shall return as soon as I can. If I am delayed do not worry. I shall come when I am able.'

'Take no risks for me, my love,' he began but she silenced him with a kiss on her finger which she transferred to his lips.

'If I am not hindered I shall be no more than a few minutes.'

She turned and ran swiftly through the formal gardens, slowing her pace only as she reached the house. Her one fear was that Margaret would see her and demand her attention, but she was fortunate enough to reach her bedroom without discovery. There she made a bundle out of a silk neckerchief, adding the pot of poultice her mother had pressed on her, which, she said, helped to draw the poison from an infected wound, and linen to tear into strips. Going downstairs, she glanced into the small back parlour and found it empty, making a swift dash to take a flask of wine from the buffet, together with a dish of sweetmeats that had been placed there, emptying the little cakes into a corner of her shawl.

Knowing that she would find it difficult to explain why she had stolen the wine and the cakes, she fled the house before she could be discovered, running towards the shelter of the hedge where she had left Nicolas. He was not there, having taken her advice to seek shelter in the summerhouse, which was an English gentleman's idea of what a Roman temple might have looked like centuries before.

He was waiting as she went inside the stone building, which had no doors but was large enough to hold a bench and table, made of some kind of marble. He was sitting on the bench, trying to look at his wound, and he frowned as she went to him.

'You should not have risked so much,' he said as he saw the wine bottle and the bundle she carried. 'What if you had been seen?'

'I thought the wine might help you,' she said. 'And you may be hungry for it cannot have been safe for you to stop at an inn.'

'I brought food with me, but these will be welcome and the wine is very much so,' he said and drank a good draught of it. 'I cannot get my shirt off for it is too painful. Lift it and see what you can do, Caroline.'

She eased his shirt back carefully. In places the blood had dried and the linen had stuck to his flesh. She moistened a little of her linen with the wine and dabbed at the flesh, peeling the material back bit by bit until she could see the wound, which was festering and very raw.

'I must clean it with this Brandewine,' she said. 'It will sting, I do not doubt, but I have no water and this may help to wash away the infection.'

'Do what you can,' he muttered, his mouth closed tight against the gasp of pain that her ministrations caused.

Caroline worked as kindly and swiftly as she could,

smearing a liberal portion of the poultice on his wound when she had finished, and binding it with strips of linen. Then she eased his shirt back into place and gave him the flask of wine. He drank deeply this time and she knew she must have hurt him though he had made no sound.

'There, it is done,' she said. 'I fear I have nothing for the pain, though I will try to get something from Margaret. She may have a tisane I could have for a headache.'

'It is best that you do nothing to arouse her suspicions,' Nicolas said. 'I came only to see you, to let you know that I lived, and to tell you I love you.'

'But you will stay . . .' Her voice broke on a sob. 'You are hurt. You should rest. I would take you to the house if I dared.'

'It will do now,' Nicolas told her. 'The wound was healing but it broke open again, but now it will heal. I shall go as soon as it is dark, Caroline, for if I stay I risk being discovered – and that might mean trouble for you as well as me. You could be accused of helping a spy.'

'You did not come here to spy?'

'You know that I came only to see you,' he said and reached across to touch her face. 'I wish that we might be together – that we might marry – but I know it would break your heart if your father disowned you. We must be patient a little longer, dearest. Our time will come and then I shall speak to your father.'

'Yes . . .' Her heart ached for she knew that this brief moment had cost him dear and was proof of his love, of his brave, true heart that had risked so much for her sake. 'But if he should not relent – I shall marry you and none other, Nicolas.'

'Then I am content,' he said. He reached towards her with the arm that was not injured, touching her cheek. 'Sit with me for a little, here close by my side. Let me feel your warmth, your nearness. The scent of you lives with me, Caroline. I seem to smell it always when I lay waiting for sleep, the freshness of meadow flowers and honey.'

of hers. She ached to heal his wounds, to have him where
she could tend him, ease him, but she knew that this short
time was all they were permitted. She must savour these
moments to the full, hold them in her heart until the time
came when they could be together once more.

Caroline would not leave him until it was dark. He kissed
her once more before they left their place of refuge, and then
he walked away from her and she ran towards the house. It
was as she was walking through the last of the knot gardens
that a man came towards her, calling her name.

'Caroline! I have been searching for you. Margaret feared
that you were lost.'

'I have merely been walking,' she said, outwardly calm,
though her heart leaped with alarm. If he had been searching
for her others might still be looking. She prayed that Nicolas
had made his escape. 'But it was kind of you to look for
me, Captain Benedict. Unnecessary, as you see, but kind.'

His eyes went over her as they walked into the house and
the lights of the candles together. They narrowed for a
moment and she remembered the blood spot that she had
forgotten to sponge in her urgency to help Nicolas.

'You have a mark on your gown.' His hand hovered and
she thought that he would touch her breast but then they
heard the sound of footsteps and he pointed to the spot on
himself.

'I pricked my finger while sewing,' Caroline said and
turned from him to her hostess as she came into the hall.

'So there you are, Caroline,' she said. 'I wondered where
you had got to, my dear. We were all beginning to worry.'

'I am sorry if I made you anxious,' Caroline said. 'I
walked further than I had intended and the darkness came
suddenly. I lost my way for a little, but as you see I found
it again . . .'

'Well, that is a relief,' Margaret said. 'Walter was worried

132

that you might have come to harm. There have been reports of a Roundhead spy in the area and I thought that something might have happened to you – that is why Walter offered to look for you.'

'It was thoughtless of me to worry you so,' Caroline said. 'Please forgive me.' She glanced at Captain Benedict and saw a suspicious look in his eyes. He was looking at the bloodstain again and a cold chill went down her spine as she realized that he did not believe her story of having pricked her finger sewing.

'If you will excuse me, I shall run upstairs and make myself tidy,' she said. 'I shall not keep you waiting long for your dinner.'

She hurried upstairs, her heart beating wildly. Thank goodness that Nicolas had gone. If Captain Benedict had happened to come across them . . . it did not bear thinking of!

When she took off her bodice, she saw that the bloodstain was larger than she had imagined and understood why he had not believed her story of pricking her finger. She laid it down and replaced it with a darker bodice, which was front lacing, then smoothed her hair and went down to join the others in the large parlour.

It did not matter whether Captain Benedict believed her or not. Nicolas had gone now and it was unlikely that he would return for many months, and Caroline was well able to bear any suspicion that might fall on her, for nothing could be proved.

Mercy sat gazing out at the night sky. She placed her fingers against her lips, a little smile forming beneath them as she recalled the kisses Harry had given her that afternoon. He had been so gentle with her, so loving, promising that he would do nothing to harm her, but they had become a little carried away in their loving and she had done nothing to stop him when he pushed down the bodice of her gown to kiss her breasts.

'Harry . . . we should not,' she had whispered when his

hand crept beneath her skirt. 'I love you but . . .'

'I want you so much, my darling,' he had whispered close to her ear. 'I cannot love you here for someone might come but we must be alone together. Properly alone so that I can love you.'

'Oh, Harry,' she said, her eyes wide and shining as she looked at him, for surely no woman had ever been wooed so passionately. 'You know that I love you, but I am a little afraid . . .'

'There is no need,' he promised her, kissing her nose and then her lips as his fingers caressed her breast. 'I would never do anything to harm you, Mercy. You are the only woman I have ever loved – and we shall be married soon. It cannot be just yet for I must speak to my father and at times like these it is awkward. But trust me, my darling. I shall always love you and nothing but death or duty shall part us.'

How sweet his words were, Mercy thought as she sat dreaming, brushing her long hair as she stared out at the sky. He had wanted her so much but she had resisted when he wanted to bring their loving to its final act. Yet she had longed to be his, truly his. Surely there was no shame in it, for she would be his wife as soon as he could arrange it.

Smiling, she went to bed to dream of the happy days ahead when the war was over and she was living at Thornberry Manor as its mistress.

'That is a nasty stain,' Mercy said the next morning when she visited Caroline in her room and saw her trying to sponge the mark from her green silk bodice. 'How came you by it? If it is blood I do not think it will come out.'

'It does not matter,' Caroline said carelessly. 'Tilly will see to it. Perhaps we can place a pretty appliqué design to cover it.'

'You were gone a long time yesterday.' Mercy looked at her oddly, for even though she had met Harry, she had been back long before her cousin.

'I walked further than I expected,' Caroline said, then

lowered her voice. 'Will you swear to keep my secret on your sacred honour?'

'You have seen Nicolas,' Mercy said. 'I am so glad, Caroline. Need you ask if I will keep your secret? You must know that I would never betray you. You have been such a friend to me and I would never do anything to harm you.'

'I know that you would not,' Caroline replied. 'He was in the gardens when I went out yesterday and he had been wounded. I took bandages and I stole a flask of wine from the small parlour, also some sweetmeats.'

'Margaret remarked that a flask was missing yesterday, though I do not think she noticed the sweetmeats, but she has so many guests who make free of her house that I dare say she did not find it strange. Gentlemen often take a flask to drink somewhere else, do they not?'

'Yes, sometimes,' Caroline said and bit her bottom lip. 'I think Captain Benedict suspects something, though he cannot know for sure.'

'Did Nicolas take the flask with him?'

Caroline stared at her in horror. 'No! I left everything in the summerhouse. We sat together and talked until it was dark and then . . . I just forgot.'

'Then you must recover what was left,' Mercy said. 'For if these things were discovered it might prove awkward.'

'Yes, I know. Nicolas was worried that I might be accused of harbouring a spy, but I did not think it likely.'

'Surely Captain Benedict cannot suspect you of anything so wicked?'

'Nicolas is not a spy. He came to see me, nothing more.' Caroline sprang immediately to his defence, for in these uncertain times she must be viglilant, even with those she loved.

'Then we shall walk to the summerhouse this morning and fetch the things you left,' Mercy said. 'Come, let us go now before they are discovered.'

They gathered their cloaks and went out together, their steps hurried as they moved closer to their destination.

However, when they went inside there was no sign of the flask or of Caroline's neckerchief.

'But I know I left them here on the floor,' she said, feeling a chill at the nape of her neck.

'Are you sure that Nicolas did not take them with him?'

'I – I do not know,' Caroline said uncertainly. 'I cannot recall him picking them up, but it would be like him to return and take them if he thought of it.' Yes, it could easily have been Nicolas for she knew that he would take risks rather than have her come to harm.

'Then I suggest that that is what must have happened,' Mercy said. 'At least we must pray 'tis so for otherwise . . .'

She left the rest unsaid and Caroline looked at her in dismay. If someone else had found the things it might cause trouble for her. She had made it clear that she was not wholeheartedly for the King and perhaps that might be used against her.

Yet what conclusive evidence could be gleaned from a neckerchief and an empty flask of Brandewine? But then she remembered that there was also the pot of poultice and a few scraps of linen, some of which might be bloodstained.

Taken together they might constitute proof that she had met a Roundhead spy in the summerhouse, and had tended his wounds. She might be arrested and at the very least imprisoned, for this was war and such acts were treason.

But who could have taken the flask and neckerchief? No one came here in winter and it was unlikely that servants would have bothered to visit to clean for it was too far from the house. It must surely have been Nicolas. Unless . . .

Caroline recalled the look in Captain Benedict's eyes the previous night and knew that he had suspected her. Could he possibly have taken the evidence? And if he had, what use did he intend to make of it?

Seven

Caroline was nervous when they returned to the house, but Margaret was calmly working at her sewing. No mention of the stolen Brandewine was made, nor of the discovery of suspicious items in the summerhouse.

'Have you been walking together, my dears?' Margaret asked. 'It is too cold for me of late. I do not care to walk when the wind is so bitter.' She smiled at them. 'But I am glad that you have returned for I wanted to tell you of my plans for Christmas.'

'Yes, of course, it will not be so very long,' Caroline said. 'I would like to send my parents gifts, ma'am. Do you think the carrier would deliver them in time?'

'We have time enough and I dare say it may be arranged. For ourselves, I plan a large entertainment here on Christmas Eve, though we shall of course pass the day itself quietly as is fitting. On the following night we are invited to a masque ball at Lady Henrietta Symonds' house.' She looked at the girls in anticipation of their delight and instead saw consternation. 'Is something wrong, my dears?'

'Neither of us have suitable gowns for such a grand occasion, ma'am.'

'But that is the fun of it,' Margaret told her with a smile. 'We shall all dress up in costumes from the storerooms. I have chests containing clothes that my grandparents wore as well as some that were made to resemble Greek or Roman styles, and have been used before for such masques. I am certain that we shall find something to suit us all. And we may make any alterations ourselves.'

'It sounds as if it will be entertaining,' Caroline said, her eyes bright with pleasure. She looked at Mercy and saw her delight echoed there, for it would be the first ball her cousin had attended. Her stepfather had thought dancing an abomination. 'When may we choose our costumes?'

'I shall have the trunks brought down this very afternoon,' Margaret said and smiled at Mercy. 'There is one gown in particular I think would look well on you, my dear. It is made of green velvet and in the French style. I believe it will suit you.'

'Harry says I should always wear such colours,' Mercy said and then blushed. 'But I dare say it is all nonsense.'

'Green becomes you,' Margaret told her. 'Harry Mortimer is right. He admires you, Mercy. You would do well to encourage him. It would be an excellent match for you.'

'Oh no . . .' Mercy's blush deepened. She remembered her last meeting with Harry, his passionate avowal that she should be his wife, but it would be immodest in her to speak of something that was still so private. He had not yet written to his father for it was difficult to send letters in these times of war. To speak of his promise before Lord Mortimer had been informed would be improper. 'That is . . . I should not mind but . . .'

'We shall be busy with our costumes,' Caroline said, thinking to spare her blushes. 'But we must not neglect our gifts. I have been making a pretty cutwork bodice for my mother and a sash for my father. I have also worked a fine sword belt of soft leather for Rupert but I know not if he will manage to visit us before Christmas.' She had been embroidering the cuffs of a pair of beautiful leather gauntlets for Nicolas, but it might be many months before she was able to give them to him.

'Have you heard from your brother, Caroline?' Margaret looked at her oddly for she had been aware of the girl's anxiety for him.

'Oh, Harry told me that he was well and stationed not far from here.' Mercy stepped into the breach as Caroline hesitated. 'If he is able he will surely come to visit us.'

'Yes, I suppose Harry Mortimer may have told him you are here,' Margaret said but seemed thoughtful. 'I am glad that you have had news, Caroline, for I know you were anxious.'

'I am relieved that he is well, ma'am.'

'Yes, of course you must be. I thought you seemed a little happier this morning, my dear.' She smiled at her companions. 'Walter had hoped to dine with us today but he has been called to duty. There is a rumour of a possible attack on Oxford, and a spy hath been caught . . .'

Caroline's heart stilled. She felt a sickness in her stomach and her mouth was dry as she said, 'A spy, ma'am? Surely not?'

'So I have heard. I do not know . . .' She broke off as they heard voices in the hall and then Captain Benedict came into the room. He was dressed for riding, his boots and breeches splashed with mud.

'Ah Walter,' his aunt said. 'Now that you are here you may tell us of the spy. Is he taken?'

'No, damn it,' Benedict said, a flush of displeasure in his cheeks. 'We thought we had him but the fools had captured the wrong man. The prisoner was a Roundhead but a deserter. He had fled the field at Edgehill and was hiding out, too frightened and shamed to return to his companions.'

'Then the rumours of a spy were false?' Caroline said, heart pounding. 'You have had all your trouble for nothing?'

'No, I think not,' he replied. 'There was a spy – a clever fellow and one with friends hereabouts, I believe. He hath got away, but if he returns he may not be so lucky the next time.'

'Perhaps he will not return,' Caroline suggested. 'Why should he if he already has what he needs?'

Captain Benedict smiled at her, a cold, taunting look. 'Why indeed, Caroline? Yet I think he may come and if he does . . .' He left the sentence unfinished, shrugging his shoulders.

Caroline's stomach contorted with a spasm of anxiety. Why was he looking at her that way? Almost like a fox stalking a chicken from outside the coop, knowing it could get in if and when it wanted.

'No more talk of such things,' Margaret declared. 'We were speaking of the masque at Christmas. You will attend I hope?'

'If duty permits,' he said, his eyes dwelling on Caroline's face. 'But we are at war, aunt. That is something we must none of us forget . . .'

He knew! Caroline was certain that he knew what had taken place in the summerhouse. He must have found the things she had so carelessly left behind and now he suspected her of meeting a Roundhead spy. His looks and his words had clearly been meant to warn her and yet he had not betrayed her. She paced about the floor of her bedchamber restlessly. What was she to do? Yet there was nothing she could do for the moment because he had made no threat.

Had he wished he could have caused trouble for her. Even if she had not been arrested for treason, she would certainly have been forced to leave Oxford in disgrace, branded as a traitor. Captain Benedict had stayed his hand – why?

Caroline was nervous for a few days, fearing that he might betray her or at the very least try to blackmail her. However, he did neither. Indeed, he seemed to visit less often, though Harry came almost every day.

Mercy had confessed to him that she did not know how to dance.

'At least, I can only do very simple dances that are beloved of the village folk,' she had told him and Caroline the day after their hostess had announced the ball. 'I do not think they are what will be required at this masque.'

'Then we must teach you to dance, mustn't we, Caro?' Harry said and his eyes danced with mischief. 'Will you play on Margaret's spinet for us? If you would be so good, I shall teach Mercy the steps.'

Of course Caroline had agreed, for the eager look in her cousin's eyes would have been hard to deny. Harry came every afternoon when his duty to the King was done for the day, and each day Caroline played for more than an hour as the other two danced the various steps; the slower graceful pavane and the faster, lively country dances.

Watching them laughing together, Mercy's first stumbling steps gradually becoming a graceful and confident performance, Caroline knew that their relationship was deepening. She had always known that her cousin was in love with Harry, but now she began to think that he was as hopelessly besotted as she.

Caroline could not but be anxious for her cousin, for she believed that there would be much opposition to a marriage between them. Yet she did not want to spoil this time of happiness for Mercy and so she said nothing. Her cousin had had little joy in her life and it would be unkind to stop her enjoying herself now. If it ended in upset that would be painful for Mercy, but it was already too late to warn her now for her heart was no longer her own.

And so they passed their days in an odd kind of contentment. Visiting their friends in Oxford, the streets of the town often thronged with groups of Cavalier soldiers, they could not fail to be aware of the work going on about the town and outlying countryside to strengthen their defences, and thoughts of the war were always there in the back of their minds, and yet it was a happy time. People laughed, entertained their friends and believed that come the spring the King would vanquish his enemies and all would be well.

Rowena wiped the spittle from her mouth. That was the third morning in a row that she had been sick and she knew what the symptoms must mean, for her mother had made potions to cure it in other women. There were two kinds of potions; those that cured the sickness and those that caused a woman to miscarry her child in the early days.

The best way would be to be rid of it, for she wanted

neither the pain nor the trouble of giving birth to a child that had no father, but perhaps it would bring Harry back to her for the child was surely his. She had lain with two others since the night he had told her he wanted no more of her, but the sickness did not begin until a woman was some weeks into childbearing, therefore it must be his.

Would he believe her? Would he care?

Rowena did not know what to do for the best. Her mother would curse her for a fool if she knew that she was with child, but she was not frightened of the poor, tired woman whose life consisted of nothing but work these days. It might be best to ask for a potion that would rid her of the unwanted babe. She had found lovers easily enough and most were willing to give her money in return for favours. But she wanted more, she wanted to be Harry's wife, and mayhap if he knew that she was carrying his child he would change his mind and take her back.

Two days before Christmas, a letter and parcels arrived for Caroline. Her parents had sent presents for her and Mercy. Lady Saunders told them that all was well with her husband. His health and his spirits were improving, especially since he had received a letter from his son, asking him to try and understand why he had chosen to join the King and to forgive him.

Your father seems now to have recovered from his low spirits, but I heard yesterday that Lord Mortimer hath been unwell, though I believe he is recovered. Your letter told us that you often see Harry so please convey the news to him. We thank you for your gifts and shall hope to have you with us again, perhaps in the spring when the roads are better for travelling. However, you must not cut short your visit but return only when you feel you wish to be at home once more.

Caroline read the letter several times. She had thought it right to tell her mother that she had seen Harry, though she had not mentioned how often they entertained Royalists. It was clear that Lady Saunders had shown the letter to her husband, and from the tone of her mother's reply it seemed that Sir John was at least prepared to be tolerant towards Harry now that his first anger had faded, though that did not mean that he would be prepared to countenance her marriage to Nicolas.

She did not show the letter to her hostess, though she mentioned to Mercy that Lady Saunders hoped that they might return in the spring.

Mercy looked a little uncertain, seeming as if she wished to speak but then changing her mind again. Was she thinking that she might be Harry's wife by then and would prefer to stay in Oxford to be near him?

Caroline hoped that it might be so for her friend's sake, but she did not ask for she was sure that her cousin would tell her once there was something positive to discuss.

No letter had come from Nicolas, but she had not truly expected it – it would be too difficult to have it smuggled through enemy lines. She must accustom herself to long silences for as long as the war continued.

It seemed to Caroline that they were set for a protracted conflict. There were often Cavaliers in the house, for Margaret allowed them to come and go at will, always pleased to entertain her young men. Caroline heard at first hand of the patchwork of competing garrisons and local militia that covered the country. There was talk of what ought to be done to group these bands of fighting men together. However, it emerged that on the opposing side, the strongest of these bands was in East Anglia; the Eastern Association had been given wide powers and was apparently raising a strong army under the leadership of the Earl of Manchester, whose cavalry commander was Master Oliver Cromwell.

He was sometimes dismissed as an insignificant country squire, but Caroline knew that in fact he was a clever man who chose the habit of a Puritan but whose mind was more far reaching. Nicolas had told her that he admired and respected his commander, and therefore she thought the Royalist officers were foolish to dismiss him so lightly. However, she said nothing for as a young woman she was not expected to have an opinion on the strategy they often discussed in front of her.

At Christmas however, the talk had changed, becoming lighter, everyone entering into the spirit of the season as the visitors helped to bring in greenery with which to deck the halls. A large chunk of a fallen tree was brought in by the servants and set to burn in the huge fireplace in the great hall. It was seldom used for they preferred their smaller parlours, which were warmer in the bitter days of winter. However, Christmas Eve was to be a day of celebration and so many guests were invited that only the hall would be big enough to hold them all.

The banquet was to be given at two in the afternoon, and would go on until late into the evening. A roast boar's head with an apple in its mouth was carried in to begin the feasting, but after that the rich dishes were many and varied. Venison swimming in a thick, aromatic gravy, capon, geese, pork and roast beef were just some of the meats served at the table. Besides, there were sweetbreads in a cream and wine sauce, neaps, cabbage and plums in a dish that was delicately flavoured, removed with dishes of preserved fruits, nuts, quince tarts, dates and sweetmeats. All these were washed down by quantities of sack, cider, ale and mead, a very sweet drink that was much stronger than it seemed and must be treated with caution.

For entertainment there was a band of strolling players, who acted a Christmas play, did acts of tumbling and juggling and a minstrel who sang sweetly of love and betrayal. Towards the end of the evening, when everyone had eaten and drunk their fill, some of the guests formed rings in the middle of the huge room and played foolish games. One of them was to pull their unfortunate victim into the middle and form a ring around him. The man or woman so captured was then forced to sing or recite a poem before he or she was released, and if the performance did not please they might be beaten with a pig's bladder on a stick.

Caroline watched, torn between amusement and a sense of nostalgia, for it brought back memories of other times, particularly the previous year when Nicolas had promised that she must pay his forfeit one day. If only he could be here, how much happier she would feel. It was only when the hall began to empty that she realized she had not seen Mercy for some time. Glancing round, she saw that Harry was also missing.

A little chill started at the nape of her neck and slithered down her spine. Mercy would not be fool enough to go somewhere to be alone with Harry, would she? At a time like this when the blood was heated with wine, good food and excitement, it would be foolish to welcome temptation by providing opportunity.

Worried that Harry might have led her cousin astray, she left the hall and went in search of Mercy in the small parlours that they often sat in together. It was possible that her cousin had sought a little solitude because of the noise and the heat in the hall. Some minutes spent searching produced no result, and Caroline was headed towards the stairs when someone came towards her.

'Mistress Saunders,' Captain Benedict said. 'I saw you leave and wondered if you were ill?'

'No, I thank you. I – I just came to find my cousin.' His eyes had narrowed in suspicion. 'But as you see, I have not managed to come upon her.'

'I am not surprised for your cousin is in the hall.'

'Is she?' Caroline was truly surprised for she had not seen Mercy return. 'Then I shall go and join her.' As she moved to pass him, he reached out and caught her wrist, his strong fingers pressing deeply into her flesh. 'I pray you let me pass, sir.'

'I wanted to give you a Christmas gift,' he said. 'Mayhap you would care to take it from me now?'

'I . . .' Caroline's mouth was dry as she looked into his

eyes and sensed something that made her tremble inwardly. 'I fear I have none for you, sir.'

'None was expected,' he replied, reaching inside his doublet to bring out something she recognized immediately. It was the neckerchief she had left behind the day she had tended Nicolas's wounds.'

'I . . . Where did you find that, sir?'

'Do not try to lie to me, Caroline,' he told her. 'I know that you met someone that day and that you bound his hurts. I suspect that he was a Roundhead spy and . . .'

'No, you are wrong,' Caroline said, knowing that there was no longer any point in pretence. 'He was a friend. He came to see me, not to spy on you or the King. I give you my word of honour that he came only for my sake.'

For a moment Captain Benedict's fingers tightened their grip. His eyes seemed to sear her flesh. 'You swear to me that you speak only the truth?'

'Yes, I swear it. He was wounded at Edgehill and came to tell me that he lived, but his wound opened and I helped him, that is all.'

Benedict nodded, loosening his grip. 'I shall believe you, for I wish it to be true,' he said, his voice slightly hoarse. 'I once hoped that you might come to care for me, Caroline, but what you tell me makes me realize that it cannot be. However, I would have you know that I care for you and that if you should ever need me I should be glad to serve you. To wed you if you would have me.'

'I thank you for your gift and your forbearance,' Caroline said and her throat was tight with emotion. 'Had my heart been free we might have suited well enough.'

'Then I am satisfied,' he said. 'I shall not see you again for some months, for I leave in the morning. There is much to be done before the spring and my duty calls me to the west of the country where we hope to gather much support. I ask you to think kindly of me and to remember that I would serve you. My loyalty is first to the King, and then to you. Please believe that I speak truly.'

Caroline hesitated, then moved towards him. Reaching up, she kissed his cheek. 'You could have harmed me had you wished,' she said, 'but you have been a friend. I shall not forget and should I ever be in the position to help you, you may come to me in safety.'

He smiled at her, inclined his head and walked away. Only when he had gone, did Caroline notice that there was something hard caught in the folds of the neckerchief. When she opened it, she saw that it was a beautiful pendant consisting of a large baroque pearl hanging from a garnet and pearl knot – a lover's knot.

It was not a gift she would knowingly have accepted from him, but she could not refuse it now, for it would be insulting. He had hidden it in the folds of her neckerchief because he had known that she would not take such a priceless thing from anyone but the man she was to marry.

Her thoughts turned to Nicolas as she went up to place the neckerchief and pendant in her room before returning to the hall to say goodnight to Margaret. Where was he and had he good company for this night? She wondered if he was remembering the previous Christmas, when if truth be told she had begun to realize that her feelings for Nicolas were more than friendship. She had refused to admit it for she had not understood her own heart, but now she knew. She knew that she loved him more than life and longed to be with him, but it could not be.

Only when she returned to her home would it be possible for Nicolas to find a way of seeing her. She had become restless of late and longed for home and all that was familiar. Perhaps now that her father had recovered his spirits he might consider a match between her and Nicolas.

Mercy glanced at her face in the beautiful silver-backed mirror that Harry had given her as a Christmas gift. Did she look different? Could anyone tell just by looking at her what she had done that night?

He had teased her and courted her with soft words, singing

to her in his pleasant tenor voice, his eyes telling her so much more than the words of that beautiful song.

'Drink to me only with thine eyes . . . and I'll not ask for wine . . .'

The words were echoing in her head as she remembered each look, each touch, each kiss – and what had happened afterwards.

When Harry had given her such a wonderful gift, kissing her so tenderly, so sweetly that her body cried out to his, she had not been able to resist him, for she loved him with all her heart, all her being. And so she had let him love her in a way that no decent woman ought before she was a wife.

Their coupling had been sweet and Harry was a considerate and gentle lover, but her guilt had prevented her from truly enjoying herself. She had been happy while he was content to kiss and touch her, but afterwards when he had . . . her mind sheered away from what she had let him do and the feeling of shame that had swept through her afterwards.

She must be a wanton! No modest woman would have behaved as she had. If her stepfather found out what she had done she truly thought that he might kill her. He would certainly despise her. She was afraid that Harry would think the less of her, for she had clung to him and wept, but he had kissed her tenderly, told her not to worry, promised that all would be well.

He was going to write to his father and tell him of his intention to wed and they would be married very soon, before Harry had to leave Oxford. He had promised her as he stroked her thighs, drawing her along the path to pleasure.

She had wept a little more then and begged him not to leave her, to take her with him to his lodgings, but he had kissed her tears away, telling her that she would be better with her cousins until he could come home for good.

Sighing, Mercy traced the smoothness of the silver trinket. She told herself she must not be foolish. These were difficult times and Harry had his duty to the King. She could not expect him to take time off to marry her and then accompany her to his home.

She would just have to wait and pray that he would arrange their wedding before he left for the spring campaign.

The masque ball was proving to be very pleasurable, Caroline thought as she glanced around at all the smiling faces. Everyone had been asked to wear a mask over their face when they arrived, and it had caused a great deal of amusement as people tried to guess the identity of various characters.

Mercy's costume was the French one that Margaret had recommended to her, fashioned in the style of a hundred years earlier and worn with a pretty hood that covered her hair. However, Harry, dressed in the costume of an Elizabethan pirate captain, guessed it was she almost at once.

'How could I not know those eyes or those sweet lips?' he said to her softly. 'For they are my constant companions when I sleep.'

Mercy blushed a delicate pink but looked delighted with the compliment.

Caroline, dressed in the costume of a lady of the fourteenth century, noticed that they were together most of the evening, and that for a period of almost an hour they were missing from the ballroom. She hoped that no one else had noticed their absence, for it would do Mercy's reputation harm if it was known she had gone somewhere private with Harry. Of course she might simply have gone to the bedchamber that had been put at the ladies' disposal that evening, but instinctively Caroline knew that Mercy and Harry were together, just as they had been for a time on Christmas Eve.

It worried her for she could not be certain of his intentions towards her cousin. She did not doubt that he felt some strong emotion for Mercy, but was it in his mind to wed her?

Caroline wished now that she had voiced her doubts from the start, but she had been afraid that her cousin might interpret her warning as jealousy. Of late she had begun to feel real concern, but there was nothing she could do for the moment. If she should have a chance to speak to Harry alone one day, she might use the familiarity of old friendship to ask him what he intended, but that could not be here or now. This evening was meant for merriment and everyone was making the most of it, their spirits lifted by the wine and laughter.

Caroline herself was asked to dance constantly by a variety of young men dressed in costume. She knew most of them at once, but one or two escaped her. Just before the unmasking was due to take place at midnight, one of the many gentlemen in medieval costume suddenly grabbed her hand and drew her into the merry whirl of a country dance.

Caroline suspected his identity, though she could not be certain until at the hour of midnight the music stopped and everyone took off their mask.

'Did you know me?' Rupert demanded, mischief in his eyes. 'I have been waiting for this moment all evening, Caro. You looked my way once or twice and I was almost certain you knew me.'

'Only when you touched my hand and drew me into the dance. There was something then that made me think it might be you.'

He grinned at her, well pleased that he had escaped her all evening. 'Have you heard anything from Mother?' he asked, his smile fading now. 'Is Father better?'

'I had her letter for Christmas,' Caroline told him. 'She says that since he had your letter, he is very much better in spirits than he was.'

Rupert looked a little conscious. 'It played on my mind that we had quarrelled, and when Nicolas told me that he had been ill . . .'

'I thought it must have been because of that,' Caroline said and smiled at him. 'I am glad that you have made your peace, dearest.'

'I could not, would not, do other than I have in matters of conscience,' Rupert declared. 'But I have grown up since

I left home, Caroline. I have seen men killed, others dying slowly in agony, and there will be many more such deaths before the war is over. I might even be amongst them.'

'Pray do not!' Caroline said, though she knew that it was true.

'You would not have me lie to you?' She shook her head. 'I shall do my best to survive,' he said and the merry smile was back in his eyes, 'but I would have you know that I care for you, Caro. You have always been the best of sisters.'

Caroline's throat caught. 'Rupert . . .' she whispered, feeling the sting of tears she must not shed. 'You will take care?'

'Of course. We leave tomorrow,' he told her, his eyes holding hers. 'There will be a big campaign in the spring, Caro, and we hope to settle this once and for all.'

'I shall pray that it will soon be over,' she said, but the laughter and smiling faces had faded away and she seemed to stand alone on a moor where all about her were the dead and dying, and amongst them her brother. She could see his face, his eyes open and staring, and for a moment the vision was so strong that she was seized by terror. She wanted to hold him, to prevent him leaving with his commander, but she knew that nothing she could say would sway him. 'I love you, Rupert. May God be with you.'

'And with you, sister,' he said and once again the teasing light was back in his eyes. 'And when I next see you I hope that you will be a certain gentleman's wife.'

'If you mean Nicolas, it is my heart's desire.'

'Be happy, Caro,' he said, 'and be certain you name your first son for me.'

'He shall certainly have your name,' Caroline promised and then turned as Mercy came up to them. 'I think it is time for us to leave.' A wave of emotion rushed over her and she hugged him impulsively. 'God be with you, dearest.'

Glancing round the room, seeing the expressions on the faces of some other ladies, Caroline knew that she was not the only one saying goodbye to someone she loved. And some of the gallant gentlemen who rode out so bravely for the King would never return.

Harry came to the house the next morning. Caroline was in the parlour, Mercy was still upstairs checking the linen cupboards with one of the servants.

'I shall call Mercy for you,' Caroline said and then hesitated before making up her mind. 'May I ask you something that presumes upon our friendship, Harry?'

He looked at her warily. 'If it concerns Mercy . . .'

'I must be concerned for her. She is my cousin and it was through me that you met.' Caroline's eyes met his in a challenge.

'I love her. You cannot doubt it?' Harry looked uncomfortable. 'Damn it, Caro! In God's name how can I marry her? I have debts I cannot pay and Father has already sold land to pay others. I must marry a fortune, if I survive, and who knows that I shall?'

'None of us can know that for certain,' Caroline replied. 'But if you cannot wed her, then you must tell her so. Unless you wish to break her heart at the end?'

Harry swore softly. 'You know I would not hurt her – yet what can I do?'

'You have been selfish,' Caroline said, 'to encourage her hopes.'

'She is so beautiful and I do love her . . .' His eyes begged for understanding. 'I never meant to harm her. She is such a gentle girl, Caro, not like you. How can I tell her something I know will hurt her?'

'I do not know,' Caroline said. 'Could you not find some means of paying your debts?'

'I cannot go to my father. Nicolas might help me – but it would never work, Caro. I am expensive.' A rueful smile touched his mouth. 'Father has told me often enough and I fear it is so.' He was silent for a moment. 'I shall be leaving Oxford soon. You will not tell her? May we not have this little time together?'

'I cannot forbid either of you,' Caroline said. 'And I shall not tell tales behind your back, but you must find a way. Do not leave without telling her, Harry. It is not fair that she should wait for your return believing that you mean to wed her . . .'

'I shall find a way,' Harry promised and then they both turned as they heard footsteps and in another moment Mercy entered the room. Her face lit up as she saw Harry. Caroline's heart sank. How could either of them tell her that her dreams of becoming Harry's wife were impossible?

'Ah there you are,' Caroline said. 'Excuse me if you will. I have something I must do.'

She left the room feeling sore at heart. It seemed inevitable that the future held only heartbreak for her cousin. If Harry behaved decently he would find a way to tell Mercy the truth, and yet in her heart she knew that he had not the courage.

In the end it would be Caroline who would have to tell her.

Three weeks had passed since the ball and the town was becoming emptier as each day passed, for the Royalist troops were leaving for different parts of the country, a few at a time, though some remained to guard the King's stronghold.

'Harry says that he may be here longer than he thought,' Mercy told Caroline that morning. 'He expected to leave soon after Christmas but he has been asked to remain with the garrison for the moment. Is that not good news?'

There was such hope, such pleasure in her eyes that Caroline's heart caught, and yet perhaps her talk with Harry had done some good for her cousin's next words surprised her.

'I think we shall marry quite soon,' she said. 'You will not speak of this to anyone please, for it is not settled. But I believe it will be arranged within a few weeks.'

Caroline got up at once and embraced her. It seemed that Harry had decided to put love before all, and no doubt he would find a way to curb his expensive habits once he had a wife to care for.

'I am delighted for you both,' Caroline said. She glanced at the beautiful skeleton clock on Margaret's mantle. 'You must excuse me now, Mercy, for I have promised to meet friends in Oxford this afternoon and I must go now or I shall be late. Do you care to come with me?'

'Thank you, but I think Harry may come this afternoon,' Mercy said, a faint colour in her cheeks. 'I have asked him to call and I believe he will.' Surely he would not let her down once he read her letter? She had told him of her suspicions in the belief that he would keep his promises to her. He must know that she would otherwise be an outcast, shamed and branded as a wanton. The very thought of having to return to her stepfather in disgrace was enough to make her sick to her stomach.

Caroline nodded, thinking that she had misjudged Harry. It seemed that he was ready to behave properly after all.

'I shall see you at supper,' she said. 'Excuse me now.'

Rowena waited outside the house where she knew Harry was staying. She had come before but there had been no sign of him. However, today she was luckier for she saw him leaving with two of his friends. He noticed her but she thought he meant to ignore her until she moved towards him. Something in her manner must have alerted him for he stopped, frowned, made some laughing remark to his companions and came to greet her.

'What do you want?' he asked. 'Did I not tell you it was over? If you have come for money I have none until the next time I receive my allowance, and that is months away.'

'I didn't come for money,' she said. 'I be with child, Harry Mortimer, and it be your child.'

'If this is one of your tales . . .' He stopped as she shook her head and knew instinctively that it was true. 'Then I am sorry for it. Can you not find someone to get rid of it?'

'Is that what you would have me do?' Rowena felt the

anger stir inside her. 'Do you care nothing for your child?'

'How can I be certain that it is mine? You have been with others – do not deny it, Rowena, for I know it is the truth.'

'There were none until you threw me over,' she told him. 'And the child be too far on not to be yours.'

Harry nodded, eyeing her thoughtfully. He was not sure how he felt about the possibility of a child. He had never given it a thought until now. He could never marry her but the child might be the only one he would ever father if he were killed. Despite himself, the thought of a son to live after his death was appealing.

'Come to the inn with me,' he said and smiled at her in the old way, the way that had always made her heart leap so wildly. 'We'll have a drink for old time's sake and talk about the child. It makes no difference to what I said before, because I could not marry you. But my father might take the babe, especially if it should be a boy, if I should die on the field of battle. If so, you must take the child to my home, Rowena, tell Lord Mortimer that it is mine and he may take it from you. I make no promises but he will give you money if nothing more. I fear that I have only pennies to offer you but my father will do the right thing if I am dead.'

'And if you do not die?'

'Then I shall give you money when I have some,' he said and laughed. 'Stop looking as if you could curdle the milk, Rowena. Soon I shall be going to fight and mayhap to die. Surely you will drink with me for the sake of what has been?'

Rowena scowled for he had given her nothing but pretty words as he always did, but she would go with him because she loved him.

Caroline spent the afternoon shopping with Lady Symonds and her two daughters. Afterwards she stayed to take refreshments with them, and so it was beginning to get dark when she was taken home in her hostess's carriage. She had protested that she did not mind the walk for it was not much more than half an hour's distance, but Lady Symonds had insisted.

'There are some rough elements in the town,' she said. 'There has been trouble at one of the inns and you must pass it on your way. Much better that you should be protected by my servants.'

Caroline thanked her and allowed her to have her way. She enjoyed walking and the dark held no fears for her, but perhaps it was safer if there had been trouble in the town.

Night had fallen by the time they reached the inn of which Lady Symonds had spoken, and the only light came from lanterns hung outside various houses and the inn. Hearing some shouting, she glanced out of her window and saw that some men were fighting in the street. Her kind hostess had been right and she was glad to be inside the coach, for it would not have been pleasant to walk past something like this, and it would have been impossible to avoid.

It was only by chance that she happened to look towards the inn itself, and as she did so, she saw a man and a woman coming from it. The man's arm was about his companion's waist as she looked up at him and laughed. They appeared to think the fighting amusing and Caroline suspected that they had been drinking rather too much. She suddenly felt shocked and upset for she saw the man was Harry Mortimer and the woman with him was Rowena Greenslade.

Sickness stirred in Caroline's stomach. How could he? How could he do this when he had encouraged Mercy to believe she was soon to be his wife? It was cruel and thoughtless, but as she thought about it she realized that it was no more than he had done when she had expected to be betrothed to him herself.

It was as she had suspected for a long time. Harry was not to be trusted. He was a rogue and a cheat. He spoke of loving Mercy, but in truth he cared only for himself. Caroline wondered how long he had been meeting the blacksmith's daughter, and just what was going on between them. Had Mercy any idea of what he truly was? Even if he married her he would not be faithful and she would end up grieving.

Caroline's heart ached for her cousin as she sat back against the squabs and thought about what she had just seen. What ought she to do about it? If she told Mercy the truth it would break her heart – and yet she would be broken-hearted anyway when she learned that Harry had cheated and lied to her.

Somehow Caroline must find a way to tell her the truth.

It was not until later that evening that Caroline had a chance to be alone with Mercy, and that was when her cousin came to say goodnight to her.

'Did you chance to see Harry?' she asked without waiting for Caroline to speak. 'When you were with Lady Symonds, did you happen to see him in the town?'

'No . . .' Caroline hesitated, gathering her courage. If she confessed what she had seen it would break Mercy's heart. 'Did he not call as you asked?'

'No. I have had no word from him,' Mercy said and looked distressed. 'Do you think that perhaps he did not receive my note?'

'I do not know,' Caroline said, and the look in her cousin's eyes made her want to weep. How could she tell her when she was already in such distress? Perhaps if she waited something would happen and everything would be right again. Perhaps Harry would come another day. Maybe he had forgotten that Mercy had asked him to call?

'I must see him,' Mercy said, her face white. 'It is very important. I think I shall go into Oxford tomorrow and see if I can speak to him at his lodgings.'

'Are you sure that is a good idea?'

'No, it is not a good idea,' Mercy said, a break in her voice, 'but I must speak to him, Caroline. I must . . .'

Caroline stared at her. Her eyes were dark with an emotion that went deeper than distress. She was frightened! Upset and yes, even . . . ashamed. Something terrible must have happened to make her look so!

'Mercy, are you in some trouble?' she asked. 'Is there anything I can do to help you? You know that I am your friend and that I care for you?'

'Yes, I know you are my good friend,' Mercy said, a tearful smile on her lips. 'But you cannot help me. No one can help me, unless Harry will marry me very soon.'

'Unless . . .' Caroline stared at her in silence. She felt shocked and angry – angry with Harry. It seemed that there could be only one explanation for Mercy's distress. Yet it was so terrible that she could not bring herself to believe it. 'Are you saying . . .'

Mercy looked startled, as if realizing that she had said too much. 'I am saying only that I cannot bear it if he does not love me,' she whispered, tears brimming in her lovely eyes. 'Forgive me . . .'

Caroline stared after her as she left the room in a hurry. Ought she to go after her? But what could she do, what comfort could she offer?

For a moment she had thought that Mercy was carrying her lover's child, but Mercy had seemed to deny it. And yet she had seen fear in her cousin's eyes – fear of what would happen to her if Harry would not marry her.

If she were indeed with child it would be the end of everything for Mercy. She had been brought up so strictly and it must be playing on her conscience, she must consider herself to have sinned, and would be frightened and ashamed. She would never be able to return to her home, for, from what she had told them of her stepfather, he would sooner see her dead than bearing the evidence of her shame.

By unfortunate chance, Harry was given Mercy's note only when he returned to his lodgings that evening. He was in no state to read it until the morning, and by then his head was spinning, his stomach churning. He read it through and tossed it to one side, feeling wretched, a taste of ashes in his mouth as his conscience smote him. Mercy must have been desperate to leave a note asking him to call – and he could only think of one reason why she might do so. He acknowledged that although she had not said it in plain words, she seemed to hint that she was with child.

Damn it! How could this have happened? It wasn't possible that both she and Rowena could be carrying a child! And yet Mercy's note was clear enough if he considered it. Of all the cursed luck! He put a hand to his throbbing head, trying to think clearly. He had fobbed Rowena off with vague promises and a few tankards of ale, but Mercy was another matter. How could he refuse to wed her? She was innocent and beautiful and he had taken shameful advantage – and he loved her.

Despite himself, he loved her but he could not marry her. After sending Rowena off he had gone on to another inn with friends and there he had gambled recklessly. He owed more than two thousand pounds and had no hope of paying it, now or in the near future. He was ruined and the last thing he needed to worry about was a wife.

Besides, it was only a few weeks since he had made love to Mercy, just twice in all. It couldn't happen so quickly. He'd been with other women and none of them had claimed to be carrying his child before this. It was just ill luck!

What should he do? Harry cudgelled his brains but could come up with no simple solution. His father would accept the marriage to Mercy if he chose to wed her. He could send her back to the Manor and . . .

Hearing a knock at his door Harry went to answer it. It was a sealed note, a message from his commanding officer. Breaking the seal, he saw that he was under orders to leave for the West Country at once.

'Thank you,' he said to the soldier who had brought the note. 'I shall carry out my orders as commanded.' As he turned back into the room a feeling of relief flooded over him. After Caroline had taken him to task on Mercy's behalf, he had asked for a transfer to the army in the west of the country and his request had been answered most opportunely. He would write Mercy a note, telling her that he was called away. It was unlikely that he would return to Oxford for months or years, if at all.

In the meantime Mercy would either discover that she had

made a mistake or throw herself on the kindness of her friends. Caroline would stand by her. Yes, of course. There was no need to worry. Caroline would make sure that Mercy was well cared for. Relief swept over him. There was no need for him to do anything at all.

Caroline spent a restless night, and in the morning when she went to look for her cousin, it was to be told that she had gone out very early.

She did not return before luncheon and Caroline worried about her. She would not do anything foolish, would she? She must know that Lady Saunders would stand by her?

Caroline was certain that her mother would do what she could to help Mercy, but there was nothing they could do to prevent the shame and scandal that would fall on her. She might be denounced from the pulpit as a wanton when she attended church; some young women in a similar situation had recently been made to stand at the front of the church wearing a plain white shift while the parson denounced them to his congregation and damned them as sinners. Margaret Farringdon had thought it a shame, for it was the Puritan way not hers, but even she would be shocked at Mercy's plight, would think the less of her for being foolish.

What could Mercy have been thinking of to allow it? Caroline understood how easy it would be to lie with the man you loved, for she had experienced such longings in Nicolas's arms, but he had refused to dishonour her, despite their need.

Harry had taken disgraceful advantage. He should be made to marry Mercy!

It was after supper that Mercy finally returned to the house. She went straight upstairs to her room and locked the door. When Caroline followed and asked to speak to her, she would not answer.

'Please leave me,' she begged at last. 'Go away, Caroline. I need to be alone.'

'Remember that I love you,' Caroline told her through the

locked door. 'It does not matter what your trouble is, Mercy. I shall stand by you. I give you my word on it – and so will my mother. Please believe me. I am your friend, your cousin, and I think of you as my sister.'

She heard a sob of despair from the other side of the door but still Mercy did not unlock it.

'I know you are grieving,' Caroline said, 'but he is not worth your tears, Mercy. This is my fault for I should have warned you of his nature but did not want to hurt you. I would make reparation if I can. I will help you in any way you choose.'

There was no answer. Caroline realized that she could do no more, for Mercy's grief was too raw. She could not know what had passed between them, but it was clear that Mercy was in terrible distress.

'I shall speak to you in the morning,' Caroline said. 'Do not despair, my friend. Whatever must happen I shall share with you.'

She walked away with a heavy heart. Oh, why had she not spoken at the start? It would have been better that Mercy should think her jealous and spiteful than that it should come to this.

Mercy sat staring out of the window at the night. It was dark and filled with shadows, or was that only in her mind? She felt numb as she tried to make sense of what had happened to her. After much searching of her conscience and humbling her pride, she had called at Harry's lodgings only to be given a note and told that he had gone away. His note telling her that he was going away and did not know when he would return was in her purse. How could he have been so unkind? How could he have deserted her when she needed him so? She had taken a desperate chance sending him her own letter for if anyone else had read it, they might have guessed her shame, and he had ignored it.

The pain curled inside her, tearing at her so that she almost cried out, but there was no one to hear her pleas, no one to comfort her. Harry had gone and she had sent her cousin away. She could not ask Caroline for help, she was too ashamed.

She stood up and took a turn about the room, facing the bitter truth. She had been mislead and harshly betrayed by the man she loved and now she must accept the consequences. A rush of anger swept through her as she realized what a fool she had been.

How could she have been so stupid? She had known that what she did was wrong, was against all that she had been taught to respect, and yet she had given herself completely to Harry. She loved him so much, loved him more than she could bear, and now he had deserted her.

Her world was falling to pieces about her. All Harry's promises had been false. He had meant none of them. He had probably not loved her – at least not enough to wed her.

'Oh, Harry,' she whispered through her tears. 'Why did you do it – why did you treat me so cruelly?'

The tears were slipping down her cheeks now. She let them fall. Tears would not help her. Nothing could help her. Her shame was too terrible to be borne. She could not confess it to Margaret Farringdon nor yet to Lady Saunders for they would be so disappointed in her.

Caroline would not censure her, for she understood how much Mercy loved Harry. She would understand and she would not desert her, but she could not accept the hospitality her friend offered her any longer as she would bring shame on Caroline and her family.

She could not return to her home. She would not be wanted there. Her stepfather would drive her from his door with bitter words and if he did not, he would beat her. He would make her life and that of her child unbearable so that death would be her only escape.

There was only one choice left to her. She must leave this house while her friends slept, for she must not bring disrepute on them. Her sin was such that it would reflect on Caroline, the friend she loved. For Caroline's sake she must leave before her shame was known. She must go somewhere that no one knew her and she must find work of some kind, at least until her innocent babe was born. After that, she would not care whether she lived or died.

Caroline was dressing the next morning when Margaret came to her bedchamber. She knew at once that something was wrong and her heart missed a beat.

'What is the matter?'

'Mercy has run away,' Margaret said. 'Her things have gone and she left this for you on her bed.'

Caroline took the sealed note and broke it open, scanning the brief message and giving a little cry of distress. 'She says that she has left rather than . . .' Her throat closed and she could not go on. Mercy had written that she had gone rather than bring shame on those who had been good to her. 'She begs us not to look for her.'

'Has she run off with Harry Mortimer?' Margaret was stunned. 'The foolish girl!'

'No, I do not think she has gone with him,' Caroline said.

'I was told yesterday that he had volunteered for duty in the West Country,' Margaret said. 'I imagine the worst of the fighting may be there this summer. I had thought he was assigned to garrison duty. Why do you think that he changed his mind? Do you think he went and took Mercy with him? Perhaps he means to wed her . . .'

Margaret had not guessed it all then. Caroline shook her head for she did not wish to reveal her cousin's shame.

'Perhaps she has gone home,' she said. 'If she and Harry have quarrelled . . .'

It was the best she could do for she did not know how to explain Mercy's actions without ruining her reputation, and she did not know for sure that her suspicions were true. She was torn with emotion, her fears for her friend mixing with distress and regret that she had not warned Mercy of Harry's nature. He was handsome and charming, but underneath he was a selfish rogue who could not be trusted.

163

'I think she has gone with him,' Margaret said, 'for he rode out yesterday afternoon with some others. I dare say he persuaded her to this reckless behaviour. It is quite disgraceful of her – after all your good will, to say nothing of my own.'

'I do not think she meant to behave badly, ma'am.'

Mercy must have felt she had no option. She had not been able to accept Caroline's offer of help and so she had run away rather than embarrass her friends.

But where could she go? She would not dare to return to her home and she had no friends who would take her in. She must be desperate for she had little money of her own. It would not be long before that was gone and then she must find work. And who would take on a girl in her circumstance?

Caroline's heart ached with pity for her cousin. It was a terrible situation. She herself could do nothing, but her father could cause a search to be made for Mercy. He would be shocked and he might think badly of her, but for pity's sake he would do what he could to find her.

'I think I ought to go home,' Caroline told her hostess. 'My father is much recovered now. If he and my mother should learn of this from another, they would worry.'

'I feel I have let you down,' Margaret said. 'I should have warned her but he seemed so charming . . .'

'You have been all that you ought,' Caroline told her. 'But I have been away from home long enough. I think that I must return.'

'I had such hopes for you . . . and Walter,' Margaret said looking sad. 'I thought he would speak before he left.' She gave a sigh of exasperation. 'Are none of them to be trusted?'

'Captain Benedict has been nothing less than a gentleman,' Caroline said. 'He would have spoken but I . . . prevented him. I like him well enough but not enough for marriage. And besides, I do not yet know him properly.'

'Ah, I thought that must be the case,' Margaret said and shook her head ruefully. 'He seemed to be fond. I shall not repine though, for it may be that you will change your mind.'

Caroline thought it prudent to smile and say nothing more. She was not in a position to tell her hostess the truth, and must say nothing to distress her, for she was already upset that Mercy had gone without so much as a word to her.

'Well, I shall arrange your journey,' Margaret said. 'You shall go in my own coach, Caroline, with three of my most trusted servants to escort you. Will next Monday be soon enough?'

It was four days hence and Caroline could not ask to leave sooner for that would be an insult to her hostess. She agreed that she would be happy to leave the following Monday, and thanked her for arranging to make her journey comfortable.

Caroline knew she must not show it, but in truth she would be glad to be home again. She wanted the comfort of her mother's arms about her, and the security of her family's love.

Eight

'Caroline, my dear!' Lady Saunders came out of the house to greet her daughter with a cry of pleasure. 'How came you here? You did not send word . . .' She looked towards the coach and then frowned. 'Mercy did not accompany you?'

'No, she did not come,' Caroline said and embraced her mother. She was overcome with emotion, a little shiver running through her as her mother's arms closed about her. The journey had been long and arduous for the roads were filled with soldiers, sometimes Royalists and sometimes Parliamentarians, moving from one place to another, and their coach had been stopped several times by one side or the other, and papers demanded. 'I shall explain it all when we are more private.'

'Yes, of course, my dearest,' her mother said and patted her back soothingly, for she had sensed her daughter's distress. 'What matters is that *you* are here. We have missed you sorely. Your father has been talking of travelling to Oxford himself to fetch you. He will be overjoyed to have you home. Do come in and greet him for he is working in his library and may not have seen the coach arrive.'

Caroline smiled at her mother, relief washing over her as she saw the familiar things of home and her family embraced her. 'I have enjoyed my visit,' she told her mother, 'but I am so glad to be here.'

Lady Saunders looked anxiously at her daughter for there were shadows under her eyes and it was plain that something was troubling her, but she did not ask as she led the way to her husband's library. Sir John had heard the commotion in the house and was on his feet, about to investigate, when they walked in.

'Caroline, my dearest child,' he said and came towards her, taking her into his arms to embrace her warmly. 'I have missed you sorely.'

'And I you – and mother,' Caroline said. She looked over her shoulder and saw that the solid oak door was firmly shut behind them, for she did not want what she had to say to be overheard by anyone. 'And now I have some upsetting news for you both about Mercy. As I believe Mother guessed, she had deep feelings towards Harry Mortimer. Forgive me, Father, for I was unable to obey you. We saw much of Harry at Oxford, for Margaret kept open house for her friends and you must know that the King hath stayed in the city these past months. Mercy has run away and I believe she may . . . be carrying Harry's child.'

'No!' Lady Saunders gasped, her face turning pale. 'Surely you must be mistaken, Caroline? She would not be so foolish?'

'Has she gone with him?' Sir John said, his expression grim.

'I cannot be sure but I think not,' Caroline replied and explained that she had asked Harry his intentions towards her cousin. 'He said that he had no money and that when he wed it must be for a fortune. I believe that he wanted Mercy, perhaps he loved her in his way, and I suspect that he seduced her. She left a letter for me, saying that she had gone because she did not wish to bring shame on us . . .' Lady Saunders sank down on to the nearest chair, looking distressed. 'I had told her that we would stand by her if she was in trouble, as I believed you would do so no matter what she had done.'

'Poor, poor child,' Lady Saunders whispered. She put a hand to her face, hiding her grief. 'What will she do? Where can she go? Her stepfather would kill her if she went to him in her shame.'

'I think she would rather starve,' Caroline said, her eyes

sheened with tears. She turned her gaze to her father with a look of mute appeal. 'Father . . .'

'What would you have me do, Caroline?'

'Could a search be made for her, please? Would you bring her here, at least until her child is born and she has more chance to fend for herself?'

'You know that she would be scorned by many?' Sir John said. 'The goodwives would point the finger of shame at her, some might even stone her or drive her from the village. She would not be accepted in company by our friends, but be forced to stay here in the house for most of her life.'

'Perhaps in time she would be accepted again,' Caroline said, though she knew that the stain of Mercy's disgrace would never be forgotten. The finger of shame would be pointed at her forever. No matter if she wed, it would still be whispered that she was not modest, a girl of loose morals. 'If it was seen that she was actually a good modest girl who had been let down, Harry might even be brought to marry her.'

'I do not think it,' Sir John said, his mouth a thin line of anger. 'He is a scoundrel and a rogue and I am glad that I forbade the marriage between you.'

'I am also glad that you did, Father,' Caroline replied. 'I had been uncertain of my feelings toward him for some while before the breach. I think Harry is a charming man to know casually but would not make for a comfortable husband.'

'Why could Mercy not have had your good sense?' her father growled. 'If it were up to me I would say that she hath chosen her path and must follow it. However . . .' He saw the distress in the faces of the women he loved. 'For your sakes I shall do what I can to find her. I shall send a man I trust to make enquiries in Oxford and the surrounding villages, and if she can be traced she shall be brought back here.'

'Oh, Father, I do thank you,' Caroline said joyfully. 'As soon as it happened I knew that I must come home to you, and that you would know what to do.'

Her father smiled for he could not help but be pleased by her faith in him. 'I shall do my best, Caroline, but I cannot promise she will be found, for she may have taken another name. It is likely that she will try to pass as a widow in the coming months, for that way she might be allowed to settle and find work.'

'It will be so hard for her,' Lady Saunders said. Her eyes filled with tears for she was as distressed as her daughter at Mercy's probable fate. 'You must try hard to find her, husband. Imagine how you would feel if it were your daughter.'

'I thank God that she has more sense and respect for her family,' he said gruffly. 'Now, let us speak of other things. Did things go well for you at Mistress Farringdon's, Caroline?'

'Yes, Father. I made many new friends, though they were mostly Royalists. Yet I reserved my opinions to myself and sought no confrontation . . .' Except that she had helped bind the wounds of a Roundhead spy, for that is what Nicolas would have been branded if caught. 'Most of them were good, kindly people and I liked them.'

'This war is all the fault of intemperate men,' her father said, 'and I am no longer sure where my sympathies lie. As you know, I would always have wished the King to come to terms – and yet now I have begun to realize what may be our fate if he should lose the war.'

'What do you mean, Father?' Caroline was surprised for her father had been on neither side in this quarrel and it seemed that he had had a change of heart.

'It is that jumped up jack, Richard Woodville,' her father said, a flush of dark red creeping up his neck. 'He returned to the village last week with a troop of men who are to be stationed here – for our safety, according to him. To see him strutting about as if he owned the place, laying down the law to others who are above his station . . . it is beyond all bearing!'

'Now then, my dear,' his wife said distressed. 'You know

169

the physician said you were not to upset yourself. Master Woodville is pleased with his new position in life that is all.'

'All! The pompous ass thinks he is God's lieutenant!'

Caroline looked at her mother, who shook her head. 'Poor Reverend Blackwell is constantly harried by the man,' she explained. 'He has been forced to remove all the beautiful trappings from the church. We are to worship in plain surroundings now, and only a simple wooden cross upon the altar. Nor are we allowed cushions for kneeling. All those that we sewed last winter have been taken out and burned. The Reverend was nearly in tears when he came here to tell us. His sermons were criticized for not being stern enough, and he may not use his prayer book but only the strict doctrine of the Puritan faith. He fears that he may be turned out of his living and replaced with another.'

'Oh, the poor man,' Caroline said for she had always liked the gentle man who told them beautiful stories of love and hope, and was fairer than many to those who strayed from his flock. 'But can Lord Mortimer do nothing to stop Master Woodville, Father?'

'He is Captain Woodville now,' Sir John said. 'And Mortimer hath had his powers all but stripped from him. He is a known Royalist, his son a Cavalier officer and fighting for the King. Most pay him lip service still, but it is known that he is not capable of holding the Manor if it was attacked. There is talk that they may try to take Thornberry Manor for their own uses. Imagine that, Caroline. That insufferable man lording it up at that house!'

'Now, now, my dear, you must not upset yourself,' his wife said again. 'Lord Mortimer has good, loyal friends who will not desert him. Captain Woodville hath not yet been given the power to take over the Manor or he would have done so.'

'Oh, you may be certain of that,' he agreed. 'Woodville hath always been envious of his betters, and this war is a good excuse for him and others of his ilk to steal what belongs to others.'

Lady Saunders shook her head, for this was not the first time she had heard her husband in a passion over the new order. The men of Parliament were growing stronger and more powerful in this part of the country, and they must all of them give at least lip service to the new order unless they wished to pay heavy fines.

'Well, we shall trouble you no more for the moment, my love,' she said. 'I am sure you have work to do and Caroline is tired after her journey. I shall take her away now and give her a little time to refresh herself.'

'Yes, yes, I am sorry, my dear,' he said gruffly. 'I know nothing can be done for the moment, but that man tries my temper.'

Lady Saunders drew her daughter away. When they were out of the room, she turned to Caroline with a worried look.

'Your father cannot abide that man, Caroline. They fell out when he came here to tell us of his appointment and the new rules that we were to follow. And I must admit that I do not like him. He – he frightens me.'

'He is a most unpleasant man,' Caroline agreed, remembering the day that Nicolas had saved her from Master Woodville. 'I do not like him.'

'But did you meet a gentleman you could like?' Her mother looked at her fondly. 'I wished you home often, my dearest, but I hoped that you might find happiness.'

'There is someone I care for deeply, someone I would marry if I had my father's blessing, and yours.'

'Then that is good news . . .' Lady Saunders frowned. 'But something troubles you, Caroline?'

'The man I would marry is Nicolas Mortimer,' Caroline told her. 'I think that I have loved him a long time, Mother, though I would not allow myself to think it. Only after Father had forbidden the match with Harry did I begin to understand. When Nicolas told me that he loved me, had always loved me, I knew why I had not been broken-hearted that I could not wed his brother.'

'You love Nicolas . . .' Lady Saunders stared at her for a

171

moment in silence and then smiled. 'Oh, my dear, you could not have chosen better. I have always thought him the best of his family. He is quieter than Harry and perhaps not so pretty a fellow, but he is thoughtful and generous, and I like him. He will make you a far better husband than his brother ever could.'

'But will Father allow it?' Caroline looked at her apprehensively.

'You leave your father to me,' Lady Saunders told her. 'As you have witnessed for yourself, he has begun to change his mind about the war and its causes. I believe he would like to make up his quarrel with Lord Mortimer if it could be done easily. Besides, Nicolas is not a Royalist.'

'Neither is he a Puritan,' Caroline told her. 'He fights for Parliament because he believes in the rights of the common man. I think he would be as angry as Father if he knew what Captain Woodville does here.'

'I am certain of it,' her mother said. 'They are very much alike – do you not think so?'

'Yes . . .' Caroline looked at her in dawning realization. 'I had not thought of it before, but I suppose that they are. Perhaps that is why . . .'

'You chose him instead of his brother?' Her mother nodded. 'I believe your choice is wise, my love, and I am sure your father will be brought to see it too. It is merely a matter of time, and we have that in plenty for it may be many months before Nicolas is able to visit us here.'

'Yes, I am afraid it may be, for there will surely be a new campaign very soon.'

She thought of the many dangers that lay ahead. The future seemed dark and frightening for all of them. Nicolas and Rupert, two of the people she loved most in the world, now fighting on opposing sides but both dear to her. She wished fervently that the war would end and they would come home, but in her heart she knew it would be a long time before she saw either of them again.

And there was Mercy, too. Caroline's thoughts were often

with the girl she loved like a sister. Where was she? How was she faring in these dangerous times?

Mercy paused to rest on a wooden bench in the village square. It was bitterly cold, the wind icy as it cut through her thin cloak. Dusk was falling fast. In a moment she must get up and look for somewhere she might find shelter for the night, but she was so weary.

She was a stranger in this place and had been walking constantly since she left Oxford, buying what food she could from her small store of money, but as yet she had been unable to find work. Everywhere she tried she was turned away, either by the lady of the house, who thought her too beautiful and therefore a danger, or by a suspicious-eyed man who thought her too slight and pale to be of use in the kitchen. There were few indeed inclined to be charitable in these unhappy times.

She sat down on a wooden bench provided by some charitable soul for the poor and took out the crust of bread that was all she had managed to buy that day. As she sat wondering whether she should eat it or save it, a young boy ran up to her. He was thin and dirty, and his eyes were large as he stared at the bread. She instinctively knew that he was hungry and her heart went out to him.

'Are you hungry?' He nodded, his face wearing such a look of longing that she held out the bread to him. His need was greater than hers and she could not help thinking of the child she was to bear and what might happen to it in the future. As the boy snatched the bread and ate ravenously, Mercy made a mental vow that she would secure a safe future for her child. Somehow she would live – and she would give her child a home. She was conscious of a rumbling in her stomach but suppressed it. She would rest for a few moments and then she would go and look for some kind of work to earn her supper.

'Good morrow, mistress.' A woman dressed neatly in grey, with a black steeple hat and a plain linen neckerchief to proclaim her as a woman of modest habits, stopped to speak to her. She was elderly and carrying a heavy basket on her arm for she had been to the market. 'What ails you?'

'I mean no harm,' Mercy said, for it would not be the first time that angry wives, who thought her a wanton plying her trade, had driven her from a village with stones and insults. 'I have walked a long way and I need to rest for a little. I shall be on my way as soon as I am able.'

'Where are you going?'

'I . . . I am going home,' Mercy said, for a more truthful answer would have brought her a scowling glance. 'My husband was killed at Edgehill and I had only a little money. I cannot afford to pay to ride on the coach.'

'And where is your home?'

Mercy thought of the kindness she had been shown in the home of her mother's cousin; in truth Caroline's house had been her home. 'It is between Huntingdon and the Isle of Ely.'

'And was your husband a Royalist or a Puritan?'

'He fought for . . . Parliament,' Mercy lied for she could see by the woman's dress that she was of the Puritan faith.

'Then you shall come home and rest with me this night,' the woman said kindly. 'I had a son and he was killed at Edgehill. For his sake I shall offer you charity.'

Mercy thanked her, feeling grateful for a kind face and a generous welcome. She knew that she dared not stay more than the one night, for she had lied to this kind woman, but at least she could sleep in comfort for one night.

And then where could she go? Mercy had learned the hard way that the world was an inhospitable place for a young woman alone. There was nowhere she could go yet for she would not bring shame on her friends, but when the time came she would go to Caroline. She would beg her to take the child and then . . . it did not matter what became of her then for her heart was already dead.

'Stay close to me, Tilly,' Caroline whispered as she saw the man walking along the village street and knew that they could not avoid him. Her stomach curled with the repulsion he never failed to arouse in her, though she had been forced to hide it these past weeks since her return home. It was impossible to avoid him when they attended the church, and he strutted about the place as if he were the King himself, making it his business to interfere in the lives of everyone. 'Whatever happens, do not leave me alone with that man!'

'He'll have to kill me first,' Tilly vowed and scowled ferociously, for she was devoted to her mistress and would defend her with her last breath.

'Good morrow, Mistress Saunders,' said Captain Woodville as he drew near. 'It is a fine spring morning is it not?'

'Yes, sir, the morning is well enough,' Caroline answered, for the bitter weather had suddenly broken that week. She neither smiled nor curtsied for she preferred to keep him at a distance. 'I pray you will excuse us; we must return as swiftly as possible. Lady Saunders is waiting for a message from Reverend Blackwell.'

His eyes narrowed to menacing slits and she felt he would have prevented her from going on if he dared, but though he had sweeping powers against those who broke the rules, he was not yet strong enough to openly defy Sir John, who had powerful friends. It was well known that Rupert had defied his father when he joined the King and that the family had taken neither one side nor the other. There were many families of moderate views in the district, and it would have caused much unrest if the daughter of a man like Sir John were molested while going about her lawful business.

However, as she passed him, Caroline was conscious he was watching her and knew that he would not forget the insults, as he considered them, that had been offered by her father and herself.

'I do not like that man,' Tilly said when they were safely out of hearing. 'He has evil in him.'

'He makes me sick to my stomach,' Caroline told her. 'But it would be dangerous to show any disrespect. For the moment he is in control here and we must all go carefully.'

'I heard as he and his men arrested someone the other day for being a suspected Royalist spy,' Tilly said. ''Tis said they beat him and would have hung him, but somehow he escaped while Captain Woodville was absent. He was furious when he discovered the prisoner had gone, and he had the two men who were supposed to guard him flogged.'

Caroline's eyes darkened with horror, for she did not doubt that Tilly was right. Woodville was a brute and would use what force he considered necessary to break a man he suspected of spying. She felt cold and frightened for there was no telling what trouble a man like that might cause. It was no wonder that the villagers looked at each other suspiciously these days. People were in fear of their new masters for it seemed that Woodville had the power to do as he pleased.

She wished that Nicolas would come home, though she knew that it was not possible. He had risked so much to come to her at Oxford, which had proved to her beyond doubt that she meant more to him than his very life. But she was worried, a shadow hung over her for she had an odd feeling, a premonition that something terrible might happen if things went on this way.

Mercy stopped to drink water from the well in the village she had just reached. It was much better on the road now that the cold weather had passed, and two days ago she had found work helping a woman spring-clean her house. She had enjoyed the task of beating carpets and washing windows, but once the work was done the woman had sent her on her way.

'I do not know who you are, mistress,' she had told Mercy. 'You have worked well and I would keep you here but my husband bid me tell you to leave. I am sorry for it, but I think he suspects you are not what you seem.' She had pressed a bundle of food and some small coins into Mercy's hand. 'If I were you, I should return to your family. 'Tis not safe for a young woman to be on the road alone in these days.'

'I have no family,' Mercy said, 'but I thank you for your good advice and your help.'

She had walked all morning to the next village and she was hungry and tired. As she straightened from the well she saw a troop of horsemen arrive at the inn in the village. They were laughing, clapping each other on the shoulder and talking of some fighting they had apparently been involved in recently. Mercy wished that she dared approach them and ask for news of the war, but even as she hesitated, she saw that a woman was glaring at her.

'Be off with you, harlot,' the woman said and picked up a handful of dung from the road, flinging it at her. 'We don't want your sort here.'

The dung missed Mercy, but the soldiers were staring at her and she could see that one or two of them were giving her looks that made her nervous. If they thought her a whore they might seek to take advantage of her. She had hoped that she might find work in this village, but it was clear that she must be on her way again. She had been walking for weeks now and her feet were sore. Her shoes had holes in them and she had stuffed them with rags to protect the soles of her feet, but they had rubbed and made a blister.

She turned away, walking faster as she heard one of the soldiers call to her. She would starve rather than become what so many of the village goodwives thought her . . .

Caroline glanced out of the window. It was night and the gardens were shrouded in darkness. She was not sure what was on her mind, but she had been unable to sleep. She could not help wondering where Mercy was. Had she found somewhere to live? Or was she alone and in trouble? Several months had passed since Mercy had run away, and it must be getting harder and harder for her to find someone to give her work.

If only she had stayed with them, allowed them to take care of her. Caroline sighed, her thoughts turning to Nicolas and her brother once more. She knew that there had been a battle at Adwalton Moor in June but she was not sure whether either Rupert or Nicolas had been involved in the fighting. The armies were split, and there were so many small battles in various parts of the country that it was impossible to know how things stood.

'I pray that you are well and happy, Mercy,' she whispered. 'And that all those I love are safe.'

'It will soon be your eighteenth birthday,' Caroline's father said one summer morning. 'What would you have me give you, daughter?'

Caroline was silent for a moment, then replied, 'While I was in Oxford Mistress Farringdon suggested that I might have my portrait painted. I thought that I would like a miniature done on ivory.'

'That is an excellent idea,' her father said, looking pleased. 'It has been in my mind to have your likeness taken. I shall commission it, Caroline. You shall have your miniature and I shall have a splendid portrait to hang in my library where I may see it every day.'

Caroline smiled and thanked him, thinking that one day she would have the miniature framed in silver and give it to Nicolas on the day of their wedding.

'I shall look forward to sitting for my portrait, Father.'

'Then I shall send for Master Whitfield at once, my dear.' He looked at her with approval for she was a good and dutiful girl and he was proud of her.

'I fear I have been a restless subject for you, sir,' Caroline apologized to the young man as he put his brushes away and declared his work done for the day. They had been working in her mother's front parlour for her father had been as good as his word, commissioning an artist of whom he had heard much praise from his friends.

Master Whitfield smiled and shook his head. 'Your face is so expressive, Mistress Caroline. You looked sad and that is not the emotion I would capture.'

Caroline sighed. 'Forgive me. I was thinking of someone.'

'You have a friend away fighting perhaps?'

'Yes. My brother and . . . friends. Of course I am not the only one, sir. The war has split families apart.'

'My brother was killed earlier this year. It was merely a skirmish, a squabble between neighbours who were friends until a few months ago. I fear the whole country is in turmoil because of this wretched war.'

'I am sorry,' Caroline said. 'But you do not fight, sir?'

'I have no love of bloodshed, Mistress Caroline, but I think that when I have finished your portrait I may be driven to it. This war will suck us all in, in the end.'

'I do not think you should fight, sir. Your talent should not be wasted. I was much pleased by the miniature you did of me.'

'I am honoured to have been chosen for the task, Mistress Caroline, but still I shall fight. There are times when a man must do his duty even though it pleases him not.'

'Yes, you are right,' she agreed and her heart ached for all the friends she had known who had already been killed or injured. And for Mercy who would be finding life hard unless she had found a good home.

Where was Nicolas? Where were her brother and Harry? If only she could know that they were safe.

The battle was almost won. Harry felt no sense of elation, for he had long wearied of the smell of blood and the stink of death. He had joined the Royalist forces on a wave of enthusiasm, but that had gradually faded to a fatalistic sense of futility. Why did Englishmen kill other Englishmen when this quarrel might have been settled in another manner?

It seemed to Harry then that he had a clearer vision than he had ever had, and he saw that his own life had been one of selfish pleasure, never thinking of the harm he did. Of the harm he had done to Mercy.

He felt a wave of regret wash over him as he remembered

the cruel manner of his leaving. She would not have told him she was with child if she had not been sure. Rowena might have lied to gain advantage but not Mercy. She had begged him to love her, to wed her and restore her honour, and he had deliberately left her to her fate.

'God forgive me!' he groaned.

If he survived this day, and it had seemed he bore a charmed life these past months, he promised himself that he would find her and, if she would have him, he would wed her.

Hearing a cry for help close by, he turned to see that a group of Roundhead soldiers had surrounded a young Cavalier. He was fighting for his life, outnumbered four to one and – by Heaven – it was Rupert Saunders! He had been unhorsed and was in danger.

Harry acted instinctively when he saw that Rupert had been wounded, though he was valiantly fighting on against all hope. He charged into the fray, striking to left and right, killing three of the Roundheads as he fought his way through to Rupert's side.

Rupert grinned at him, staggering from the wound to his thigh as the remaining Roundheads joined their comrades in flight. It had been a victory for the Royalists and the Roundheads were fleeing.

'We beat them,' Rupert said, swooning as Harry moved to catch him. He was only vaguely aware that he was being carried from the battlefield to a place of safety. As he lay on the ground, barely conscious, he heard the sound of an explosion very close to him. 'Harry . . .' He cried out in fear, but there was no answer.

'Master Whitfield did you justice,' Sir John said. They were in his library watching as the portrait was hung in place above the wooden mantle. 'I am well pleased with his work.'

'It is very like you, Caroline,' her mother said, smiling at her.

'I believe he hath flattered me,' Caroline said and laughed. It was embarrassing to see her own picture hung. 'Poor Master

Whitfield hath put away his paints and gone to join the King's army.'

'I dare say they will find work for him other than with his sword,' her father said. 'He will be of more use recording the conflict for history than on the battlefield.'

'Yes, perhaps. He is a gentle soul.' Caroline sighed and looked at her father. 'I had hoped we might have some news of Mercy before this.'

'I would have told you,' he said with a chiding look. 'She has been searched for, Caroline, but as yet there is no sign of her.'

'I do not think she wants to be found,' Lady Saunders said. 'We can only trust that she will come to us when her child is near.'

'Do you think she will?' Caroline looked at her optimistically.

'Where else can she go?' her mother asked. 'Do not lose hope, my dear. We can but pray for her . . .'

The news came more slowly to their tiny Cambridgeshire village than it had to Oxford. Caroline and her parents were not the only ones who waited fearfully for word of what was happening in the wider world, for most families had someone fighting on one side or the other.

There were constant rumours, many of which proved false. Small battles were taking place all over the country, though it was only the news of the larger conflicts that reached them, skirmishes between trained bands raised by local gentry, some of which had been won by the Parliament forces, though in most the Royalists had been successful.

The first important battle of the year had been in July at Roundway Down in the south west of the country. The Royalists had been retreating before Waller but at Salisbury they had turned north to seek help from Lord Wilmot. This time when the Royalists attacked there was no counter charge, and after two further charges the Parliamentary cavalry fled. However, the infantry held firm until a force led by Hopton attacked them from behind. Trapped between the two Royalist forces, the Parliamentarians fled.

When at last the news came, Caroline was torn with anxiety for both her brother and Nicolas. Had they both been caught up in the fighting – and had either of them been hurt?

As yet they had had no news of any of their loved ones and they could only pray that both had managed to survive such a terrible battle.

Rowena screamed in agony as her mother bade her push harder. Her hands gripped the knotted rope that had been tied to the bedpost for her to hold on to, but it hardly helped against such tearing pain. She twisted this way and that in her distress, but it seemed as if her child would never be born.

'Damn you, Harry Mortimer,' she muttered, writhing on the bed as she struggled to push once more. 'I hate you! I wish I had never set eyes on you. I hope you know agony such as this and that you die from it.'

'Hush, girl,' her mother told her. 'Cursing him will not help you now. You should have told me at the start, then we might have been rid of the brat the easy way.'

'No!' Another scream broke from Rowena's lips, which were drawn back like a terrified animal that would fight for its life. 'He owes me for this. I would have the child live. I shall take it to his father and demand payment for what he did to me.'

Sally Greenslade wiped the sweat from her forehead with a cool cloth, shaking her head over her. 'Vengeance will gain you little, girl. Accept that you have a bastard child and make a new life for yourself. There is plenty of work here. We can put the child with someone while you work or better still get rid of it.'

Many an unwanted babe found a watery grave, and Sally was not above getting rid of a child that would be nothing but a burden to them.

'No!' Rowena caught her wrist. 'If it lives when 'tis born

I want it to live,' she muttered. 'It will buy me the things I want – the things he promised me when he said we would be wed.'

'Maybe he will wed you yet,' her mother said to ease her, though she knew it was a hollow hope.

'He is a liar and a cheat and I hope that he rots in Hell!'

She screamed again as the pain tore through her once more and then in a rush of blood and gore the child came thrusting from between her legs. Sally seized it with a cry of triumph, lifting it for her daughter to see.

''Tis a boy, Rowena. You have a son.'

'Harry said his father would take it if it was a boy,' Rowena said and lay back with a grunt of satisfaction. 'Well, his son damned near killed me but I gave him birth and he will bring me my share of the wealth that Harry Mortimer would have inherited from his father if he had lived.'

'You do not know that he is dead,' her mother told her.

Rowena smiled, her eyes as black as night. 'I ill wished him,' she said. 'He will die and his father will pay me to take the boy. Have a care for him, Mother, for he will make our fortunes.'

'Go to Thornberry if you will,' her mother said,' but I shall not accompany you. I have had enough of that accursed place and it will bring you nothing but ill luck if you return there.'

Rowena took the babe in her arms, looking down at the tiny screwed-up face. He was red and ugly and nothing like his father, but when he opened his eyes and looked at her she saw that they were a wonderful shade of blue. Oh yes, he was Harry's son all right, and Lord Mortimer would pay handsomely to have him.

Caroline was restless. It was a hot and sultry August night and she had found it impossible to sleep. She threw back the linen sheet that was all she had to cover herself and got out of bed, going to look out of the window. In another hour it would be light and she thought that she might as well go down and find a book to read for she would not rest further.

She did not bother with a candle for the first ray of dawn light was slanting through the windows and she knew her way so well that she had no fear of falling. She made her way to her father's library, for he had recently purchased a copy of some poems that she wished to read and she knew he would not mind her taking the book to her room. However, as she approached the door, she heard a slight noise coming from inside and stiffened.

It sounded as if someone had almost knocked something over. Was someone in the room? She did not think that any of the servants would be up this early, and her father certainly would not be here at this hour. She felt a slither of unease down her spine. Looking for something to use as a weapon, she seized a heavy iron candlestick and opened the door very carefully. In the faint light of early dawn, she could see a man standing by the long oak table that ran the length of the room. He appeared to be trying to pour himself a drink from the flask of Brandewine that was always kept on the table with two drinking cups, but he was making a poor job of it for she heard him swear beneath his breath.

'May I ask who you are, sir – and what you are doing in my father's house?' She sounded remarkably cool, though her heart was pounding.

The man cursed louder this time, and swung round, levelling a pistol at her. Caroline gripped the candlestick tighter, though it would offer little protection against his pistol.

'Damn it,' he muttered and gasped again, clearly in pain. His arm dropped to his side and he slumped into the chair. 'I pray you, ma'am, do not attack me. I am as helpless as a kitten and at your mercy.'

'Sir . . .' Caroline approached warily but something was telling her that she knew this man and as she drew near enough to see his face, she recognized him. 'Captain Benedict!' she exclaimed. 'How came you here – and why are you in my father's house?'

He stared at her, a look of amazement and then relief

coming to his face. 'Is it truly you, Mistress Saunders? I did not know whose house it was, only that I needed somewhere for rest, food and drink. I have been shot – from the back as I escaped my enemies – but fortunately it was a poor shot and only my shoulder was wounded.'

'You are injured?' Caroline set down her weapon and moved closer. 'May I look? I would willingly bathe and bind it for you – if you will trust me?'

'You offer to help me?' He stared at her for a moment as if in disbelief, and then smiled. 'You are truly an unusual and brave lady, Caroline. First a Roundhead spy and now a Royalist one. I believe this area is a Parliamentary stronghold. Have you any idea of what they would do to you if I were found here? Of what they would say if you were known to have helped me?'

'I think it would go hard with us, sir,' she said, 'for we have a most unpleasant man as our commander here. Captain Woodville is his name. I do not like him and I know it would please him to harm my family for my father once refused him my hand in marriage. Therefore I can only offer you temporary shelter.'

'I ask no more of you,' he said. 'Indeed, I wonder that you are so good as to help me.'

'You might have betrayed me once, you did not,' she said. 'We do not need to be enemies, sir. I have no love for your cause but neither do I hate you. But we waste time. Rest as much as you can while I fetch food, water, and linen to bind you.'

He nodded and slumped back into the chair, his face pale and sweating. Caroline hurried away to the kitchen. As she entered, she saw that Tilly had begun her morning chores. Tilly turned as she saw Caroline and would have greeted her had she not placed a finger to her lips.

'Say nothing yet! Will you risk punishment to help a wounded Royalist officer?'

'If you wish it,' Tilly said and her eyes widened. 'Is it Master Rupert?'

'No – but we know him. It is Captain Benedict.'

'Then I would help him for his own sake,' Tilly said. 'For he was always good to me at Oxford and I know he loves you, Mistress Caroline.'

'He has been shot in the shoulder, and he needs food, water and linen. I shall fetch linen and salves from the still-room if you will see to some food and wine.'

Tilly nodded and began to collect what they would need while Caroline sped away to her mother's stillroom. She collected a jar of the poultice she had used to ease Nicolas's wound, some herbs to make a tisane that he might take with him for the pain, and linen to bind him.

When she returned to the library, Tilly was already there and Captain Benedict was drinking the wine she had poured for him. Between them, Caroline and Tilly washed away the blood, though neither of them could remove the ball for it was too firmly embedded. They made a thick pad of linen and bound him as tightly as they could. He was clearly in some pain, but apart from the healing herbs mixed with the wine and poured into a small flask that he might take with him, there was not much more that they could do for him.

'I shall leave you before anyone comes to look for me,' he told them. 'I doubt not that a search will be made once it is light and I must be far away by then. I shall take the food with me for it will be impossible to find food until I am clear of this nest of traitors – no offence to yourselves or your family, ladies.'

'I wish I could offer you a bed to rest in until you are well,' Caroline said. 'But to do so would risk your safety and mine.'

'I thank you for having done so much,' Captain Benedict replied and smiled oddly. 'You have not asked me why I came this way.'

'It is not my business,' Caroline said, 'and perhaps best that I should not know.'

'A part of it you may know, though it would be best to keep the news only to those you trust for the moment. Your brother is alive, though he was injured at Roundway Down. But my news is not all good. One of the reasons I rode this way was to bring word of Harry Mortimer to his father.'

Caroline's sense of elation at the news of her brother was swiftly stilled. 'Has Harry been wounded?'

'At Roundway Down,' Captain Benedict replied and his face was grave. 'He lingered for a few days but died two weeks ago. I am sorry to tell you, Mistress Saunders, but I know that he and your cousin were close for a while.'

'Harry dead . . .' Caroline felt the tears burning behind her eyes. She had not wanted to marry him, but she had once cared for him deeply as a friend and she knew how much the death of his son would hurt Lord Mortimer. 'That is sad news, sir. It was kind of you to deliver it in person.'

'I had other business,' he said, 'and that business makes me a danger to you every moment I stay. Forgive me for using your house, Mistress Saunders. I would not bring harm to you.'

'I dare say you have not,' she said. 'And when we meet again in happier times, you must call me Caroline, for we are friends, are we not?'

'I thank you, Caroline,' he said again, 'for your kindness in all things. I think your Roundhead is a lucky man.'

'You have no news of Nicolas Mortimer?'

'None,' he said and there was a flicker of something in his eyes. 'He will live somehow. If I had you waiting for me so should I . . .' And then with an elegant bow, he turned and clambered back through the casement window that had given him entry.

Tilly was collecting up the things they had used. 'I had best get rid of these,' she said. 'I think the linen we used to bathe him had best go on the fire, for we want no evidence if they should come to search the house.'

'No, indeed,' Caroline agreed, for Tilly was more thoughtful than she had been on another occasion. 'I shall take the salve back to the stillroom . . .'

*   *   *

187

Caroline rejoiced in the knowledge that her brother was alive, but knew that for the moment she could not tell her parents. They would want to know how she had come by the information, and it was best that they did not know until Captain Benedict was safely away.

However, the shocking news of Harry Mortimer's death lingered at the back of Caroline's mind that morning, dimming her pleasure of her own news. Her heart ached for a lost friend and for Mercy's feelings if she should learn of his death. And of course for his father, because Lord Mortimer must be grieving terribly.

She felt drawn to the man who might one day be her father-in-law, and as the day wore on she knew that she had to visit him. She could not simply ignore what she had learned from Captain Benedict. She must pay a visit to the Manor.

Should she tell her parents or keep her secret? Caroline debated it for the rest of the day and throughout a sleepless night, but in the morning she had made her decision. She would go to the Manor alone, for the fewer people who knew of Captain Benedict's visit in the early hours the previous morning, the better.

She told her mother that she was going for a walk because it was too warm to stay in the house and set out across the meadow and over the rise to where the old manor house lay basking in the sunlight. Its old stone walls were warmed by the sunshine, yet it looked forlorn and lonely, forgotten as it dreamed of glories past, and she had a sense of desolation as she walked into the courtyard.

A couple of dogs were chasing a farm cat, while a boy worked in a desultory fashion at clearing the debris from the cobbles. When she hammered on the front door with the heavy iron knocker, some minutes passed before it was answered by a surly-looking servant. His expression lightened a little as he saw her and he stood back immediately, inviting her inside.

Caroline was shocked as she saw the neglect in the hall, for there was a cold chill about the place and no sign that it had been cleaned in recent times. Just what was going on here? It had not been thus when she was last in this house.

'The master is in his chamber,' the servant muttered. 'Wait here and I'll see if he will come down to you.'

Caroline nodded. She began to look about her more closely after he had gone, noticing that some pictures were missing from the walls and the great silver-gilt salt that had always sat on the long trestle and board at the far end was also gone.

She knew that many families of the Royalist persuasion had given their silver to help His Majesty's cause, but she believed the ravages here were due to another reason entirely.

The sound of a man's footsteps made her turn and she was shocked as she saw Lord Mortimer's face. The ravages of grief and illness had changed him greatly in these few short months and her heart caught with pity and with regret. Her own father had suffered because of the breach between them, but this man looked as if he had stood at the edge of Hell's fiery pit.

'Caroline . . .' He stared at her sadly. 'You have heard the news, of course?'

'Yes, sir. I came to tell you how sorry I was to learn of Harry's death.'

'And you see me in a sorry state,' Lord Mortimer said. 'I am shamed for it, Caroline. You have been given a poor welcome in my house and I know it must have cost you much to come here.'

'I grieve to see you brought to this, sir,' Caroline replied, her throat tight. She felt close to tears but held them in check, knowing that to see her distress would only add to his grief. 'I know that you have not been well . . .'

'Half my servants have run off,' Lord Mortimer told her. 'Some went to join the King with my blessing, others sneaked away in the night to join those scurvy knaves that fight against him, I dare say. I have been ill of late and the neglect is my fault for I have not bothered to order those that remain to do more than bring me food and wine.'

'And now you have this grief to bring you down,' Caroline

said, her heart wrung with pity. 'I would help you if I could, sir. You may ask anything you wish of me and if it is within my power I shall do it.'

'My dearest wish is to repair the breach between your father and myself . . .' He hesitated, his face working with anguish. 'And to see Nicolas again. If he would see me . . .'

'I am sure he would, sir,' Caroline said and hesitated, then, 'If you had not quarrelled with my father I could not have married Harry, sir. I love Nicolas and he loves me. I pray that he will return and that one day we shall marry.'

'You love Nicolas,' Lord Mortimer stared at her, his face working with the depth of his emotions. 'And he loves you? Does your father know this?'

'Not yet, sir – but my mother does and she approves. She likes Nicolas very much.'

'And I dare say she did not much approve of Harry? No, no, you need not answer. My eldest son was a wastrel and a rogue. The ruin of this estate was as much his fault as mine. I paid his debts again and again and then . . . he stole from me, from his heritage. It was Harry who took the heirlooms. I discovered their loss the day after my quarrel with Nicolas, but in my heart I knew that they must have gone with Harry. He needed more money for gambling debts and when I refused to give him any he took the jewels.'

'I am glad that you have come to that conclusion for yourself, sir,' Caroline said. 'I always knew it could not be Nicolas and that therefore there was only one other person that might have taken them; only one other who knew where the key was kept.'

'Have you seen Nicolas since he left home?' Lord Mortimer's voice was harsh with grief.

'Yes, sir. He came to my house a few days later, and then I saw him again after Edgehill. He was wounded then and I bound his shoulder. He asked me to believe that he would come back to me and I do.'

'If he should come . . .' Lord Mortimer choked on the tears he was struggling to hold back.

'I shall ask him to visit you,' Caroline promised. 'And my offer stands. If I can be of help in any way I am able . . .'

He smiled at her. 'You cannot know it but you have done much already. I was drifting in a fog, uncaring of what happened to the estate, but now I shall do what I can to put it to right. It is Nicolas's heritage now and he shall not find a ruin when he returns.'

'Then I must go, sir. For I have told no one of my visit here.'

'I would make up my quarrel with your father, Caroline. Do you think he would accept my apology?'

'I think he might meet you halfway, sir.' She smiled at him. 'I shall tell my mother of my visit and my reception here and I believe she will find a way to mend the breach, sir.'

'Then we must put our trust in her, my dear. I thank you for thinking of me, but you were always a good, generous girl. Too good for that rascal we would have had you wed.'

Impulsively, Caroline moved towards him. She put her arms about him, holding him, feeling the shudder that ran through him, sharing his grief. For no matter his harsh words, she knew that he had loved Harry deeply. He had been the image of the wife that Lord Mortimer had adored, whose death had made him a fragment of the man he once was. And Nicolas was like his father.

'God bless and keep you, my dear friend,' she whispered as he put her from him with a little shake of his head. 'I shall come again. I promise you.'

'Go then for I would not wish to bring harm to you.'

Caroline smiled and walked away, leaving him in his hall, a place of shadows now that it was empty of all those who had been precious to him. The loss of his treasures could not hurt or maim him as had the loss of his wife and son.

As Caroline crossed the meadow, she saw a troop of Parliamentary cavalry on the high road that led to the Manor, and noticed that Captain Woodville was at their head. She wondered what mischief he was up to now and hesitated –

but what could she do? Lord Mortimer was suffering from grief, but her visit had given him heart and he would surely find a way to stand up to the vindictive Roundhead captain.

When she returned home she went to her mother's parlour and found that Sir John was with her. She knew at once that something had happened for they were both clearly disturbed.

'What is it, Mother?' she asked.

'It was that damned upstart!' her father answered. 'He came here and demanded to know if we had harboured a Royalist spy. He wanted to search the house but I soon told him that I would have none of it.'

'He threatened your father,' Lady Saunders told her. 'If we did not have good friends, who would stand by us and report him to his superiors, I believe he would have forced his way inside.'

'I saw him and his men as I walked through the meadow,' Caroline said. 'I think he was on his way to the Manor . . .' She hesitated, then, 'I have seen Lord Mortimer this morning. Forgive me, Father, but I had to go. Harry has been killed.'

'You . . .' Sir John looked at her, his face registering both shock and dismay. 'How did you know this, Caroline?'

'I helped a wounded Royalist,' Caroline admitted, raising her head and meeting his stern look bravely for he must be angry. She had defied his wishes and risked their safety. 'It was yesterday morning, before the house was astir. I knew him from my stay in Oxford and he told me about Harry. He also told me that Rupert had been wounded but was alive when he left him.'

'You did not think fit to mention this to your mother and I?' Sir John's tone was harsh. 'And then you went to the Manor to see Lord Mortimer without telling us?'

'Forgive me, but I thought it best to keep it to myself,' Caroline said. 'I did not want to bring harm to you and Mother. It was as well I did go, Father. Lord Mortimer is in a sorry state. Half of his servants have run off and the house and grounds are neglected for he has not been well.'

'I had heard some such tale,' her father said and cleared

his throat. A little surprised, she realized that he was not angry but merely distressed. 'It is a sad state of affairs.'

'He is so lonely in that great place,' Caroline said. 'I know he regrets his quarrel with you and would mend it if he could.'

'Well, it was foolish after all,' Sir John said. 'In the circumstances I think I ought to visit him. We have been friends a long time and I would . . .' He left his sentence unfinished as one of the servants burst into the room. 'Yes, Ned, what is it?'

'Fire, sir,' the man cried. 'The Manor be afire.'

'What?' Sir John was shocked but then his shock turned to rage. 'This is the work of Woodville! Get our men together, Ned. We must go to help Lord Mortimer.'

'Husband, think what you do,' Lady Saunders implored him but he walked hurriedly from the room without glancing at her. 'Oh, John, do take care . . .'

'We cannot stop him, Mother,' Caroline said and a terrible fear started in the pit of her stomach. 'You know how he has regretted that foolish quarrel, and now Lord Mortimer is in trouble.'

'I know that he must do what he can,' her mother agreed. 'I would not have it otherwise, Caroline. But I fear Woodville. He hates your father for refusing his offer for you and would do us harm if he could.'

'Yes, I know.' Caroline was pale. She wished fervently that there were something that she might do, but knew she must wait patiently for news. 'But Father could not live with himself if he ignored this.'

'No, I know it,' her mother said. 'We cannot stop whatever is to happen, but I pray that it will not end in tragedy for us all.'

Caroline and her mother had an anxious wait; three hours passed without news of any kind, though they could see that the smoke hanging over the Manor did not seem to be greater. When at last Sir John and his men were seen returning,

Caroline rushed out to greet her father as he dismounted.

'What happened, sir?'

'It is bad news,' he said and his face was grey with sorrow. 'They tried to fire the Manor but there was only some small damage done for the walls are thick stone and would not catch. Inside the Great Hall woodwork hath been scorched and there is some destruction otherwise, but that is not the worst . . .' A great shudder went through him. 'When we got there those devils had already left. Mortimer lay on the floor of the hall, a bloody wound to the side of his head. We carried him out and I held him as he breathed his last.' Tears were trickling down his cheeks. 'He knew me, Caroline. I begged him to forgive me and he squeezed my hand and then . . .' His face worked with the depth of his grief. 'I shall not forget the man who did this, daughter. One day he shall be punished for his sins, believe me.'

'Oh, Father,' Caroline said, the tears running down her face as she embraced him. 'If only we could have done something.'

'It was too late when I got there . . . too late.'

She saw the regret he felt, and hugged him tighter, knowing that he would always blame himself for not mending the breach sooner.

'Nicolas will not let this pass,' she said. 'One day he will return to us and then . . .' She left the words unfinished as she saw that they were bringing Lord Mortimer's body.

'He will lie with us until he is buried,' her father said. 'It is all we can do for him now, Caroline.'

She nodded and went to where the men had laid Lord Mortimer upon the ground. They had borne him home on a gate torn down from the estate and covered him with a blanket. Kneeling on the ground beside him, she drew back the cover, and then bent to kiss his lips.

'God keep you now, sir,' she told him. 'Nicolas shall know of your love. That I promise you on my honour. If he comes back to me, he shall know.'

Nine

Caroline turned away from the graveside, her face pale with grief for the man who might have been her father-in-law one day. She had brought flowers, standing in silent prayer for several minutes. There had been a huge gathering for Lord Mortimer's funeral; as if the people of not only Thornberry but surrounding villages had turned out to show respect and perhaps also anger for the way that he had met his death.

England was at war, but most of her people did not wish it thus. They suffered from the ravages of marauding soldiers of both sides. In some cases their harvests lay rotting in the fields for there were only women, children and old men to gather in that which they had sowed. In many homes there would be hardship and even starvation this winter because of the war between the King and Parliament.

As yet no one had dared to accuse Captain Woodville of murdering Lord Mortimer, though there were whispers and some that named him guilty. The finger of shame was pointed at him, but always behind his back for he was feared and hated by most.

As Caroline left the churchyard that morning, she saw a woman walking along the street carrying a bundle in her arms, and the wailing sound issuing from the torn and dirty shawl told her that a baby lay inside. As she met the woman's eyes and saw her angry, defiant stare, she sensed that the child was Harry Mortimer's.

'Good morrow, Rowena,' she said. 'How long have you been back in the village?'

Anne Herries

'What be it to you?' the girl answered her with a scowl.
'I be entitled to live 'ere if 'tis my wish.'

'I would not deny your right,' Caroline told her. 'I merely
wondered if you knew that Harry had been killed?'

'Aye, I know it,' Rowena said and for a moment her eyes
were bright with anger and resentment. 'And his father, thanks
to that devil Richard Woodville.' Hatred glittered in her eyes
then. 'Harry told me his father would take my child if anything
happened to him. May all the goblins in Hell plague
Woodville! May a curse be upon him and all he does!'

Rowena swept past her, her head held high. Caroline
watched her go. She understood the girl's hatred of the man
who had killed Harry's father, for no doubt she had hoped
to find help at the Manor, and remembering Lord Mortimer's
loneliness, Caroline believed that he would have been glad
to take Harry's son had he lived.

It would be difficult for the blacksmith's daughter with a
bastard child. Many would scorn her and she would find it
difficult to get work here where she was known.

Caroline's thoughts turned to Mercy as she made her way
home across the meadow. Where was she? If Caroline had
been right and she was carrying Harry's child, the birth must
be very close now – perhaps it had already been born.

Rowena had returned to the village that she knew so well,
to seek help. But where was Mercy? Caroline wished that
her friend might come home but she was afraid the girl was
too proud and too ashamed.

Rowena saw the gypsy girl as she was gathering herbs and
berries from the hedgerow. Her child, as yet unnamed, lay
in a shawl of cloth that she had fastened across her shoulders so as to leave her hands free for her work.

Carlina smiled at her, coming to meet her. 'There is a
heavy crop of elderberries over yonder,' she said. 'And I
found a goodly amount of mushrooms and fungi this
morning.'

'I am looking for blackberries,' Rowena told her, 'but I

196

have found only unripe ones. I think the birds must have been there before me.'

'You have the child then,' Carlina said. 'It was as written. You should give him a name fit for a prince for he will be one.'

'A prince?' Rowena mocked. 'His father was a lord's son but I doubt mine will ever rise above his station.'

'Have faith,' Carlina said. 'The hour of your trial is near now. Choose wisely when it comes for it is the way . . .'

'You speak in riddles like your grandmother,' Rowena said and yet there was something about the girl that chilled her, and despite herself she half believed what she had been told. 'Is Roald here with you?'

'He has been on his travels as always,' Carlina told her. 'But 'tis the autumn fair next week and he will join us then as is his habit. We await his coming and when he does, be ready.'

Rowena nodded. She was thoughtful as they went their separate ways. She had always liked to tease Roald for he made her laugh inside. While she had had hopes of Harry, her thoughts were all of him, but now she felt a flicker of hope inside her. Would Roald still want her once he knew that she had born a bastard child to the lord's son?

She had intended to approach Lord Mortimer and get him to take the child, but he was dead and she did not know what to do next. If Carlina spoke for her people, perhaps the gypsies would take the boy? Otherwise she might be driven to simply abandon him, perhaps on the doorstep of Mistress Saunders . . .

The rattle of stones at her window awakened Caroline early the next morning. She lay for a moment wondering what had disturbed her, and then got up to investigate. Looking down, her heart took a great leap as she saw the man below. He was gazing up hopefully, and she opened her window to call down to him.

'Nicolas,' she cried joyfully. 'Wait for me. I shall come down.'

Snatching up a wrapping gown, she pulled it on over her

nightrail, running down the stairs in bare feet and fumbling with the bolts at the door in her haste. Then she was outside as the first rays of sunshine began to streak the dawn sky and running towards him. He swept her up into his arms, crushing her in a hungry embrace as their lips met in a long, sweet, needy kiss.

'Nicolas, my dearest love,' she whispered when his mouth released hers at last. 'When did you come? I have longed for you so often and now that you are here it seems like a dream.'

'No dream, my darling,' he told her with a teasing smile. But the smile faded swiftly, his eyes clouded by grief. 'I came last evening and I have been to the Manor and to my father's grave. There were fresh flowers there though 'tis a week since he was buried. God rest his soul – and Harry's. They tell me he was buried near the place he fell . . .' His eyes reflected his sadness. 'Though we fought on opposite sides we were never enemies.'

'I know it,' she said putting a loving hand to his cheek. 'I have said prayers for him, though I cannot take him flowers as I do your father.' Her throat cought with emotion. 'I am so sorry, Nicolas. My father did what he could but he was too late. Your father died in his arms and they forgave each other. He forgave you too. He told me when I saw him earlier that day that he hoped you would visit him, and that you would find it in your heart to forgive him.'

'The breach between us was not of my choice,' Nicolas said, his face working with grief as he struggled against the useless tears. 'I know it hurt him when I took up arms against all that he believed in, but I tried to explain. I had no quarrel with him, Caroline. It grieved me that we parted in anger, but I had to follow my conscience. The King was wrong to impose unjust taxes and to try and bring foreign troops here, Catholics at that, but I do not like what is happening in some parts of the country. Men like Woodville are not why I took up arms against the King.'

'He is an evil man,' Caroline said. 'He threatened my father but we have good friends and have taken no part in the fighting and he dare not carry out his threats – though Rupert declared for His Majesty.'

'Woodville has exceeded his authority here,' Nicolas said, his expression grim. 'I have come to send him about his business and to establish another regime here.'

'Are you to take his place?' Caroline stared at him with a mixture of hope and uncertainty.

'No, only to send Woodville back to join Cromwell,' Nicolas replied. 'I was given leave to attend to my father's affairs and to request that Woodville explain himself. If I choose, I may have him arrested for the unlawful death of Lord Mortimer.'

'Be careful of him, Nicolas,' Caroline warned. 'He is a jealous, evil man and will not take kindly to losing his authority here.'

'I do not fear Woodville or his ilk,' Nicolas replied. 'But I shall not take petty revenge. He shall answer to Cromwell for his actions, not to me.'

'Oh, Nicolas,' she said and laid her head against his shoulder. 'I do love you so.'

'Then will you wed me?' He looked down at her, his eyes warm and teasing. 'I have but six days before I must return, but I have a dispensation to do away with the banns.' He touched her cheek. 'Do you think that your father will permit it?'

'I believe my father would like it of all things,' Caroline said, with emotion. 'It pleased your father also to know that we planned to marry. We spoke just a little time before his death.'

'You saw him on the day he died?'

'I had heard of Harry's death. I knew that he had been told of it and must be suffering, so I went up to the Manor to see him. He had been ill, Nicolas, and there was much neglect, but he told me that my visit had given him new heart and that he intended to make sure that you did not return to a ruin. As I crossed the meadow, I saw a troop of Roundhead cavalry passing by and Captain Woodville was at its head. I was with my parents when the news came that they had tried to fire the Manor. My father took men and set out to help yours, but it was too late. I believe he has since been to assess the damage and see what may be done to repair the house.'

'Then I must thank him for his efforts,' Nicolas said. 'I came early to see you, my love, lest nothing had changed, but now I shall leave you and return later this morning to speak with Sir John.'

Caroline was loath to let him go, but she knew that he was right. She ought not to be here with him and dressed only in her nightrail.

'Go then,' she said, 'for you have business to attend. I shall see you later.'

She kissed him again, letting him leave reluctantly before she turned and ran into the house. It was a small parting for she would see him before many hours had passed, and yet she was impatient for his return.

'You are a whore and a disgrace to the village,' Richard Woodville said as he faced Rowena outside the blacksmith's cottage. His eyes glittered with anger as he saw her proud and defiant, for she had once refused him, told him that he was the last man she would ever lie with, and he hated her for it. 'I am giving you twenty-four hours to leave. If you are here tomorrow at this hour, I shall have my men drive you out.'

'Who gave you the right to order what I do?' she demanded defiantly, for she did not fear him as others did. Rowena knew a secret that would bring him to his knees if she chose, but for the moment she would let him rant on. 'You be nothing, Richard Woodville. I be wed to the lord's son and the mother of his child. I be entitled to live at the Manor now.' She lied boldly for how could he know the truth?

'You are a slut and a wanton,' he said giving her a

murderous look. 'If I give the order they will stone you to death in the street . . .'

'So say you,' Rowena smiled, a sly, knowing look in her eyes. 'Well, you'd best keep your mouth shut, Richard Woodville, for I do know something that would hang you . . .'

She saw his start and knew that she had made him think. He had believed himself safe all these months, but she knew who had killed Tom Greenslade, and why. She had held little love for the man most had thought her father, and his death had released her mother and her from a tyrant, but she would use her knowledge to gain advantage for herself if she could.

'I could kill you . . .'

'Aye, you could,' she said, her eyes ridiculing him. 'But I be your blood kin, Richard. You be my half-brother for your father got me on my mother by rape. She be still living and if I should die at your hand she will speak it out and all shall know that you be my brother – and what your father be.'

His eyes bulged and his face turned dark red. 'You are a lying whore!'

'I may be a whore, but you be a murderer, Richard Woodville,' she spat at him. 'You killed Tom Greenslade because he saw you rape the gypsy girl. Others saw you that night and they will swear to it. Deny it all you will, 'tis true.'

He moved towards her threateningly. 'I shall not let you live to spew your lying poison . . .' He raised his hand as if he would hit her, but a shout from behind gave him pause.

'Woodville! I would have words with you if you please, sir.'

The colour drained from his face as he saw Nicolas striding towards them, and he glared at the girl, stepping back.

'Off with you! I shall finish this another time.'

Rowena gave him a mocking smile, turning to go into her cottage. She had wondered if someone would have taken it over while they were gone, but it belonged to them by right and few would dare to live in the house of a witch. The fools would think it haunted and fear the consequences of taking Mistress Greenslade's property.

Her child was crying in its cot. She stared at it moodily, weary of its demands. She had hoped to bring her son to Harry's father, believing that her claims of being wed would find her a home and a life of ease, but Richard Woodville had killed her hopes when he killed Lord Mortimer.

'Stop crying,' she muttered as she took the babe and held it to her breast. 'You be a trouble to me, that's what you be, and I would be rid of you.' And yet there might still be some profit to be gained through the babe.

Hearing the sound of shouting from outside, she went to the open window and listened. Two men were fighting and calling each other something terrible. As she watched, Nicolas Mortimer knocked Woodville to the ground and stood over him.

'That was for my father,' Nicolas was saying. 'And now you will get on your feet and ride out of here. You are relieved of your command here and will report to Cromwell immediately.'

Woodville stood up, rubbing his chin. He stared sullenly at Nicolas, as if tempted to defy him.

'I am in command here.'

'You were. I have an order rescinding that commission. You will leave this village at once and if you come back I shall order that you be arrested for the murder of my father.'

'He was a traitor, harbouring a Royalist spy,' Woodville said. 'I told him I intended to search the house but he tried to stop me. We struggled and he fell awkwardly.'

'I have witnesses who will testify that your act was deliberate and knowing,' Nicolas said. 'You killed through jealous spite and anger. You are a murderer and shall be judged by your peers. I could hang you now if I chose, but I shall send you to Cromwell for justice. You may have a chance for mercy if you report to him and put your case as best you may.'

'I'll see you in hell for this, Mortimer!'

'If I see you again I'll kill you.'

Rowena watched as the two men glared at each other, and

then Woodville's eyes dropped and he turned, walking away, his shoulders stiff with anger. She smiled slyly. With Woodville gone from the village there was none to frighten her away. Some would call her names but she had only to look at them and they would back away. The fools believed that she was a witch like her mother and might curse them.

She would move on when she was ready, but for the moment she wanted to stay here. Lord Mortimer might be dead but his younger son lived. He was a good man with a conscience so folk said.

A little smile touched her mouth as she realized that perhaps she had found the answer to her problems. If she could find some way of getting Nicolas Mortimer to accept her child as his brother's son, there might yet be some advantage for her here.

'Caroline told me that you were coming,' Sir John said as Nicolas knocked at the door of his library. 'It is good to see you, sir. I thank God that you are alive and safe. I would that you will sit with me a while, tell me how things go and your opinion of the war.'

Nicolas smiled and sat on the hard settle by the fire. 'You are generous to receive me, sir. I know that there has been a feud between our families, but it is my hope that it will end now and that we shall be good friends in the future. Mayhap more than that if you will give me permission to wed Caroline.'

'It was naught but a foolish quarrel and much regretted,' Sir John said. 'I was given the chance to make my peace with your father before he died, but the guilt lies heavy on me. Had I done so earlier I might have been able to protect him from those who wished him harm.'

'It was as much his fault as yours, sir. I begged him to make his apologies before I left but he was too proud. I am glad that he did so before he died, and I thank you for trying to aid him at the end. And for seeing him decently buried.'

'I could do no less, Nicolas. We were friends for many

years,' Sir John said. 'But enough of this sad business. My daughter tells me that there may be happier news?'

'It is my wish to marry Caroline,' Nicolas told him. 'I have loved her for a long time, though when I thought her content to marry my brother I made no effort to dissuade her. We have discovered our love is mutual and would wish to wed as soon as may be possible, for I must return to Cromwell soon enough.'

'I see no reason why you should not be married,' Sir John said. 'I shall speak to the Reverend Blackwell about it. We need no more than a small private ceremony for it would be impossible to summon our families here in time. We shall celebrate quietly in our own way, and then, when you return another time, we may hold a proper feast to toast your future.'

'I believe many weddings are thus in these difficult times,' Nicolas replied. 'If Caroline is content, then let it be so.'

Mercy felt the wave of exhaustion wash over her as she paused, leaning her back against a tree. She had walked so far and she had eaten nothing for three days. She knew that her child was almost ready to be born and she felt that she could not put one foot in front of the other, her body so weary that she wanted only to lay down and die.

But she must not give up now, she thought, her eyes wet with tears. Harry would want his child to live. It was only this thought that had kept her going these many months. Harry was dead. She had felt it as it happened, felt the light drain out of her, and the knowledge was like a stone inside her, weighing her down every step of the long journey she had made. But his child must live. He had seduced her and deserted her after she had told him that she was with child, but her love for him remained. He might have been a rogue and ruthless, but he was her love. She would never love another, and now she thought only of the release the birth of her child would bring.

She had struggled all this way for the sake of the child

she carried. At times she had felt like giving up, but there was something inside her that would not let go. Sometimes she had been so hungry that she had eaten roots from the fields to still the ache in her belly, at others she had stolen eggs from the nests of farmyard hens, eating them raw. And now she was so tired . . . so very tired.

If only she could lie down and sleep. If only she need never wake again! Mercy whispered a prayer, asking for God's justice for her child. She was a sinner and she had no wish to live, but she must deliver her child safely to the one person she knew would help her.

Caroline had told her that she would stand by her no matter what, but Mercy had not wanted to confess her shame, to see shock and condemnation in the eyes of people who had been her friends, but now she knew that she could not do this alone. If she gave birth at the side of the road, as she had lived for months, eating only berries and roots or bread begged from a kindly soul, she would die, and so would her child.

There had been times when she was able to earn her supper but in these past weeks, when her shame was evident for all to see, the chance had come less often. Most women called her a harlot and threw stones at her, driving her from their village.

Her eyes stung with tears, but she brushed them away, lifting her head and gathering what strength she had as she prepared to walk the last few leagues of her journey. She must get to Caroline and then at last she could rest.

It had been arranged that the wedding should take place in the private chapel up at the Manor. Sir John had sent his servants to restore what order he could and the bride and groom would spend their first night of marriage there. However, Nicolas could stay only two days with his love, and Lady Saunders had begged her daughter to come back to them when he left.

'You will not want to stay in that great barn of a place

alone,' she told Caroline. 'It will please your father and I if you will return home, dearest. When Nicolas returns the next time you will of course go with him, but for now you might be happier with us.'

Caroline kissed her mother's cheek. 'I do not think we shall live at the Manor as it is,' she told her mother. 'Nicolas has his own estate, which he says is a good house much like this, and will suit us better. When he can find the money, he intends to pull down the Manor and build a new house, though that may not be for many years to come.'

'That will be much more comfortable for you,' her mother said and looked pleased. 'His estate is not so very far away and we may visit each other often enough.'

And so it was all arranged for the Friday morning. On Sunday Nicolas would have to leave, but Caroline tried not to think of that as she dressed for her wedding that morning. She had chosen a gown of pale green silk with a scooped neckline and a band of rich Brussels lace to cover her shoulders. The sleeves were full and nipped in tight below the elbow, a froth of lace falling to her wrists.

Around her throat she wore a rope of large creamy pearls fastened with a blood red ruby hanging from it which was a gift from her father. A bracelet of pearls and rubies adorned her wrist, and matching earrings hung from her lobes. Nicolas had given her a simple ring of cabochon rubies and pearls.

'It is but a token of my love,' he told her. 'One day you shall have the jewels my wife deserves, but for the moment this is all I can give you.'

'It is precious to me,' Caroline answered, lifting her face for his kiss. 'I need nothing but your love, Nicolas.'

She was smiling as she saw her mother waiting for her.

'You look beautiful, my love. I am very proud of you,' Lady Saunders said as she took her hands to kiss her cheek.

'Caroline is as lovely of face as she is of nature,' her father said looking at her proudly. 'Are you ready to leave, my dear?'

'Yes, Father,' Caroline said and smiled at him. 'Very ready.'

She took his arm and they went out into the pale autumn sunshine, Lady Saunders following behind. Several of the servants had come out to shower her with rose petals as she got into the coach. However, as she put her foot on the steps that had been let down for her, a woman stumbled towards her, holding out her hand in supplication.

'Caroline . . .' she cried. 'Help me, I beg you.'

Caroline stared at her, seeing her filthy rags, her hair matted about her face, her body swollen and heavy with child and the despair in her eyes, and her heart ached with pity.

'Mercy, my dearest,' she shouted and went to her at once, catching her as she swayed, clearly near to fainting. 'Oh, my dear cousin, why did you not come to us before this?' Tears stung her eyes, her throat tight with emotion as she felt how thin her cousin was, and sensed her frailty. She was, she feared, close to death.

'Forgive me . . .'

Caroline called for help and Tilly came running. Between them they helped Mercy into the house, easing her on to an oak settle in the hall. She opened her eyes and looked at Caroline.

'My child,' she said. 'Harry's child . . . will you take him? Will you promise to care for him?'

'Yes, of course, you know that I will,' Caroline told her. 'Rest here for a little, Mercy, and then we shall have you carried up to your room.'

'Caroline . . .' Lady Saunders came into the hall. 'They will be waiting for you at the Manor. Leave Mercy to others for the moment, my dear. She will be safe enough now that she is home. You must not be late for your wedding.'

'Nicolas will understand.' Caroline was torn between the man who waited to make her his bride and Mercy, who needed her sorely. 'Send someone to the Manor and ask Nicolas to come here,' she said. 'I cannot leave Mercy like this. The wedding must be postponed for a few hours.'

'No!' Mercy clutched at her arm, looking distressed. 'I must not keep you from your wedding, Caroline. I shall be all right now I am here. I just need to rest for a while. If you give me your promise I may die at ease.'

'You have my promise, but you shall not die,' Caroline said, her heart racked with grief. How much her dearest friend had suffered these past months! She wanted to weep for the pity of it.

'Come along, my dear,' her mother said. 'Tilly and the others will care for Mercy now, and you may see her later.'

Reluctantly, Caroline allowed herself to be ushered out to the waiting coach. She felt uneasy in her mind, though she knew that her father's servants would take good care of her cousin, and that the physician would be called. There was nothing she could do if she stayed and yet she was loath to leave Mercy.

As she got out of the coach and saw that Nicolas had gathered his servants in the courtyard to greet her, she did her best to put thoughts of Mercy to one side. This was her wedding day and she was to marry the man she loved so much.

She walked into the chapel on her father's arm, and the look that Nicolas gave her as she moved to stand by his side made her heart leap. The Reverend Blackwell smiled at her, his wife and her eldest daughter there in their best gowns to act as witnesses to the happy union.

The sun was shining through a high window, casting rays of colour on to the stone flags. Caroline could smell the scent of flowers as she turned to look into the eyes of her beloved.

'Let those who have been joined by God,' the Reverend's voice boomed out the joyful words. 'I now pronounce thee man and wife.'

Caroline lifted her face as the Reverend bid her husband kiss her, gazing up at him, knowing that now only death could part them, for they were as one, united in heart and mind.

'You were late,' he said to her as they went arm in arm to the small feast that had been provided for them and the few friends gathered there to see them wed. 'I began to wonder what had happened.'

'I almost didn't come,' she admitted, and as he frowned she explained, 'It would have been a mere postponement, my dearest. Mercy has come home to us at last. She is ill, Nicolas, very ill, and her child is very near. She begged me to take Harry's child and I told her that we would. You do not mind that?'

'It is what I would expect of you,' he told her, his expression grave for he had known nothing of this. 'Of course we shall take my brother's child. We could not do otherwise. You must be worried for her. We shall go and see her when the feasting is done.'

'How well you know me,' Caroline said and took his hand. 'I knew that you would understand – but Mercy bid me leave her. She will be cared for as if I were there and I do not think the birth is imminent. She has a few more days perhaps.'

'Yet still we shall go,' he said, 'for then you may be easy in your mind.'

She nodded, loving him the more for his compassion and his understanding. But she made no reply for the guests were calling for a speech from the groom and ready to make merry. The celebration had begun and despite its impromptu nature, it was a goodly feast that was brought to them. Ham and capon, a stuffed pike, and a good rib of beef along with a dish of pickles, cabbage and plums, junkets and tarts, both sweet and savoury, and fine wines, together with all manner of sweetmeats.

After the guests had eaten their fill, a fiddler began to play for them and there were calls for Nicolas and Caroline to dance. They were very ready to oblige and delighted their guests by putting a deal of energy into the lively gavotte, an old-fashioned dance but still much enjoyed at country weddings and such gatherings.

It was almost dusk when the guests began to depart, wishing them happiness and peace. Caroline and Nicolas waited until most had gone, and then accompanied her parents back to Hillgrove House.

Caroline left Nicolas to talk with her father while she and

her mother went up to Mercy's room. Her hair had been washed and was spread on the soft linen pillow as she lay half sleeping, her hands moving restlessly on the covers as though her dreams distressed her. However, as Caroline approached, she woke and saw her.

'You should not have come on your wedding night.'

'We have time enough yet,' Caroline told her. 'Nicolas knew that I would not rest until I saw you settled.'

'If I had known, I should not have come today,' Mercy said. 'Forgive me for spoiling your wedding day, Caroline.'

'You did not spoil it,' Caroline told her, blinking back tears for her friend's plight. Mercy was so weak and so ill. 'It made everything better to know that we have you safe at last, dearest. You must rest now for we shall take care of you. And Nicolas will take the child into his home, and you shall live with us if you choose, for we love you.'

Mercy closed her eyes against the tears, but one escaped her, trickling down her cheek. Caroline wiped it away and then bent to kiss her cheek.

'Sleep if you can, Mercy. I am going home with Nicolas now, but I shall come to see you tomorrow, and after my husband leaves to return to the war I shall be here with you. You will be better soon, I promise you.'

Mercy made no reply and Caroline left the room. Her mother stayed behind, for she was to sit with the sick woman for a while and she knew that Caroline did not need her.

Nicolas looked at her as she came back to him. His eyes searched her face. 'Is all well?'

'As well as we can hope for,' Caroline told him. 'She has suffered terribly, Nicolas. I do not know if she will live beyond her child's birth for she is very weak. I wish that she had come to us long ago, but she was too proud, and too shamed.'

'We must pray for her,' he said and took her hands, his eyes seeking hers, trying to see into her heart. 'Would you rather stay here tonight?'

Caroline smiled as she saw his compassion, the goodness

he hid behind his stern manner. Why had she ever been afraid of him? She was afraid no more for now she understood that he was honest, sincere and thoughtful in all he did, and she loved him more than life itself.

'No, my dearest husband, I would go with you. Mercy would have it so, for she has my mother and the others to care for her. I can do no more if I stay, but I shall visit again tomorrow.'

Nicolas put his arm about her waist as they left the house and began to walk back towards the Manor. It was a still, warm autumn night, the scent of late summer flowers caught upon the air. The sky was dark but for a sprinkling of stars, but it was enough to light their way. They were at peace, happy in a quiet way, content in the love that wrapped about them.

Once back in the Manor, they took a glass of warm, mulled wine in the room that was most comfortable and had been Lord Mortimer's book room. Then Caroline went upstairs to prepare for bed. Tilly was waiting for her; for after she had settled Mercy comfortably, she had attended the wedding and was to stay with them while they dwelled at the Manor.

'You look lovely, mistress,' she told Caroline as she brushed her long hair loose on her shoulders. 'Lord Mortimer is a lucky man.'

'Lord . . .' Caroline was startled for it had not occurred to her until then that Nicolas was now the lord of the manor. She smiled, shaking her head for it seemed so strange. 'No, you are wrong, Tilly. I am the fortunate one to have so good a man as my husband.'

The girl smiled and kissed her cheek, leaving her mistress to greet her husband alone when he came, which was soon after for Nicolas was eager to claim his bride.

Their loving was as sweet and tender as Caroline had known it would be, for she learned the meaning of passion that night in her husband's arms. His kisses and caresses drew her carefully along the path to its passionate conclusion, and she cried out at the end and clung to him as waves of pleasure broke over her.

211

'I love you,' she whispered against the salty dampness of his shoulder. 'I am so happy, Nicolas.'

'No happier than I,' he told her, his hand caressing the smooth arch of her back as they lay side by side, warm, content, satiated for the moment. 'I did not believe that such happiness could ever be mine. I loved you for so long when you seemed not to like me, and I thought it was hopeless.'

'I was a foolish child,' Caroline said and stroked his strong back, feeling the muscles ripple beneath, the iron hardness of him. He was a man she could respect and love, and she would do so her life long. 'But now I am a woman and I am yours, Nicolas.'

Her words aroused him to passion once more and he made love to her with an urgency that took them to the heights of passion, and then they slept.

Richard Woodville stood in the darkness looking at the Manor, a brooding hatred festering inside him. He had ridden off when Nicolas Mortimer bid him, but he had no intention of leaving Thornberry or of joining Cromwell, for he knew what fate would await him. Cromwell had hung men for lesser offences. He had not meant to kill Mortimer, merely to frighten him, to teach him a lesson, but his rage had carried him too far. Just as it had the night he killed Blacksmith Greenslade.

That bitch Rowena had seen him. Her sly look and her taunts had told him that, though he did not believe her when she said that his father had raped her mother. She must be lying! His father had been a godly man, strict and pious. He had beaten Richard without mercy for any small fault. He would never have raped a woman . . .

If that lying bitch told her tale in the village he could never return here. He had hoped that he might find some way to avoid Cromwell's justice and fight elsewhere. After the war he might return here and no one be the wiser but only if Nicolas Mortimer was dead. He must find a way to kill him, and that lying bitch Rowena!

This day Nicolas Mortimer had married Caroline Saunders, another source of anger upon which his envious soul might feed. It would serve that proud wench right if she became a widow before she had hardly been a wife!

His instinct was to enter the Manor while they were sleeping and shoot both Nicolas and his wife, but he hesitated for if he were discovered it was a hanging matter. Might it not be better to follow Nicolas when he left to return to his commander? A shot in the back in some lonely place and none would be the wiser. As for Caroline – he might yet have her once she was a widow.

He licked his lips as he thought of the revenge that he would like to take on the haughty Lady Mortimer. He had not been good enough for her or her father, but they might still rue the day they had slighted him.

That bitch Rowena should not live to tell the tale of her birth. He knew her habits, knew where she went to pick herbs and berries. He would follow her and then . . . a little smile curved his mouth. Be damned to her lies! He would have her first and then he would kill her.

Mercy seemed a little better when Caroline visited the next day. She was sitting up, propped against a pile of fresh pillows which smelled of lavender, feeding herself with good, nourishing broth that one of the maids held for her.

She smiled as she saw Caroline and offered her hand. 'It was good of you to come, but you should not neglect your husband. They tell me Nicolas must leave tomorrow?'

'Yes, I fear so,' Caroline replied ruefully. 'We do not wish for the parting, but we know it must be. However, I could not rest easily without coming to see you, my dear cousin.'

'I am rested now,' Mercy told her. 'I feared that my child might be born by the side of the road, and die with me, but now I am content for I know that you will care for him.'

'Are you so sure that it will be a son?'

'Yes,' Mercy said and laughed softly. 'Do not ask me why, but I have felt it these many months.'

'And what would you call him?'

'I should like him to be named for his father.' A look of sadness came to her eyes. 'You will care for him, Caroline?'

'I have given you my word but you will care for him yourself.'

'I do not think I shall live,' Mercy told her. 'I am not afraid and you should not grieve for me if I die. I have lived this long only to give my child his life. There is nothing left for me, Caroline. I believe that Harry is dead, and indeed I saw it in your good Tilly's eyes when I asked if she had news of him, though she denied it. I felt it a few weeks ago.'

'I fear it is so, Mercy,' Caroline told her. 'I am sorry, my dearest.'

'I knew it was so. I grieve for him but in truth I have lost nothing. Even if he had lived he would not have wed me. When I went to his lodgings that day I was given a note he had left for me. He told me that though he loved me more than any other woman he had known, he could not marry me. He was a gambler and deeply in debt. He said that if he lived he must marry a fortune for otherwise his estate would be ruined.'

'I believe that Harry could not help himself,' Caroline said, taking Mercy's hand. 'He was charming and I liked him, but I knew that he was not honest. I should have warned you at the start. Forgive me, Mercy.'

'There is nothing to forgive,' Mercy said. 'If you had warned me I should not have listened, Caroline. I loved him from the first time he smiled at me.'

'Then it was your fate,' Caroline said. 'But you must put your grief behind you, dearest. Live for your son and for me, please. I would not have you die for shame.'

'You are kind and generous,' Mercy said, 'and I do love you. Leave me now and return to your husband, for you have only a few hours before he leaves. And we shall talk again another time.'

Ten

The gypsy caravans had begun to gather in the far meadow. Roald was expected at any time, for the hour was near. It had been foretold and their true prince knew that he must be there by that night.

Carlina sat with her grandmother as she threw the bones and peered into the fire, reading what it told her as she had so many times before.

'Is it tonight?' she asked, for she knew that she too would be called upon to play her part if the prophecy was to come true.

Greta looked at her, the deep lines of her face heavy with grief for she knew that if what was written was to be fulfilled she would lose the person that she loved most in the world.

'It is tonight,' she said. She spoke the words without tears or emotion for they had talked of this often before and Carlina knew that she must make the sacrifice to bring them what they wanted. 'May the gods of old protect and keep you, my child.'

'I am not afraid,' Carlina told her. 'I have waited my chance. After the evil one despoiled me I would have gone willingly to my death, but you bade me wait and I have obeyed you. I am not afraid for through me the child will come to you and the destiny of our people shall be as it is written.'

Greta nodded encouragingly. The girl was young and brave, a true daughter of the Romany blood. It grieved her that she must die for one who was of so much less worth, but it was the only way.

'You shall not be forgotten,' she told the girl. 'Roald will sing of you. It shall be done.'

'Yes,' Carlina said and smiled sadly. 'It shall be done.'

Mercy felt the pain soon after Caroline had left her, but she tried not to cry out. Caroline had only a few hours before her husband left her and if she knew that Mercy had gone into labour she would return to be with her. So she bit her lip and held back her cries. She would bear it in silence for as long as she could, and only then would she ask for help.

Her hands gripped the covers for the pain was terrible. She closed her eyes and thought of the man she had loved, now mouldering in a soldier's gave.

'Oh my dearest love,' she whispered. 'I did love you so, why did you desert me?'

For a moment it seemed to Mercy that she saw the face of her beloved, that he was there beside her, comforting her, telling her that he loved her and hoped to be with her again one day.

'It will be soon now,' she whispered. 'I shall be with you soon, my love, for in Heaven we shall surely be together.'

Rowena looked at the child in the cot, a surge of resentment building inside her. Would he never stop screaming? He was so demanding, sucking her breasts until she was sore and still he wanted more. He was too like his father! Sometimes she felt like throwing him into the ditch and leaving him to die, and she had wished a thousand times that she had asked her mother for a potion to be rid of him in the first weeks of her quickening.

'Be quiet, you trouble,' she said. 'That's what you be, nothing but a trouble to me. Carlina says you will be a lucky charm for her people, but what of me? What profit is there for me if I let them have you?'

She had been pondering the problem all day, and she had almost made up her mind. If Roald wanted her she could go with him and his people, but she knew she would be expected to care for the babe and do all manner of rough work. It would be a hard life – travelling the roads – for the gypsies were never welcomed and could stay nowhere for long. She had hoped for something better when she lay with Harry Mortimer, and though she liked Roald well enough, she did not want the life he could offer her.

Yet if she took the child to Nicolas Mortimer, would he take it? Would he believe it was his brother's son?

She knew that Harry was the father of her babe. She had carried him full-term and he had been born too soon to be the child of any of the others she had lain with later, but would his brother believe her? Richard Woodville had branded her a whore and a liar, but he had been driven from the village and would bother her no more. Besides, she knew his secrets and he feared her because of it.

As the day wore on and it began to grow dark, Rowena reached her decision. She would carry the child to the Manor and demand that they took it in, and that they gave her some recompense for her trouble. With money in her pocket she could go to London. She had liked Oxford and she thought that London would be even better.

If she had enough money she might pass herself off as a lady, and then she could take the lovers she wanted. She would choose rich lovers who would give her costly presents.

It was a tempting future, but she did not want or need Harry's son to complicate matters. She needed to get rid of her trouble and she would make certain that she never carried another brat to its full term. She had learned the secret of the cure from her mother now and she would use it.

Caroline looked at Nicolas when the news came that Mercy had gone into labour, her eyes pleading for understanding. He smiled at her, reaching for her hand and turning it up to kiss the palm.

'Of course you must go to her, my love,' he said. 'I shall come with you. We may as well spend the night at your house, for I leave early in the morning as you know.'

'You know that I would not be apart from you a single moment if I could help it?'

'Mercy is having my brother's child. She has no one but you to love her, Caroline. Your mother and the servants will tend her with Christian charity but it is you she needs.'

'Yes, I believe she does,' Caroline said. 'We must go to her for I would not have her suffer alone.'

'We shall take our horses and go by the highroad,' Nicolas said. 'It will be quicker than walking through the meadow and I shall need my horse in the morning.'

'Then let us leave at once for I wish to waste no time.'

Rowena reached the Manor just as Nicolas and Caroline were leaving. She saw them canter out of the courtyard on their horses and called out to them but they did not hear her. She frowned as she watched them go, for she had no idea of where they went and she was afraid that she might have missed them altogether. Perhaps they were going to Nicolas Mortimer's other estate, and she did not know where that was, though she had heard that it was near Ely.

Now what was she to do? It was ill luck that she had been foiled in her plans for now there was only one way open to her. She must go to the gypsies. It was the child they wanted so perhaps they would take him and leave her be. The money she might have gained from Nicolas Mortimer might have made her new life easier, but she was resourceful. She would find some other way to get money once the child was gone.

Rowena frowned as she turned her footsteps towards the woods. The gypsies were camped in the far meadow for they had gathered for the autumn fair as usual. It was quicker through the woods for she knew them well and she did not fear the dark. Other folk might be frightened by the tales of goblins and spirits that haunted the woods, but Rowena laughed at such tales. She had always loved the woods, and she knew all the secret places that most did not for she had learned them as a child.

*   *   *

Richard Woodville heard the horses approaching and moved behind the shelter of a tree. He had made up his mind to break into the Manor that night and kill both Nicolas Mortimer and his wife as they slept. For after consideration he had decided that once the new lord had left the Manor he might miss him, and his hatred had risen to such a pitch that he could wait no longer. But now, as he saw the riders come into view, he realized that his quarry had made it easy for him. He would kill them and then he would find that whore Rowena and kill her too. He would be rid of them all within a single night.

He drew back as the riders came nearer, hiding, and then, as they passed, he took a step forward and fired. His first shot was for Nicolas and he smiled as he saw that it had found its mark, embedding itself in his back. Nicolas's body slumped forward over the horse but Woodville had no time to finish his work for even as he took aim, a shadow came out of the gloom, startling him.

For a moment he thought he had been caught in the act of murder, but then he realised it was only a girl; slight and pale, a wraith in the darkness. He paused for a moment as he looked at her, his attention turning from his quarry as he recognized her. It was the gypsy girl he had raped the night he killed Blacksmith Greenslade.

'What do you want, whore?' he snarled at her. 'More of the same I gave you last time?'

Carlina smiled at him, moving closer. Her eyes were dark but glittering from some inner excitement as she came to stand before him and he thought for a moment that she wanted him to take her. And then, as he felt his blood stir with lust, her arm came up and he felt a surge of alarm as he saw that she was carrying a knife.

It flashed silver in the moonlight as she plunged it deep into his side. He groaned but did not fall as he struck out at her with his pistol butt, catching her at the side of her temple and causing her to pitch forward to the ground.

She was lying face down. He turned her over with his booted foot to look at her and instantly knew that he had killed her. A pity, he thought, that he had not done it before she managed to plunge her blade into his side.

The knife was still embedded in his flesh, a sharp stinging pain causing him to catch his breath. Damn the bitch! But he was not done for yet. He took hold of the bone handle of the knife and pulled it out, cursing as the pain almost sent him reeling. Blood was dripping from the wound and he knew that he must bind it. He had been camping in the woods for some days and there were things that he could use to tend his wound if he could reach his hidden retreat.

'Curse the whore,' he muttered as he turned and began to stumble in the direction of Thornberry Woods. 'Damn her and all her kind to hell!'

Caroline gave a little cry of fear as she saw Nicolas slump over his horse. Acting instinctively, she brought her horse in closer and reached across to catch the reins of his, slowing the pace of both mounts to little more than a trot. It took all her strength to hold them, for they had been unnerved by the shot and would have bolted had she not acted swiftly to calm them. Yet somehow she managed to rein them in, talking to them softly, though she was terrified, barely controlling the scream that built inside her. But she knew she must not give way to her nerves. Everything depended on her managing to bring them safely home.

She could see that Nicolas was still alive, though he must be in terrible pain, for she knew that he was still conscious as he was somehow managing to keep in the saddle. She realized that she took a risk by making the horses walk so slowly, for the man who had tried to shoot her husband might follow, might try to finish his evil work. However, she had no choice but to go slowly for Nicolas was barely hanging on to the reins and any faster pace would cause him to fall.

Her heart was thudding, her strength near exhausted as she manoeuvred the horses into the courtyard of her father's house and shouted for help. Her concentration had been all on getting her husband here, but now the thoughts began to crowd into her mind. How bad was Nicolas's wound? And who had fired on them from the woods? She had seen only the shadow of a man by the tree and as yet she could not be sure who might have wanted to kill her husband, though she had her suspicions. Richard Woodville hated him and this might be his revenge for what he saw as his humiliation at Nicolas's hands.

Caroline's shouts for help were answered soon enough as servants came running. Eager hands reached out to ease Nicolas down from the saddle and carry him to the house. He was barely conscious, though he managed to smile at her once before he closed his eyes.

'Someone must go for the physician,' she said, seeing her father come from the house as they approached. 'Quickly, for Nicolas is hurt.'

'What has happened, Caroline?' Sir John asked as he came hurrying to greet them. 'How came Nicolas to be hurt?'

'Someone shot at him as we rode here,' Caroline said. 'I saw the assassin but briefly, for I knew that his ball had gone home and I had to help my husband.'

'We shall send men to investigate,' her father promised her. He signalled to the hovering servants. 'Take Lord Mortimer to the room next to my daughter's. We shall do what we can for him before the physician comes.'

'Is my mother with Mercy?' Caroline asked in distress. She was torn between concern for her cousin and fear for her beloved husband. 'We were on our way to see her when this happened.'

Even as she spoke a terrible scream echoed though the house and Caroline shuddered as she thought of her cousin's suffering.

'Go to her for a while,' Sir John said, seeing that she was much affected by it. 'I shall see that Nicolas is settled in his bed and then you may come to him.' He shook his head sorrowfully as they heard Mercy scream again. 'I fear this shall be a long night, Caroline. '

'Yes, I think you are right,' she said and a cold fear clutched

221

at her heart for now two of those she loved most were in mortal danger. 'I shall go to Mercy, but in a little I shall come to Nicolas.'

'Where are you going, Black Eyes?' Rowena started as she heard the voice she recalled well enough, and then she saw the tall, powerful figure of the gypsy coming through the trees towards her. 'And where do you take the child?'

Rowena paused, looking up at him, her head to one side as she considered. It was best to lie to him, for if he guessed the truth he would not help her. 'I was coming to your camp,' she said. 'Carlina told me that your people wanted my child. I was going to offer him to them.'

'And what then?' Roald asked. 'Where would you go after that?'

'That depends . . .' She pouted her lips at him, her eyes bright as she taunted him. 'What would you have me do?'

'I would have you come with me,' he said, his eyes fixed on her face with an intensity that sent a shiver though her. 'I would have you as my woman.'

'Then perhaps I shall come with you,' she replied. He wanted her but she would not give in easily. 'Or perhaps I shan't. What will you give me if I come?'

'Nothing but the food you put in your mouth and the clothes you wear,' he said. 'That much is your right. I have nothing more. My riches are not of gold or silver, but of the sky in the morning and the sunset at night. I am rich with the beauty of a bird singing or a wild fawn nursing at its mother's teat, my gold is in the life I lead.'

'That is free for everyone.' Rowena dismissed his words with a toss of her head, but seeing his face darken, she laughed softly. Mayhap it would be wise to take what he offered for now. In time she would find something better for she had no intention of living as he did. 'I but tease you, Roald. I will come with you for it is my destiny.'

'Yes, it is your destiny,' he said. 'Give me the child then. For we must leave this place tonight.'

Rowena hesitated. Perhaps she could still have found Nicolas Mortimer. He might have gone to Caroline's house and he might have taken the child. Yet as she put her son into Roald's arms she was already thinking ahead. She would go with him for now, for she had no money and with the child to hamper her she could not find work, but when she was ready she would leave him. The gypsies wanted her son, and they could have him with her blessing, but she would not stay with them for any longer than need be.

Caroline spent the night going between her husband and Mercy, for they were both suffering; in terrible agony. Nicolas's was ended the sooner, for when the physician came he removed the ball from his back, where it had lodged in his shoulder bone. Then he bound his patient well and administered a sleeping draught that would hold him for several hours.

'He will be in pain when he wakes,' Doctor Wells told Caroline. 'But he was lucky for if the ball had penetrated further it would undoubtedly have killed him. However, your husband is a strong man and this is not the first time he hath been wounded. You must keep him to his bed for as long as you can, and I shall send something for his fever.'

'Thank you,' Caroline said, holding back the sob as it rose to her lips, for she believed that her husband would live. He could not die! God could not be so cruel as to take him from her so soon. She would not believe it. 'I shall do all I can to care for him, and I pray that he will not suffer too much.' She hesitated, then asked, 'Would you come to my cousin again, sir? The child seems not to want to be born and she grows weaker all the time.'

'I shall look at her, though I fear there is not much I can do in her case,' the physician said. 'She was weak when she came here and I feared then that she might not survive the birth of her child. I might be able to save the babe . . .' He looked at her sorrowfully, wondering if she would be brave enough to make the right choice, for if he did nothing both mother and child would die.

'Please come to her,' Caroline begged, her throat tight with tears. He was only saying what she feared, but it was so painful to know that they could do nothing for Mercy.

The doctor made his examination of Mercy as she writhed with agony. Her body was soaked in sweat, her hair plastered on her forehead. She was trying to push when the pains came but her efforts grew weaker as her strength waned.

'I can save the child, but not the mother,' Doctor Wells told Caroline and her mother after he had examined Mercy. 'The child lives but if we leave it much longer it may die. Would you wish me to use my instruments to bring the babe out? I think the mother is so far-gone that she will hardly notice what I do. I can give her a strong dose of laudanum to make her drowsy.' It was a drug he used only sparingly for it was as expensive as it was dangerous; it could ease Mercy's pain but it would also kill her if the dose were too strong.

'I think we have no choice, Caroline,' Lady Saunders said looking at her daughter anxiously. 'Otherwise we shall lose them both – Mercy and the child.'

Caroline fought down the tears that threatened to overwhelm her. 'Give me a few moments alone with her please?'

'We shall wait outside,' Lady Saunders said. 'Come, sir. Let me give you a hot posset before you begin your task for you must be weary at this hour of the night.'

'It would be most welcome, ma'am,' he told her with a smile. 'For I have come from the deathbed of another patient and need something to sustain me.'

Caroline went to sit on the bed as they closed the door behind them. She reached forward to bathe Mercy's forehead with a cool cloth. Mercy opened her eyes to look at her.

'I am such a trouble to you, Caroline. You should be with your husband for he leaves in the morning.'

'No, no, my dearest,' Caroline replied, swallowing the sob that rose up. 'He will stay a little longer. Do not distress yourself. I am here with you, but in a while I shall leave you to the doctor. He has things he must do to help you . . .'

Mercy's eyes widened for she knew that the doctor must cut her to get the child out and that she would die. She was already so weak that she could not survive so much loss of blood. And it was her destiny to die young. Had it not been foretold her long ago, from the gypsy at her door?

She smiled at Caroline, her fingers tightening about hers for a moment. 'He will save the child, won't he? He will save Harry's son?'

'Yes, he will save your baby, Mercy, and he shall be named for his father as you asked.' Caroline's eyes stung, her throat ached with the grief that was tearing her apart. 'I promise he shall be loved and cared for as my own.'

Mercy's lovely eyes were bright with tears. 'You have forgiven me for shaming you?'

'There was nothing to forgive, dearest. Harry should not have taken advantage as he did. But I shall not blame him or you. I shall always love you and your child. I promise you that with all my heart.'

'Then I am prepared,' Mercy said and made the sign of the cross over her breast. 'Tell the physician to do what he must – and do not come to me again, Caroline. Grieve not for me but be happy with your husband and think kindly of me. Let this be our farewell.'

Caroline bent to kiss her on the forehead. As she rose and left the room, the tears were sliding down her cheeks. Mercy was prepared to die, wanted to die – but it was so very painful to know that there was nothing they could do to save her.

'Mercy is dead?' Caroline asked when her mother came to her as she sat by Nicolas's bed, watching over him. He had been sleeping peacefully for some time but now he had begun to toss and his skin was hot when she touched him. 'God rest her soul.'

'Her child was a boy just as she said it would be,' Lady Saunders said and she wiped a tear from the corner of her eye. 'This is a terrible night, daughter. Yet the miracle is that the child seems healthy. I thought that he might be a weakling and that the doctor's work would be in vain, but 'tis not so. He cries lustily and we have been trying to feed him on cow's milk. Doctor Wells says there is a woman in the village with milk enough to spare after the birth of a child that has not survived more than a week, and he will ask her to come to us. The babe will thrive with a wet-nurse, I dare say.'

'We must take good care of little Harry,' Caroline said and got up to bathe her husband's forehead as he moved restlessly. She looked at him anxiously, the fear catching at her heart. She had lost Mercy, she could not bear it if she were to lose Nicolas too. 'He is very hot, Mother. I think he hath a fever.'

'Yes, I believe you are right. I shall bring him some of my own fever cure, Caroline. Doctor Wells has promised to send him something, but I think my own may work as well. I shall go down and prepare it now.' She touched her daughter's hand. 'This has been a sad night, Caroline, for I know how much you loved Mercy – as I did in my way. We have lost her but we have her child, and she did not wish to live. However, your husband has everything to live for and he will.'

Caroline nodded, for she believed it in her heart, even though it tore at her to see him lying there, his body damp with sweat, his face contorting now and then with the pain he was beginning to feel as he came out of his drugged sleep.

'Please be well soon, my love,' she whispered as she bent to kiss his lips. 'I do love you so very much. I could not bear to lose you too. I beg you do not leave me.'

It seemed to her that Nicolas stirred as he heard her voice and his hand moved as though he would reach out to her. She took it in hers and his fingers tightened about hers, as if even in his fever he knew that she was there.

He would be well. Caroline clung to her belief as she watched the sweat break on his forehead again and he moved restlessly, crying out her name.

'I am here, my love,' she whispered. 'I shall not leave you in this life.'

But the next morning she was persuaded to leave him for an hour or so to rest upon her bed. When she came back she saw that the fever seemed to be waning a little and by the evening he was cooler and resting more peacefully. Caroline sat in the chair watching over him until her mother made her go and sleep for a while, but she was back with him by dawn and it was just after that he woke and looked at her.

'How is Mercy?' he asked. 'Were we in time?'

His first thought was for another! Caroline's heart caught with love for him, her smile warm and tender as she took his hand.

'Yes, my dearest. I saw her, comforted her.' She would not tell him yet that Mercy was dead. Time enough for that when he was better.

'What happened to me?' he asked. 'Was I shot? I must have been for the pain in my shoulder is damnable.'

'The doctor left you something for the pain if you will take it,' Caroline said and got up to fetch a small bottle from the chest nearby. 'But you asked what had happened; someone shot at you from the shadows as we passed. I saw him only dimly, for I was concerned to slow the horses lest you fall, but I have considered and I think it may have been . . .'

'Richard Woodville?' Nicolas asked and frowned as she inclined her head. 'I fear you may be right. It was in my mind that he might still be lurking nearby, waiting his chance to gain his revenge on me. It was fortunate that he fired only one shot for he might have finished me – or you, Caroline.'

'Would he have done such a wicked thing?'

'He is a jealous, evil man, and he wanted you,' Nicolas reminded her. 'You must take care if you leave the house. Do not go up to the Manor until he has been found. I think he must have been hiding in the woods and we must have a search made for him. Promise me you will not go far until we have found him?'

'If you ask it then I must obey,' she said, 'but you must promise me that you will leave his capture to others. You must rest for several days before you try to leave us.'

'Cromwell will understand in the circumstances,' Nicolas said grimly. 'I should have arrested Woodville and sent him to Cromwell under guard but I did not want to be seen to judge him in this case. I pray that I shall not yet rue the day, for if harm should come to you . . .'

'It did not,' Caroline said and bent to kiss his lips. 'I am well, as you see, and all I care for is that you may soon be well again.'

Nicolas held out his hand and she took it, smiling as he turned hers to kiss the palm. 'Now tell me about Mercy?' he said. 'She hath given birth to her child but is all well?'

'The child is well and thriving,' Caroline told him. 'Little Harry suckles at the breast of the wet-nurse and she says he is a greedy babe, but she dotes on him as everyone seems to in this house. I think he will be spoiled.'

'It seems he will take after his father,' Nicolas said with a frown. 'And what of Mercy?'

'I was not going to tell you until you were better,' Caroline said choking back a sob. 'There was nothing the physician could do to save her. She was too weak to give birth to her child and he could only save the boy.'

'May God have pity on her,' Nicolas said. His look was grave, a little angry. 'Though I did not know her, she was by all accounts a gentle girl and did not deserve such a fate, Caroline. My brother had much to answer for. It was he who brought her to this cruel end.'

'You are right, but she loved him deeply and I think in the end she was happy to die. Somehow she knew that Harry was dead when she came here though no one had told her so. Yet she knew it for she loved him more dearly than her life. I think she wanted to die to be with him. Had he lived she might have found the strength to live too, for though she was a gentle girl, she had a great deal of courage.'

Nicolas's eyes were dark with sorrow. 'Then I pray that she finds more happiness in the next life than in this.'

'Amen to that,' Caroline said. 'It is very strange, Nicolas, but at the spot near or very near where someone shot at you they have found the body of a young girl. She had a wound to her head and they say she was no more than fifteen summers. She was a gypsy. Her people claimed her and took her away with them. Do you think . . .'

'That Woodville killed her?' Nicolas frowned. 'I think it likely, Caroline, though I know not why.'

'It is very strange,' Caroline said. 'He always pretended to be such a godly man but I do not think he cares for anyone but himself.'

'We must hope that he is taken soon and brought to justice,' Nicolas said. 'But until that happens, remember that you are not to leave this house alone.'

'While you are ill, my love, I have no wish to leave,' Caroline said. 'I would be with you, to ease you as best I can . . .'

The gypsy bitch had almost done for him. Richard Woodville felt the pain in his side, and knew that he needed some treatment for the wound was festering. He had bound himself as best he could, and the blood had dried, but the wound was oozing puss and he feared that it would turn poisonous unless he could get it treated.

He would not go to his mother, for he had no wish to suffer the lash of her scolding tongue, and he had no money to pay the physician. Besides, he knew that he might be searched for even now. If there was any justice Nicolas Mortimer would be dead of his wounds, but his wife was not. She still lived and she might be able to identify him. So he dared not go to the village physician, which meant there was only one other who might help him.

That little bitch owed him something for her lies. He was weak but still had strength enough to force her to help him. Her mother had been a healer and there was no reason why Rowena should not have the same gift. She gathered the herbs so it followed that she knew how to make healing potions.

He would go to her, make her give him something to take

the poison from his wound, and then, when he was stronger, he would do something about the other one.

Rowena watched as Greta nursed the babe. All the women in the camp seemed to dote on him, and they were all willing to help look after his needs. Roald had been good to her, giving her a gold bracelet, which he said sealed their pact. She was his woman now, and it seemed that the tribe had accepted her.

She wandered over to Greta, watching as the child laughed up at the old woman, a shudder running through her as she remembered the day that she had told her fortune. She had thought that the stench of death emanated from Greta then, and it had made her fear her.

'Where is Carlina?' she asked. 'I have not seen her since I joined you. Is she ill?'

'Carlina is dead,' the old woman said. 'She died that you might live and give your child to us.'

'I do not understand you,' Rowena said. 'Why should she have died for me? I have been in no danger.'

'You did not know it, but death hovered at your shoulder,' Greta told her. 'Carlina killed your enemy. It was in his mind to punish and kill you, but she followed him and she killed him. In the struggle she was murdered, but the seeds of death are in him. He was unable to carry out his evil plans that night and now you are safe for he will not live long. You are safe for as long as you stay with us. If you break your word, your fate is sealed.'

Rowena shook her head, walking away from the old woman. All this talk of things being foretold was nonsense. And why should the child be of such importance to the gypsies?

She did not believe any of it, and she did not like Greta. Roald was a good lover and she sometimes felt that it was worth the hard living to be with him, but as the days passed she was becoming more and more dissatisfied with her life.

She fingered the gold bangle that Roald had given her. He had let her take her pick from a small casket in which other jewels were kept. Her mouth drooped sullenly. He had lied when he said he had no gold for there was enough in that casket to keep her in luxury for months, nay years.

If she had all the jewels in the casket she could go to London. She could live as a fine lady and do all the things she longed to do . . . if she had all of them.

She knew where Roald hid the casket in his caravan, but she was afraid of him. There was violence in him, and though he was good to her he sometimes treated her roughly. He was used to being obeyed, and she knew that he resented it that she had borne a child to another man, even though that child was seen as a lucky charm by the gypsies.

Well, they were welcome to keep the boy, Rowena thought. She would be happy with the gold in exchange . . . if only she dared to take it.

'I am feeling much better this morning,' Nicolas said as he saw Caroline's expression. 'Do not worry, my love. Doctor Wells was overcautious when he told you I should not get up for several days. I am still a little weak but well enough to come downstairs to the parlour and sit with you.'

'Very well, if it is your wish,' Caroline said. 'Make your way there carefully, Nicolas, and I shall fetch little Harry to show you.'

Nicolas was sitting in her father's chair when she returned, a cushion at his back, and a small stand beside him with a glass of her mother's healing posset. Lady Saunders had settled in her own chair and was at her needlework, while Sir John was standing at the window looking out. It was a happy picture and one that made Caroline smile as she brought the child to show her husband.

'Is he not a fine boy?'

'Very handsome, and his eyes are very like Harry's,' Nicolas said and looked pleased. 'I dare say he will prove a handful when he is growing up. I remember that Harry and I fought all the time.'

'He thrives and we shall do our best to see him grown to

manhood,' Caroline said, looking fondly at the child. 'It makes me wonder . . .' She sighed and shook her head. 'But I do not know for certain.'

'What do you wonder, my love?' Nicolas asked.

'It was just that I saw Rowena Greenslade a week or so ago and she had a small babe in her arms. I think, though I am not certain, but I think her child may also be Harry's.'

'Surely not!' Lady Saunders looked shocked, but she could see that Nicolas was thoughtful.

'It is possible I suppose,' he said, a harsh expression in his eyes. 'My brother had an affair with her before he left to join the King in the North but . . .' he stopped as he saw that Caroline was upset. 'What else would you tell us?'

'She was in Oxford for a while. I saw them together. He had his arm about her waist and they had been drinking . . .'

'That is terrible,' Lady Saunders said. 'Poor Mercy. To think that he behaved so badly is quite shocking. I had not thought it of your brother, Nicolas.'

'Harry Mortimer was a rogue,' Sir John said bluntly. 'Forgive me, Nicolas. One should not speak ill of the dead, but I cannot say other.'

'I know you speak truthfully, sir,' Nicolas said and looked grave. 'Harry was selfish and thought only of his own pleasure.' He was silent for a moment, then looked at Caroline as she nursed Mercy's son. 'What is in your mind, my love?'

'I cannot help thinking that Rowena's child may have a hard life,' she replied. 'We shall care for little Harry as if he were our own but what of the other one?'

'Caroline,' her mother chided. 'You cannot expect Nicolas to take the other one. You will have children of your own and . . .'

'Is that what you want?' Nicolas asked with a lift of his brows.

'I could ask Rowena if she would like to work for us,' she said thoughtfully. 'She could help to care for her child but he would grow up as a part of our family, if I do not ask too much of you, Nicolas?'

'It is what I would expect of your generous heart,' he said fondly. 'And I would not feel easy in my conscience if I did not at least offer to take her and the child in. She may refuse and we cannot compel her, but if she will not come to us, we can at least give her money.'

'Are you certain that the child is Harry's?' Sir John asked suddenly. 'A girl like that may have had other lovers. Do you think it wise to take her and her babe into your home?'

'I believe that the child is Harry's,' Caroline said. 'I would at least like to speak to her, to ask her for the truth. And I would help her if I could, give her a little money if nothing more.'

'Then it is settled,' Nicolas said. 'You shall ask her, Caroline. It is only right that we should help her if my brother fathered her child.'

'I shall go this very afternoon,' Caroline said. 'No, do not look so anxious. I shall not go alone. Tilly shall come with me. And one of father's grooms if you wish it, to make sure that we are safe.'

'Leave it for a few days more,' Nicolas told her. 'I shall be well enough to come with you then, and I should like to talk to her myself. I would like to discover the truth of the matter if possible.'

Caroline could do no other than agree. For herself she believed that Rowena's child was also Harry's, but her husband was so good and generous she could not gainsay him. Her instincts urged her to go at once, but she would not disoblige her husband. She would wait a few days more until he felt able to accompany her.

Rowena was trembling as she took the casket from its hiding place, opening it to look at the contents. How could Roald have lied to her when he said he had no treasure? The casket was full of golden items and precious jewels. She did not know the name of all the pretty stones for she had never seen anything like them in her life, but she liked the red ones particularly and picked up a ring with a large stone that glowed like

233

fire. It tempted her so but did she dare to steal it from Roald?

It was clear that he did not trust her. She knew that he often followed her with his dark, intent gaze, and she had wondered what was in his mind, but of late he had seemed to grow less watchful of her. This was the first day he had left her entirely alone. He had gone to meet someone at a horse fair and she knew that this was her chance.

As yet they had travelled only a few leagues from Thornberry for they had paused to give Carlina a ritual burial. Rowena had watched from a distance as the young girl was carried into her caravan and burned together with all her belongings. She had thought it a terrible waste to burn everything, but Roald had told her that no true gypsy would take what belonged to a member of the tribe who had died.

'Carlina died for us,' he told Rowena. 'Therefore she has been given all the honour we can give her in death.'

'It be strange to me,' Rowena told him. 'You be an odd people, Roald, that be the truth.'

'You have the true Romany blood in you and will learn to understand us,' he said, 'if you stay with us.' He gave her a harsh look as if he did not trust her. She lowered her eyes, hiding her thoughts from him for she did not mean to stay longer than she needed to.

'Where would I go if I left you?'

'I do not know,' he told her. 'But if you should leave me now I shall kill you.'

Had he meant his threat? Rowena was not certain. She stared at the gold and jewels. With this she could live as she pleased. It was too tempting to be ignored, and she would never have a better chance than this to escape.

Eleven

The next morning Nicolas was a little feverish. He was not as ill as he had been at the start, but his skin was hot and he suffered from a thundering headache. Caroline scolded him and made him promise he would stay in bed. He promised to do so if she sat with him and read to him from one of his favourite books, which she was happy to do.

After a while he grew sleepy, his eyelids drooping as he lay back against the pillows. She kissed him and left him to rest. As she reached the top of the stairs she heard voices in the hallway. Her mother and father were greeting someone and from the tone of their voices they were excited. Her heart raced as she began to guess whom it might be, and then she saw her brother and ran down the stairs to greet him.

'Rupert! How glad I am to see you.'

'Caroline, my dear sister. How well you look. I hear that you have married?'

'Who told you that?'

'I stopped in the village to speak with the Reverend Blackwell,' her brother said. 'How is your husband?'

'Recovering, though he hath a fever,' Caroline said. 'But tell us about yourself, Rupert.' She recalled her premonition when she had last parted from him, seeing again that lonely moor on which she had feared he might lose his life, and thanking God that she had been mistaken. 'We have all been worrying about you.'

'I was injured,' Rupert told them with a wry grimace, 'but

235

I have recovered and that is entirely due to Harry Mortimer. He saved my life at Roundway Down and received the injury that killed him for his pains.'

'Oh, Rupert,' Caroline said as she tucked her arm through his. 'We were told that Harry had died but not the manner of it. This makes his death so much worse for he died a hero and we none of us knew the debt we owed him.'

'I was knocked from my horse by a pikeman, and surrounded by four Roundhead soldiers,' Rupert said, his expression grave. 'I had lost my horse and was fighting for my life, but had not much hope of winning free. Harry fought his way to me and between us we dispatched them but I had received a wound to my leg and could not walk. Harry lifted me on his shoulder and carried me to safety. It was then that he was cut down by cannon fire – not from their ranks but from our own. We were firing at the enemy and one of the cannons blew up. I was lying behind a wagon and protected from the worst of the blast, but Harry took the full force of it. I was ill so I do not recall what happened then, but they told me later that he had died of his injuries.'

'Oh, Rupert.' Caroline's eyes were wet with tears as she realized how close she had come to losing her precious brother. 'I am so glad that Harry came to your aid.'

'After Harry was wounded, it was another cavalry officer that took me to be cared for by the surgeon,' Rupert went on. 'He visited me several times, and told me that he knew you, Caroline. His name was Captain Benedict and I believe you became friends in Oxford?'

'We knew each other and in the end we were friends of late,' she agreed, recalling the morning when she had bound the Cavalier's wound and sent him on his way with food and medicine. 'It was good of him to help you, Rupert.' Why had he not told her of his kindness to her brother? Perhaps he had thought it best she learn it from Rupert.

'He also did what he could for Harry, for they were friends, but though he lingered for a while, there was nothing they could do for him.'

'That was very sad,' Caroline said, her eyes shadowed for a moment and then she smiled. 'Tell me, how long can you stay with us, Rupert?'

'I have been given a month's leave,' Rupert told her. 'So I came home, though I was not sure of my welcome until I got here.'

'Now you know that you are welcome always,' his sister said and kissed his cheek. 'We all love you dearly, my brother.'

'Enough of me,' Rupert said as they joined his parents in the front parlour. 'Tell me how you all are. Is Mercy well? Harry spoke of her when he was helping me from the battle-field. He said that he liked to think of her safe with you. He told me that he meant to find her when he had the chance and that . . . she was carrying his child.'

Caroline's smile faded. 'Mercy ran away from us the night that Harry left for the West Country. She *was* having Harry's child and it was born a few days ago – but Mercy died.'

'I am sorry to hear that,' Rupert said. 'I liked her. Does the child live?'

'Yes. Nicolas and I have decided to take him into our family. He will be brought up as our own, though he will be told that he is Harry's son. And Mercy's, of course.'

'I am sure that is what Harry would want,' Rupert said. 'Had you not decided on it, it was my intention to ask Father if he would take the child, but I did not know then that Mercy had run away.'

Caroline nodded, understanding how he must feel, but the time for such confidences was at an end. Her father wanted to know more about his son's life in the King's army, and how he had fared since leaving home, for he had gone with only a handful of coins in his pocket.

Caroline sat silently as they talked. She could not help but be grateful to Harry Mortimer for saving her brother's life and it made her feel even more determined to find Harry's other child and see if there was some way of helping Rowena and the baby.

Had Nicolas not been so particular about her waiting for him she would have gone that very day, but she did not want to make him angry by going against his wishes. Besides, Rowena had brought her child home so she must intend staying in the area and therefore there was no particular hurry.

Rowena paused to take breath as she saw her father's cottage ahead of her. She seemed to have been running ever since she had left the gypsy camp, a handful of Roald's treasure in her bundle. She had not dared to take it all, just enough to see her settled. She was terrified for she knew that he would come after her, and that she must not stay here long, but she wanted to fetch some things she had left at the cottage, and then she would be on her way, perhaps to London. In London she could sell her treasure; become someone else and then Roald would never find her.

She glanced over her shoulder before she entered the cottage. There was no one behind her but she felt as if someone were watching her all the time. It was an uncomfortable feeling and made her nervous.

The sooner she had collected her things and was on her way the better!

It was dark inside the cottage, which had downstairs only a back kitchen and a front parlour, where they had sat of a Sunday evening to read the Bible, for the blacksmith had been a religious man. It had not stopped him losing his temper or hitting his wife and Rowena, but outwardly he had held the Lord's day holy.

Rowena felt for the tinderbox and the candle, which were always left on a ledge just inside the scullery. She struck the flints together several times until they sparked and she was able to light her candle. Then, as she turned, she gasped for a man was lying slumped on her floor, his face downwards. He gave a little moan as if he were aware of her but unable to speak. Setting the candle down, Rowena went to him, kneeling beside him and rolling him over on to his back.

It was Richard Woodville. She was startled and pulled her hand back as if she feared he would rear up and strike her, but then he groaned and opened his eyes to look at her.

'Where have you been?' he asked in a whisper she could barely hear. 'I need help . . .'

Why should she help him? Rowena sat back on her heels. She could see the staining on his shirt and knew that he had been wounded, for it was obvious that he had bled a great deal. If she left him here he would undoubtedly die of his wound in time.

'Please,' he begged. 'Help me to recover and I will give you money.'

'Where is your money?' she asked, a greedy gleam in her eyes. Why should she not take his money and leave him to die? He was nothing to her and had never done anything but abuse and threaten her.

'Not here,' Richard said. 'Hidden in the woods. Help me and it is yours.'

'How much money?' she asked, glancing over her shoulder as if she feared that someone was watching. For a moment she felt that Roald was very close and a feeling of terror caught her. 'No, no, I cannot stay to tend you.' She saw a bundle lying on the floor and seized it, looking for anything of value it might contain, but there was nothing other than his pistol, which she left lying on the ground, a little out of his reach. 'I will fetch water and put some salve on your wound and then I must go. You have nothing of value. If you had gold you would have it with you. Besides, I have all I need.' She dangled the bangles on her arm before him. One of them Roald had given her, the others she had stolen from his casket.

'Fools gold,' Woodville muttered. 'Your bangles are made of brass, Rowena. Whoever gave them to you cheated you.'

Her eyes narrowed as she looked at him. Roald had given one of the bangles to her as a gift and she had believed it was gold, for she had never owned or seen anything made of gold in her life.

'You lie to make me think that you have better.'

'Look at your arm, girl. See where the bangles have made black marks on your wrist. They are not true gold. If you try to sell them the merchants will laugh at you. Help me and I will give you more gold than you can spend.'

Rowena rubbed at her arm. She had noticed the black mark before but it had not occurred to her to doubt that the bangle Roald had given her was gold. She felt for a ring with a large red stone that she had secreted inside her bodice and held it out to him.

'What is this? Is it not a precious jewel?'

Woodville looked at it and smiled his scorn. 'Did you think it a ruby? It is glass with a piece of crimson cloth behind it to give it more colour. A worthless trinket.'

'You're lying,' Rowena said, her eyes filling with tears as the disappointment welled up in her. She remembered Roald telling her that he had no gold, but she had thought he was lying to her when she saw the bangles and beads in his casket. Now she understood that his treasures were only cheap trinkets for selling at the fairs. She felt foolish, angry and then frightened as she realized that she had thrown everything away for fools gold. 'What shall I do? This is all I have . . .'

'Help me,' Woodville said. 'We shall go to London together and live as man and wife. One day I shall be rich and you will have a real ruby to wear on your finger.'

'But you are my half-brother,' Rowena objected. 'My mother told me it was so.'

'Your mother lied,' he said. 'Forget her, forget everything from the past and come with me. Help me to get strong again and I shall make you rich.'

Could she trust him? Rowena considered. He was weak and it would be a long time before he recovered his strength. If he had gold she would find it, and then she would leave him.

'Very well,' she said. 'I shall help you, and when you are better you will give me real gold to prove that you are rich.'

'As soon as I am strong enough we shall go together to find it,' Woodville promised. He smiled maliciously as she turned away to fetch water. The girl was a fool. Once he was strong enough he would take what he wanted of her and then he would kill her.

'Let her go,' Greta said when it was discovered that Rowena had fled. 'She stole from you and she would do it again if you brought her back. We gave the wench her chance and we have the child, let her go.'

'She belongs to me,' Roald said, his face cold with anger. 'She is my blood kin for my grandfather and hers were brothers. Besides, she is my woman. I shall find her and this time she will not escape me.'

Greta looked at his face, shaking her head as she saw the stubborn line of his mouth. 'You will regret it if you go against what is written, Roald. It will end in sorrow.'

'You said that she would be mine when she came to me.'

'Perhaps I was wrong,' Greta said. 'I shall read the signs again.'

'I have no time for such nonsense,' Roald said and turned his back on her, striding away.

Greta sighed. He would fare ill if he turned his back on his people but he was caught in the toils of that woman – a woman who was not worthy of him. She had seen it written in the stars and the bones, but she had kept the last from him. It would be a great bitterness to him all his life, but he must follow his destiny for it was written.

'I am feeling much better,' Nicolas told Caroline as he came downstairs that day. 'No, do not look so distressed, my love. I shall not become ill again, I promise you.'

'You look better,' Caroline said. His colour had begun to return and she knew that he was eating the food they gave him. 'I am glad that your strength is gaining, my dearest, but I know that it means you will have to leave me soon.'

'Not for another day or two,' he said. 'Your father gave

241

one of my men a letter for Cromwell and I shall not be expected for a while. However, I am feeling well enough to accompany you to Rowena's cottage today. I know you have wanted to see her, to ask her if she will bring Harry's son to us here, but you kept your word and did not go alone.'

'I knew that you were anxious lest Captain Woodville was hiding somewhere near and so I did as you asked, Nicolas. I am sure that Rupert would accompany us today or perhaps one of your own men?'

'Most of them have returned to Cromwell,' he told her. 'I sent them away once I had settled things here. However, it might be best if we took someone with us, for though nothing has been seen or heard of Woodville I cannot be sure that he is not still lurking somewhere nearby.'

'I shall ask Rupert if he cares to ride with us,' Caroline said. 'And one of my father's grooms. Captain Woodville has tried to murder you once, it is best not to give him a second chance.'

'You are as wise as you are beautiful,' he said and reached out to take her in his arms. 'It was a lucky day for me when our fathers quarrelled for otherwise you might have been wed to my brother.'

'I do not think so,' Caroline said. 'I think at the last one or both of us would have realized that it must not happen.' She lifted her face for his kiss. 'We are so lucky, Nicolas. We have each other and as soon as this war is over we shall be together for the rest of our lives ...'

Rowena straightened up after binding Woodville's side. In the two days that she had been caring for him, he had made a remarkable recovery, though she knew he was still in a great deal of pain. He was capable of standing alone now and she was impatient to be on their way.

'Where is your horse?' she asked. 'Where did you leave your things? I know the woods well. Tell me where they are and I shall fetch them for you.'

'And steal what you find, I dare say,' Woodville's mouth

curved in a sneer of derision. 'I am not such a fool, wench. You will wait until I am well enough to walk there with you.'

'You do not trust me,' she said, a sullen look in her eyes. 'Well, I do not trust you either and I shall not wait any longer. I am leaving now and . . .'

She got no further for he made a lunge at her, trying to grab her arm, but failing and groaning as he felt the pain in his side. She had eased him and her cures had given him back some of his strength but he was still very weak.

'Damn you,' he muttered. 'You are a greedy bitch and if I did not need you . . .'

Rowena stared at him, understanding what he had not said. She had been a fool to stay here so long. He had no gold and he would treat her badly if he recovered enough to become her master. She must leave now while she had the chance. Better she had stayed with the gypsies than let this man rule her.

'I am leaving,' she told him and began to gather up her things. 'I should not have listened to you.'

'Give that to me!' he demanded as he saw that she had picked up his pistol with her own bundle. 'Damn you! That belongs to me.'

'And will be payment for what I have done for you,' Rowena said, her eyes glittering. 'It is little enough but you have nothing else of worth.'

'You bitch!' Woodville said and lunged at her again, trying to wrestle the pistol from her.

Rowena held on to it for all she was worth, her finger pressing down on the hammer without realizing what she was doing. She screamed and recoiled as it went off, the loud noise making her jump back and drop the pistol on the floor.

Woodville staggered back, his eyes wide with astonishment as he clutched at his stomach. He was trying to speak but only a gurgling sound came out as the blood gushed from his mouth, and then as she watched, he buckled at the knees and fell to the floor where he lay twitching for some minutes before he was still, his eyes open and staring.

Rowena felt sick. She had never seen a man die violently before and it terrified her. She backed away from him, shaking her head. She had killed him; she was a murderer and would be arrested and hanged for her crime.

She could not stay here another moment. She snatched up her bundle, leaving the pistol lying on the ground. All she wanted now was to escape from this place!

It was cooler now than it had been of late and the leaves were beginning to change colour: now it was truly autumn, the season of swirling mists and russet fruit. The small party set out from Hillgrove in a relaxed mood, laughing and talking amongst themselves.

When they reached the blacksmith's house they saw that several people had gathered in front of it and an argument seemed to be going on amongst them.

'Something is amiss here,' Nicolas said and turned to his wife. 'Stay here with your groom, Caroline. Rupert and I will go to investigate.'

'Here be Lord Mortimer,' an old woman cried as he rode up to them. 'Now we shall have justice. There be murder done here, sir. Captain Woodville be dead upon the floor and it be that wench Rowena Greenslade what done it.'

'My son has been murdered and I demand justice!' a querulous voice cried out and Nicolas recognized Woodville's mother amongst the crowd. 'She must be brought back to the village and hanged.'

'How do you know that it was Rowena?' Nicolas asked. 'Did anyone see the crime committed?'

'I heard the shot,' Granny Sorrell declared importantly. 'And then I see Rowena running away from the cottage with a bundle in her arms. She looked scared and I thought it best to fetch a witness afore I went into the cottage. I asked Baker Melbourn and Master Goodjohn to come with me – and we see him lying there, his eyes staring up at us. Dead he be, shot through the stomach and the pistol lying there for any to see. That girl was always a bold hussy! She is likely a witch as her mother before her.'

'She is a wicked girl and must be punished,' Mistress Woodville cried vengefully. 'A hue and cry must be set up to find her and bring her to justice.'

'If Rowena is taken she will be given a fair trial,' Nicolas said. He got down from his horse and went into the cottage. It took no more than a glance to see that all was as he had been told, but a brief examination showed him that Woodville had an earlier wound that had been bound and cared for.

'Rowena has been here,' he told his brother-in-law as he joined him. 'It looks to me as if she cared for him – but why she killed him I have no idea. It may be that they argued . . .' He paused thoughtfully. 'Or it may be that someone else killed him. We must find her before anyone else does, Rupert. That mob out there will stone her to death for she was not liked and they will look for no proof of her guilt.'

'I shall take Caroline home while you organize it,' Rupert said. 'You have some power here. I have none for most hereabouts are not lovers of Royalists and I may be taken for a spy.'

'I saw some angry looks come your way,' Nicolas told him. 'I believe that you should leave once you have Caroline safely home, my friend. The mood is angry and may grow ugly, especially if they are thwarted of their bloodlust.'

Rupert went outside at once. He heard the rumblings amongst the crowd and knew that Nicolas was right. It would not be safe to stay here if the mood of the villagers turned ugly. He must take Caroline back to their parents, and then he must leave. It was time he returned to his comrades and the war.

'What is it?' Caroline asked when he came up to her. 'Has something happened to Rowena?'

'I shall tell you as we ride,' he said. 'Nicolas is going to get up a search party for her but the mood here is hostile and we should leave now.'

*   *   *

245

Roald stood watching the angry scene outside Blacksmith Greenslade's cottage. He listened to the harsh words and the cries for vengeance, and knew that Rowena would receive no justice from these people. They would not ask why she had killed, for their bloodlust was aroused and the hate that had festered inside them for so long would not be appeased by anything but death.

If the militia found her she would be given a trial, but they would find her guilty even if they believed that it had been self defence. She might be given a prison sentence rather than the death penalty, but she would die in that place if her freedom was taken. For though she did not yet know it, she had true Romany blood in her – the blood of ancient princes.

He must find her himself and take her from this place. She was his woman and she belonged with him and his people, whether she knew it or not.

Caroline ran to greet Nicolas as he came into the house later that day. She could see that he was tired and was nervous lest his wound had broken open again, but after he had sat for a while and drunk the cup of restorative wine that she brought him he was able to relax and talk to her.

'Do not look so anxious, my love,' he told her. 'It is nothing but weakness and I shall be better soon. It has taught me one thing, I am not yet ready to return to my duty.'

'Then it has done some good,' Caroline told him, a little smile on her lips. 'Have you found Rowena?'

'So far she has managed to elude us. My men made a search of the woods for we thought she might go there. Some of them are out searching the roads, for she cannot have gone far.'

'What will happen to her if the villagers find her first?' Caroline's eyes were dark with the horror of what was in her mind for she had seen the mood of the people, sensed their anger. It was an anger generated by the war that had taken sons, husbands and fathers and brought hardship in their place.

246

'I do not know,' Nicolas answered truthfully. 'But I do not think she will find much justice from some of those women.'

'They have always resented both her and her mother,' Caroline said. 'I fear that they have found her guilty without trial.'

'Yes, I think you are right,' Nicolas agreed. 'It is the vengeance of the mob, Caroline, and ugly, and unless we can find her before the villagers do . . .'

'What of her child?' Caroline asked. 'Did anyone say anything about the child?'

'I questioned Granny Sorrell,' Nicolas said and she claimed that Rowena did not have a child when she left the cottage.

'She had a child with her the day I met her as I came from the churchyard,' Caroline said. 'I am not mistaken, Nicolas.'

'She must have left it somewhere,' he said with a frown. 'But unless we can find her alive we shall never know.'

Caroline shivered as a cold chill slithered down her spine. 'We must make every effort to find the child,' she said and for a moment she felt that a dark shadow hovered at her shoulder. 'It is an instinct, Nicolas. I cannot tell you why, but I feel that . . .' She shook her head. It was impossible to explain that she had a premonition of something terrible happening one day in the future that might touch all their lives. 'The child could be anywhere.'

'Surely she would not simply have abandoned it?' Nicolas said. 'Wherever it is I am sure it is being cared for.'

'I pray that you are right,' Caroline said. 'But come, my love. You are tired and you must be hungry. Let us eat our supper for you can do nothing more today.'

'Lie still,' Roald told Rowena as he heard the pounding of approaching hooves on the road behind him. 'Pull the covers over you and do not move if they stop us.'

Rowena obeyed him, for she had seen the men searching the woods for her and knew that she would be given little justice if she were taken back to her village. She had been hiding in a place deep in the woods, the crumbling ruin of an ancient Saxon church so long covered with vines that few knew of its existence. She was cold and hungry and frightened when Roald found her. She had thought it was one of the villagers and when she heard his voice calling to her softly, she had run to him, begging him to help her.

'You ran from me,' Roald said his eyes dark and intense, 'and yet now you ask for my help.'

'Yes,' she said and lifted her dark eyes to his. He was a true Romany and her way of escape from the danger that surrounded her. She believed that she carried the blood of his people in her veins through her mother and knew that she needed the freedom he offered. 'Yes, I ask for your help.'

'Why should I not give you up to those who search for you? Did you kill this man as they say?'

'I was foolish and greedy when I took what was yours,' Rowena said, her eyes wide with fear. 'I tried to help that man but he turned on me and we struggled and . . . the pistol fired by accident. I did not mean to kill him. I swear it.'

Roald was silent for a moment, then he inclined his head. 'If you had not killed him, he would have killed you. He meant you harm, Rowena. Carlina gave her life to stop him, but she was not strong enough. Her blow only wounded him.'

Rowena knew that that was not quite true. Richard Woodville would have died of his wound if she had not helped him. She had helped him because he had offered her gold, but she would not tell the gypsy that. He was her only chance of escape.

Now she lay terrified beneath the blanket and piles of old clothes that Roald had told her to pull over her if they were stopped. She could hear the harsh voices asking Roald if he had seen her.

'I am a traveller, good sirs,' he told the soldiers as they ordered him to stop. 'I do not know the woman you speak of and I have passed no one on the road. No, I beg your pardon, there was an ancient one driving his donkey towards the market town some leagues that way.'

Roald pointed helpfully back towards the crossroads. Most of the men looked satisfied, but one of them gestured towards the van.

'What is in there?'

'Nothing but my wares,' Roald said. 'I am a poor man, sir. You are welcome to look, but there are only some old clothes I bought from the lazar house . . .'

The man looked startled. 'You have been to the lazar house.' The fear of death was in his eyes for leprosy was a terrible affliction that terrified the bravest of men. Any thought he might have had of searching the van died instantly.

'We are wasting time,' one of the others said to him. 'I told you she would not come this way. She will try to reach the London road if she can.'

Beneath the clothes that were stifling her, Rowena heard the jingling of harness, the clatter of hooves that grew gradually fainter, and threw off the clothes, sitting up.

'Why did you not tell me where these things came from?' she demanded, a shudder going through her. 'Better to die from stoning than leprosy.'

Roald turned to smile at her. 'Do you think I would risk either of our lives, foolish one? I merely sought to frighten those men. By the time they have finished searching the road to London we shall have gone beyond their reach.'

'Can I come out and sit beside you?' Rowena asked petulantly. She was tired of sitting inside the van and feeling more confident now that the men had gone. Soon she would be safely beyond the reach of those vengeful fools and then . . . her mind shied away from what might happen then for something about Roald had frightened her when he'd brought her to his van. He had told her that he would kill her if she tried to leave him again, and she knew that he meant it. He had given her one more chance, but in future he would watch her closely.

'You are mine,' he had said and the fierce look in his eyes scared her. 'I shall not let them have you, Rowena, but I would rather see you dead than have you leave me.'

She was too frightened to leave him. The villagers would kill her if she was caught. She had no choice but to go with him. Besides, if she managed to escape him she had no money and nowhere to go. She was under no illusions as to her future. Roald would expect her to obey him in all things. And she might do worse, for he was not a cruel man, though she believed that he would kill her rather than let her go again. Perhaps she would stay with him for the time being. It would be a hard life, but one day she might find a way of escape.

'There is no sign of her,' Nicolas told Caroline when he came in from searching a week later. 'I have called off the search for she must be long gone by now. The villagers have forgotten her. There is a case of pox in the village and they are all saying that it was brought by one of the travelling people who were here just before all this happened.'

'It was very strange that they all went so suddenly,' Caroline said and looked thoughtful. 'Usually they stay for the fair but this year they went before the merchants came. I wonder why.'

'If it is true that they brought the pox with them it may be that they had numbers of sick and dying amongst them and went away. We did come across a caravan that had been burned. I believe it is the way of the true Romany people, to burn all the possessions of the departed ones.'

'Yes, I have heard it said,' Caroline frowned. 'Do you think that Rowena went with them?'

'What makes you ask?'

'I don't know,' Caroline said and sighed. 'It was just a thought. I dare say it was foolish, but I pray that she is well and that her child is being cared for wherever she is.'

'You have a tender heart, my darling,' Nicolas said and looked at her lovingly. 'Think no more of her. You have Mercy's child to care for. Let that be enough. We cannot know for sure that Rowena's child was my brother's. Or if it lives.'

'Yes, you are right,' she said. 'Children are so fragile and so many die in the first months of their infancy. Even if Rowena did bear Harry a child, it does not mean that it is still alive.' She smiled at him. 'At least we have little Harry and we do know that he is your true nephew. There is no doubt of who his father was in this case.'

'None at all,' Nicolas told her. 'He shall be loved as much as if he were our own.' He drew her to him, kissing the top of her head. She always smelled of flowers and honey. 'And now, my dearest one, you know what I must say to you?'

Caroline gazed up at him. He was much recovered now and he had already stayed longer than he would had he not been searching for Rowena.

'You must go to your duty,' she said. 'I know it, Nicolas. I do not wish to part from you, but I know you must go.'

'I would stay if I could,' he told her. 'But until this war is ended I must do what is asked of me.' He traced the line of her bottom lip with his forefinger. 'But I shall not go before the morning and so we shall have one more night . . .'

Nicolas was sleeping when Caroline slipped from the bed and went to look out of the window. The sky was very dark, no more than a sprinkling of stars to light the way of those who travelled.

Her thoughts were with Rowena and her child, for despite what she had said to Nicolas there was a feeling inside her that something had happened that might bring heartache and tragedy in the future. It was foolish, she knew, but she believed that they had somehow betrayed Harry's child and that one day he might come seeking revenge.

She suddenly felt icy cold and for one terrible moment she could see nothing but blackness all about her, and then her vision cleared and she saw two men fighting and one dying. No, no, she was being foolish! She had thought Rupert would die on a lonely moor, but Harry had saved his life. These visions, that she had begun to have more often, meant nothing, despite what the gypsy had told her.

Shaking her head, she ran quickly to the bed, snuggling down under the covers, welcoming the warmth of her husband beside her.

It was all nonsense! She did not even know for certain that Rowena had born Harry a son. This shadow that she could feel hovering at her shoulder was nothing but her imagination.

Nicolas reached for her in the darkness, pulling her close. As he began to kiss and caress her, she gave herself up to the joy of his loving. It would be foolish to let a premonition overshadow the happiness she had now.

For this night she would cling to her husband. In the morning she must wave goodbye with a smile on her face. He was going to war and like the other men who fought with him or against him, his life was at risk. Yet something told her that he would return.

It was not for Nicolas she feared but for the future.

APR - - 2000   SOM